Saros Cowasjee is Professor of English at the University of Regina. Before moving to Canada in 1963, he was for two years an Assistant Editor with the Times of India Press, Bombay. Educated in India and England, he has published several critical studies, novels and short stories. He is currently General Editor of Arnold-Heinemann's 'Literature of the Raj' series.

By the same author

Fiction

Stories and Sketches
Goodbye to Elsa
Nude Therapy
The Last of the Maharajas (screenplay)
Suffer Little Children
Stories from the Raj (ed.)
Modern Indian Short Stories (ed.)

Criticism

Sean O'Casey: the Man Behind the Plays
O'Casey
So Many Freedoms: A Study of the Major Fiction of Mulk Raj Anand
'Coolie': An Assessment
Author to Critic: the Letters of Mulk Raj Anand (ed.)

More Stories from the Raj and After

from Kipling to the present day

Selected and Introduced by Saros Cowasjee

GRAFTON BOOKS
A Division of the Collins Publishing Group

LONDON GLASGOW
TORONTO SYDNEY AUCKLAND

Grafton Books
A Division of the Collins Publishing Group
8 Grafton Street, London W1X 3LA

A Grafton Paperback Original 1986

ISBN 0-586-06526-1

Printed and bound in Great Britain by
Collins, Glasgow

Set in Plantin

CONTENTS

ACKNOWLEDGEMENTS

Thanks are due to the following copyright holders for permission to reprint the stories listed:

'The Story of Muhammad Din' and 'Without Benefit of Clergy' by Rudyard Kipling (The National Trust for Places of Historic Interest or Natural Beauty and Macmillan London Ltd); 'A Tale Told By Moonlight' by Leonard Woolf (The Hogarth Press); 'The Devil Has the Moon' by Christine Weston (the author); 'The Simla Thunders' by Philip Mason (the author); 'The Tea-Party', an episode from *Coolie*, by Mulk Raj Anand (the author); 'A Horse and Two Goats', by R. K. Narayan (the author and The Bodley Head); 'Javni' by Raja Rao (the author and Oxford University Press, New Delhi); 'A Woman and a Child' by Mrs Attia Hosain (the author); 'The Riot' by Khushwant Singh (the author); 'An Experience of India', from the volume of the same name, by Ruth Prawer Jhabvala (the author and John Murray (Publishers,) Ltd); 'A Prospect of Flowers' by Ruskin Bond (the author); 'His Father's Medals' by Saros Cowasjee (the author).

Every effort has been made to trace the owners of copyright material but in some cases we have not been successful. We apologize to those our enquiries did not reach and invite them to apply to Grafton Books for proper acknowledgement, if it is due.

To the memory of my mother and father

INTRODUCTION

Saros Cowasjee

This anthology is a companion volume to my *Stories from the Raj* (1982). Once again, from the vast body of literature of this period, the stories are selected primarily for their literary qualities, and once again a good many of these stories show interaction between the British and the Indian people. But such interaction, as I have discussed in my Introduction to *Stories from the Raj*, was never very frequent. The Anglo-Indian* writers were more interested in portraying physical India with its mountains and hills and scorching plains than the people who inhabited it. And much of the writings dealt with themselves – their life in the *mofussil* towns, their exclusive all-white clubs, primitive living conditions, death, disease, the breaking of families and their eternal sense of exile. Not without reason did Sir Alfred Lyall call India the 'land of regrets' – a land of 'trial and sorrow and woe, the land of tall black monuments and vainly proud sepulchral processions'. One thing alone made every hardship bearable – the belief that they were in India to govern and bring light and civilization to an 'inscrutable' people. Once the myth exploded, the Raj began to crumble and finally disappeared in 1947.

Of the remnants of the Raj, nothing is more enduring than the literature of this period. Till very recently it was believed that Kipling alone mattered and the rest, apart

* The term 'Anglo-Indian' was applied originally to the British in India, and only later to people of mixed British and Indian descent. Here it is used in its original meaning.

from a novel each by Forster and Orwell, did not count. The purpose of this anthology, like that of my previous one, is to disprove this notion. There is a large body of work of the first order, and surprisingly a good bulk of it is by women writers. I say surprisingly, for the Anglo-Indian woman has been repeatedly censured for being insensitive towards Indians and for raising social barriers that made friendship between Indians and British impossible. This may be so, but it is the Englishwoman in India who, more than Kipling himself, has given us an insight into the Indian mind. And here Flora Annie Steel and Alice Perrin occupy a high place.

As the stories in this anthology have been selected with an eye for literary excellence rather than for their social importance, certain features of British life in India are totally absent. But what does emerge from these stories is a portrait of the British rulers themselves and their attitude towards the people they governed. The attitude was patronizing, sometimes friendly, as long as their authority in India was not challenged. And thus the loyal *khitmatgar* and the hard-working *mâli* were looked upon with approval, while the Indian intellectual and the nationalist were ridiculed. Philip Mason, who has a lot of sympathy with Indian aspirations, has little sympathy with his nationalists in 'The Simla Thunders'.

British prejudice is most marked when it came to intermarriage between the two races. This had not always been so. In the days of Clive and Hastings, it was not uncommon for Englishmen to marry Indian girls or to enter into a liaison with them. But these were times when Englishwomen in India were not numerous and the Englishman had few hopes of ever returning to England. But things began to change by the second quarter of the nineteenth century and intermarriage began to be regarded with extreme disfavour. The reasons given were numerous: that the Englishman, to maintain his position of leadership, must keep the blood 'pure'; that intermarriage would isolate him from his own people and condemn him to living in this 'God-forsaken country' for the rest of his life; that the children of such a marriage would be half-castes and have no place in British or Indian society. Above all the marriage would fail because of the differences in their ways of life. The Indian woman is invariably portrayed as a sensual and emotional creature, whose depth of passion a Westerner cannot comprehend. And her single-minded devotion to the man she loves – especially if he be a Westerner – is seen as being fraught with danger.

Concubinage between the two races was looked upon with equal disfavour and the end result – even if there was profound love between the two – was shown to be disastrous. Holden in Kipling's 'Without Benefit of Clergy' buys Ameera from her mother for one hundred rupees when she is only fourteen years old. Reynolds in Leonard Woolf's 'A Tale Told By Moonlight' buys a prostitute, Celestinahami, for twenty rupees. But Kipling's story is an idyll of love, and despite his strong racial prejudices he is artist enough to view such unions from the humane point of view. Ameera is bought for money, but the love of Holden and Ameera for each other transmutes the sordid transaction into something noble. Leonard Woolf's story is directed not so much at racial misalliance as it is at debunking romantic love. But in both stories one thing stands out: the subordinate social standing of the Eastern female. In 'Without Benefit of Clergy' Ameera declares to Holden: 'I know that I am thy servant and thy slave, and the dust under thy feet. And I would not have it otherwise.' In 'A Tale Told By Moonlight' Jessop, the narrator, comments on the love of Celestinahami, 'It's the love of a slave, the patient, consuming love for a master, for his kicks and his caresses, for his kisses and his blows.' Both women die in the end. The death of the girl – never of the Englishman – seems to be the generally offered conclusion in almost all of Anglo-Indian fiction.

The Anglo-Indian writer not only killed the girl of such romantic liaisons but did away with her offspring as well. But in real life things were different and a sizable community of mixed breeds came into existence. They were called Eurasians, and later in the twentieth century the appellation 'Anglo-Indian' came to be applied to them. The community was presented unfavourably with no attempt to understand its complexities. Its members were supposed to have acquired the worst traits of both races, and were frequently referred to as 'blackie-whites'. The men were shown to lack moral fibre: they were portrayed as obsequious and ingratiating towards the English and overbearing and contemptuous of the pure Indians for their dark skins. The Eurasian women were admittedly beautiful, but passionate and unscrupulous and always manoeuvring to capture an Englishman for a husband. So strong was the prejudice against the community that even the anti-Raj humanist George Orwell reserved his most bitter scorn for the two Eurasians, Francis and Samuel, in *Burmese Days*. Of the Anglo-Indian writers of note, only Edward Thompson has spoken up for the Eurasians. 'It's perfectly vile,' he wrote in *An Indian Day*, 'the way we have treated the Eurasians. We brought them into existence, and then we tread them underfoot and despise them.'

There are two stories dealing with Eurasians in this anthology. 'The Proud Girl' by Bithia Mary Croker is the tragedy of a Eurasian, Lilias Sheene, who is adopted by an English heiress and then dumped on to her own family after twenty years in England. Herself despised by the

English, Miss Sheene has more colour prejudice than the British themselves. 'I have the most invincible horror, of darkies, and black blood,' she says of her Cuban admirer. 'He has a tawny grandmother somewhere, – and when his hand touches me – I declare it positively makes me creep!' Little does Miss Sheene know of the real horror that awaits her in India – her own mother, a 'very dark', and 'enormously fat old woman' in 'a shapeless black costume, covered with dust.' 'The Devil Has the Moon' by Christine Weston is about a sensitive Eurasian, Mr Sanderson. He is well treated by the English couple to whose children he is a tutor, but he is never allowed to forget that he is not really one of them. It is the time of the eclipse and the local population is in a frenzy banging pots and pans to frighten the devil into releasing the moon. The story makes a significant point in comparing the superstition associated with the eclipse in the native mind to the prejudices of the Whites against the Eurasians. Turning towards home, Sanderson 'wondered briefly what charms or what logic might serve to drive away another shadow from men's minds and from their hearts.' Christine Weston's story is endowed with compassion and has a fine moral edge to it while Croker's is a statement of harsh facts.

Almost Kipling's equal in the crafting of the short story, both Flora Annie Steel and Alice Perrin are in some ways his superior in their understanding of India. 'Lâl', the first story Steel sold, is evocative of the elusiveness of India:

> Who was Lâl? What was he? This was a question I asked many times; and though it was duly answered, Lâl remained, and remains still, an unknown quantity – an abstraction, a name, and nothing more. L A L. The same backwards and forwards, self-contained, self-sufficing.

The story reminds one of the scene in *A Passage to India* where Ronny and Adela see a bird and naturally want to identify it. But they fail, and the author tells us that 'nothing in India is identifiable, the mere asking of a question causes it to disappear or to merge into something else.' Steel knows, as Forster was to know later, that in India understanding comes not through inquiry but acceptance.

I have already spoken enthusiastically about Alice Perrin in my Introduction to *Stories from the Raj.* She writes precisely and with great charm and sophistication. Several of her stories are interlaced with apt Indian proverbs and idioms, and are a reservoir of Indian superstition, folklore and customs. But it is as a satirist that she excels. She is sharply critical of the Indian peasantry, but there is no malice in her portrayal. Without taking sides, she brings the two races into contact and allows them to settle the score. Her Indians, wrong-headed as they often are, are not without dignity, and their insistence on their own merit – even where there is none – and the gravity with which they dismiss the British for their simple-mindedness add to the humour.

In the story entitled 'Justice' an old patriarch tells the village elders why it is possible for a man to kill his own mother (after all she was an old hag) and for him to cut off the nose of his girl-wife (had she not been unfaithful to him!). But the British do not understand:

'Without doubt the sahib-people mean well,' he said graciously, 'and endeavour to be just in their judgments, but "The weevil is ground up with the flour," and at times can they be stupid as owls and make big mistakes.'

The point of the story is that European justice cannot be applied to the Indian, whose mind and customs remain inscrutable to the British. The Indian love of intrigue is also the theme of Perrin's 'The White Tiger' which, with superb irony, contrasts the single-mindedness of the tiger with the deviousness of the villagers. The tiger may symbolize Britain, old and tired, but determined to hold on to her empire.

Perrin's stories prepare us for the dissolution of the Raj, hinted at in Joseph Hitrec's 'Rulers' Morning' and finally executed in John Eyton's 'The Pool'. In the former Hitrec shows, as Orwell has shown, what ruling others does to the rulers themselves. It turns Edward Parsons into a neurotic: there is nothing in his life but suppressed rage. 'The Pool' is about a Hindu shrine that falls into the hands of the Muslims, who then lose it to the English. It is an allegory of the history of India from the time of the East India Company, and ends with a prophecy that comes true, but much sooner than the author anticipated: 'The English, and his Government, and his rights, and his laws have faded away as a ripple dies on water – as a wind stirs in the trees and is gone. But on the bank of the dark pool a little white temple still stands, and still the pilgrims come . . . for such is India.'

The Indian writers' portrait of India differs considerably from that of the Anglo-Indian writer. Indo-Anglian fiction (a term used for Indian fiction in English) emerged in the thirties with the novels of Mulk Raj Anand, R. K. Narayan and Raja Rao – often referred to as The Big Three. But it was not till after Independence that a whole new set of writers appeared. These writers showed little interaction between the British and the Indian people and the reason is not difficult to see. With their newly acquired dignity of being citizens of a free country, they could hardly be expected to dwell on the master–servant relationship that had been their lot. But, more important, these new writers were far less interested in the past than in the scores of problems that faced the emerging nation. They took for their subject matter the partitioning of India and its consequences, untouchability, the problem of hunger, social reforms, etc. This may not be quite evident from the eight stories I have included in this anthology (I have endeavoured to see that no two stories in this section are alike). Still, four of these stories might be said to deal with the gruelling problem of poverty.

Though Mulk Raj Anand has written close to one hundred short stories, he is represented in this selection by an episode from his novel *Coolie* (1936) which I have entitled 'The Tea-Party'. It deals with the visit of the Englishman Mr W. P. England to the house of Babu Nathoo Ram for tea. Modelled on an episode in J. R. Ackerley's *Hindoo Holiday*, the superb fiasco with which the tea-party ends has never been bettered in Indian fiction, and is equalled only by the fiasco of the tiger hunt in *Private Life of an Indian Prince*. But behind the comedy there is a stern warning. British rule not only exploited the country's natural resources but debased the Indian character as well. It created a body of sycophants, looking up to the English, fawning and cringing. And they lost their sense of humanity and human decency.

'An Experience of India' by Ruth Prawer Jhabvala could never have been written during the Raj. No white woman (Ruth herself is Polish by birth and Indian only by adoption) would have had the gall to speak about her sexual encounters with Indians ranging from stray travellers to swamis promising peace and spiritual calm. Illusion-proof, and without any preconceived notions, the narrator (wife of an American journalist) moves from one man to another and in the process reveals the whole gamut of Indian sexual habit and thought.

> There's one question though . . . that always inevitably comes up during sex, so that you learn to wait for it: always, at the moment of mounting excitement, they ask 'How many men have you slept with?' and it's repeated over and over 'How many? How many?' and then they shout 'Aren't you ashamed?' and 'Bitch!' – always that one word which seems to excite them more than any other, to call you that is the height of their love-making, it's the last frenzy, the final outrage: 'Bitch!' Sometimes I couldn't stop myself but had to burst out laughing.

To look upon this wicked, but entirely believable, story as simply a tale of sexual encounters is to misread it. The point seems to be that only when one gives oneself unreservedly to India does one see the real India – an India quite unlike what many Indians, and some Westerners, would like us to believe.

What of some of the other stories by Indians in this volume? 'A Prospect of Flowers' by Ruskin Bond tells of those men and women of the Raj who made India their home and remained there after Independence. Miss Mackenzie, now in her eighties, 'had no intention of going to England; she had not seen the country since she was a child, and she knew she would not fit in with the life of post-war Britain. Her home was in these hills, among the oaks and maples and deodars. It was lonely, but at her age it would be lonely anywhere.' Narayan's 'A Horse and Two Goats' is a hilarious account of an American tourist engaged in a conversation with a rustic who knows no English. However, failure to understand each other pays off both abundantly: the American drives away with a clay horse in his van while the starving peasant returns home with a hundred rupees in his pocket. But beneath the surface comedy there is a distressing portrait of poverty. A similar portrait emerges in Raja Rao's 'Javni', though its theme is universal fellowship that brooks no barriers of caste and creed. 'The Riot' by Khushwant Singh is a biting satire on the Hindu–Muslim feud during the partitioning of India, while Attia Hosain's 'A Women and a Child' reveals a barren woman's desperate wish to have a child of her own and her frenzied attachment to another's.

Reviewing Mulk Raj Anand's *The Sword and the Sickle* in the *Horizon* of July 1942, Orwell said it was difficult to conceive that the English language would have much of a future in a free India. 'Mr Anand and Ahmed Ali are,' he wrote, 'much better writers than the average run of English novelists, but they are not likely to have many successors.' Yet another Orwell prophecy has gone astray and English Literature is the richer for it.

University of Regina
Regina, Canada, 1986

RUDYARD KIPLING

The Story of Muhammad Din

Who is the happy man? He that sees in his own house at home, little children crowned with dust, leaping and falling and crying.
– *Munichandra*, translated by Professor Peterson.

The polo-ball was an old one, scarred, chipped, and dinted. It stood on the mantelpiece among the pipe-stems which Imam Din, *khitmatgar*, was cleaning for me.

'Does the Heaven-born want this ball?' said Imam Din, deferentially.

The Heaven-born set no particular store by it; but of what use was a polo-ball to a *khitmatgar*?

'By Your Honour's favour, I have a little son. He has seen this ball, and desires it to play with. I do not want it for myself.'

No one would for an instant accuse portly old Imam Din of wanting to play with polo-balls. He carried out the battered thing into the verandah; and there followed a hurricane of joyful squeaks, a patter of small feet, and the *thud-thud-thud* of the ball rolling along the ground. Evidently the little son had been waiting outside the door to secure his treasure. But how had he managed to see that polo-ball?

Next day, coming back from office half an hour earlier than usual, I was aware of a small figure in the dining-room – a tiny, plump figure in a ridiculously inadequate shirt, which came, perhaps, halfway down the tubby stomach. It wandered round the room, thumb in mouth, crooning to itself as it took stock of the pictures. Undoubtedly this was the 'little son.'

He had no business in my room, of course; but was so deeply absorbed in his discoveries that he never noticed me in the doorway. I stepped into the room and startled him nearly into a fit. He sat down on the ground with a gasp. His eyes opened, and his mouth followed suit. I knew what was coming, and fled, followed by a long, dry howl which reached the servants' quarters far more quickly than any command of mine had ever done. In ten seconds Imam Din was in the dining-room. Then despairing sobs arose, and I returned to find Imam Din admonishing the small sinner, who was using most of his shirt as a handkerchief.

'This boy,' said Imam Din, judicially, 'is a *budmash* – a big *budmash*. He will, without doubt, go to the *jail-khana* for his behaviour.' Renewed yells from the penitent and an elaborate apology to myself from Imam Din.

'Tell the baby,' I said, 'that the Sahib is not angry, and take him away.' Imam Din conveyed my forgiveness to the offender, who had now gathered all his shirt round his neck, stringwise, and the yell subsided into a sob. The two set off for the door. 'His name,' said Imam Din, as though the name were part of the crime, 'is Muhammad Din, and he is a *budmash*.' Free from present danger, Muhammad Din turned round in his father's arms, and said gravely, 'It is true that my name is Muhammad Din, *Tahib*, but I am not a *budmash*. I am a *man*!'

From that day dated my acquaintance with Muhammad Din. Never again did he come into my dining-room, but on the neutral ground of the garden, we greeted each other with much state, though our conversation was confined to '*Talaam, Tahib*' from his side, and '*Salaam, Muhammad Din*' from mine. Daily on my return from office, the little white shirt and the fat little body used to rise from the shade of the creeper-covered trellis where they had been hid; and daily I checked my horse here, that my salutation might not be slurred over or given unseemly.

Muhammad Din never had any companions. He used to trot about the compound, in and out of the castor-oil bushes, on mysterious errands of his own. One day I stumbled upon some of his handiwork far down the grounds. He had half buried the polo-ball in dust, and stuck six shrivelled old marigold flowers in a circle round it. Outside that circle again was a rude square, traced out in bits of red brick alternating with fragments of broken china; the whole bounded by a little bank of dust. The water-man from the well-kerb put in a plea for the small architect, saying that it was only the play of a baby and did not much disfigure my garden.

Heaven knows that I had no intention of touching the child's work then or later; but, that evening, a stroll through the garden brought me unawares full on it; so that I trampled, before I knew, marigold-heads, dust-bank, and fragments of broken soap-dish into confusion past all hope of mending. Next morning, I came upon Muhammad Din crying softly to himself over the ruin I had wrought. Some one had cruelly told him that the Sahib was very angry with him for spoiling the garden, and had scattered his rubbish, using bad language the while. Muhammad Din laboured for an hour at effacing every trace of the dust-bank and pottery fragments, and it was with a tearful and apologetic face that he said, '*Talaam, Tahib*,' when I came home from office. A hasty inquiry resulted in Imam Din informing Muhammad Din that, by my singular favour, he was permitted to disport himself as he pleased. Whereat the child took heart and fell to tracing the ground-plan of an edifice which was to eclipse the marigold-polo-ball creation.

For some months, the chubby little eccentricity revolved

in his humble orbit among the castor-oil bushes and in the dust; always fashioning magnificent palaces from stale flowers thrown away by the bearer, smooth water-worn pebbles, bits of broken glass, and feathers pulled, I fancy, from my fowls – always alone, and always crooning to himself.

A gaily spotted sea-shell was dropped one day close to the last of his little buildings; and I looked that Muhammad Din should build something more than ordinarily splendid on the strength of it. Nor was I disappointed. He meditated for the better part of an hour, and his crooning rose to a jubilant song. Then he began tracing in the dust. It would certainly be a wondrous palace, this one, for it was two yards long and a yard broad in ground-plan. But the palace was never completed.

Next day there was no Muhammad Din at the head of the carriage-drive and no '*Talaam, Tahib*' to welcome my return. I had grown accustomed to the greeting, and its omission troubled me. Next day Imam Din told me that the child was suffering slightly from fever and needed quinine. He got the medicine, and an English Doctor.

'They have no stamina, these brats,' said the Doctor, as he left Imam Din's quarters.

A week later, though I would have given much to have avoided it, I met on the road to the Mussulman burying-ground Imam Din, accompanied by one other friend, carrying in his arms, wrapped in a white cloth, all that was left of little Muhammad Din.

RUDYARD KIPLING
Without Benefit of Clergy

Before my Spring I garnered Autumn's gain,
Out of her time my field was white with grain,
The year gave up her secrets to my woe.
Forced and deflowered each sick season lay,
In mystery of increase and decay;
I saw the sunset ere men saw the day,
Who am too wise in that I should not know.

BITTER WATERS

I

'But if it be a girl?'

'Lord of my life, it cannot be. I have prayed for so many nights, and sent gifts to Sheikh Badl's shrine so often, that I know God will give us a son – a man-child that shall grow into a man. Think of this and be glad. My mother shall be his mother till I can take him again, and the mullah of the Pattan mosque shall cast his nativity – God send he be born in an auspicious hour! – and then, and then thou wilt never weary of me, thy slave.'

'Since when has thou been a slave, my queen?'

'Since the beginning – till this mercy came to me. How could I be sure of thy love when I knew that I had been bought with silver?'

'Nay, that was the dowry. I paid it to thy mother.'

'And she has buried it, and sits upon it all day long like

a hen. What talk is yours of dower! I was bought as though I had been a Lucknow dancing-girl instead of a child.'

'Art thou sorry for the sale?'

'I have sorrowed; but to-day I am glad. Thou wilt never cease to love me now? – answer, my king.'

'Never – never. No.'

'Not even though the *mem-log* – the white women of thy own blood – love thee? And remember, I have watched them driving in the evening; they are very fair.'

'I have seen fire-balloons by the hundred. I have seen the moon, and – then I saw no more fire-balloons.'

Ameera clapped her hands and laughed. 'Very good talk,' she said. Then with an assumption of great stateliness, 'It is enough. Thou hast my permission to depart – if thou wilt.'

The man did not move. He was sitting on a low red-lacquered couch in a room furnished only with blue and white floor-cloth, some rugs, and a very complete collection of native cushions. At his feet sat a woman of sixteen, and she was all but all the world in his eyes. By every rule and law she should have been otherwise, for he was an Englishman, and she a Mussulman's daughter bought two years before from her mother, who, being left without money, would have sold Ameera shrieking to the Prince of Darkness if the price had been sufficient.

It was a contract entered into with a light heart; but even before the girl had reached her bloom she came to fill the greater portion of John Holden's life. For her, and the withered hag her mother, he had taken a little house overlooking the great red-walled city, and found – when the marigolds had sprung up by the well in the courtyard and Ameera had established herself according to her own ideas of comfort, and her mother had ceased grumbling at the inadequacy of the cooking-places, the distance from the daily market, and at matters of house-keeping in general – that the house was to him his home. Any one could enter his bachelor's bungalow by day or night, and the life that he led there was an unlovely one. In the house in the city his feet only could pass beyond the outer courtyard to the women's rooms; and when the big wooden gate was bolted behind him he was king in his own territory, with Ameera for queen. And there was going to be added to this kingdom a third person whose arrival Holden felt inclined to resent. It interfered with his perfect happiness. It disarranged the orderly peace of the house that was his own. But Ameera was wild with delight at the thought of it, and her mother not less so. The love of a man, and particularly a white man, was at the best an inconstant affair, but it might, both women argued, be held fast by a baby's hands. 'And then,' Ameera would always say, 'then he will never care for the white *mem-log*. I hate them all – I hate them all.'

'He will go back to his own people in time,' said the mother; 'but by the blessing of God that time is yet afar off.'

Holden sat silent on the couch thinking of the future, and his thoughts were not pleasant. The drawbacks of a double life are manifold. The Government, with singular care, had ordered him out of the station for a fortnight on special duty in the place of a man who was watching by the bedside of a sick wife. The verbal notification of the transfer had been edged by a cheerful remark that Holden ought to think himself lucky in being a bachelor and a free man. He came to break the news to Ameera.

'It is not good,' she said slowly, 'but it is not all bad. There is my mother here, and no harm will come to me – unless indeed I die of pure joy. Go thou to thy work and think no troublesome thoughts. When the days are done I believe . . . nay, I am sure. And – and then I shall lay *him* in thy arms, and thou wilt love me for ever. The train goes to-night, at midnight is it not? Go now, and do not let thy heart be heavy by cause of me. But thou wilt not delay in returning? Thou wilt not stay on the road to talk to the bold white *mem-log*. Come back to me swiftly, my life.'

As he left the courtyard to reach his horse that was tethered to the gate-post, Holden spoke to the white-haired old watchman who guarded the house, and bade him under certain contingencies despatch the filled-up telegraph-form that Holden gave him. It was all that could be done, and with the sensations of a man who has attended his own funeral Holden went away by the night mail to his exile. Every hour of the day he dreaded the arrival of the telegram, and every hour of the night he pictured to himself the death of Ameera. In consequence his work for the State was not of first-rate quality, nor was his temper towards his colleagues of the most amiable. The fortnight ended without a sign from his home, and, torn to pieces by his anxieties, Holden returned to be swallowed up for two precious hours by a dinner at the club, wherein he heard, as a man hears in a swoon, voices telling him how execrably he had performed the other man's duties, and how he had endeared himself to all his associates. Then he fled on horseback through the night with his heart in his mouth. There was no answer at first to his blows on the gate, and he had just wheeled his horse round to kick it in when Pir Khan appeared with a lantern and held his stirrup.

'Has aught occurred?' said Holden.

'The news does not come from my mouth, Protector of the Poor, but – ' He held out his shaking hand as befitted the bearer of good news who is entitled to a reward.

Holden hurried through the courtyard. A light burned in the upper room. His horse neighed in the gateway, and he heard a shrill little wail that sent all the blood into the apple of his throat. It was a new voice, but it did not prove that Ameera was alive.

'Who is there?' he called up the narrow brick staircase.

There was a cry of delight from Ameera, and then the voice of the mother, tremulous with old age and pride – 'We be two women and – the – man – thy – son.'

On the threshold of the room Holden stepped on a naked dagger, that was laid there to avert ill-luck, and it broke at the hilt under his impatient heel.

'God is great!' cooed Ameera in the half-light. 'Thou hast taken his misfortunes on thy head.'

'Ay, but how is it with thee, life of my life? Old woman, how is it with her?'

'She has forgotten her sufferings for joy that the child is born. There is no harm; but speak softly,' said the mother.

'It only needed thy presence to make me all well,' said Ameera. 'My king, thou hast been very long away. What gifts hast thou for me? Ah, ah! It is I that bring gifts this time. Look, my life, look. Was there ever such a babe? Nay, I am too weak even to clear my arm from him.'

'Rest then, and do not talk. I am here, *bachari* [little woman].'

'Well said, for there is a bond and a heel-rope [*peecharee*] between us now that nothing can break. Look – canst thou see in this light? He is without spot or blemish. Never was such a man-child. *Ya illah!* he shall be a pundit – no, a trooper of the Queen. And, my life, dost thou love me as well as ever, though I am faint and sick and worn? Answer truly.'

'Yes. I love as I have loved, with all my soul. Lie still, pearl, and rest.'

'Then do not go. Sit by my side here – so. Mother, the lord of this house needs a cushion. Bring it.' There was an almost imperceptible movement on the part of the new life that lay in the hollow of Ameera's arm. 'Aho!' she said, her voice breaking with love. 'The babe is a champion from his birth. He is kicking me in the side with mighty kicks. Was there ever such a babe! And he is ours to us – thine and mine. Put thy hand on his head, but carefully, for he is very young, and men are unskilled in such matters.'

Very cautiously Holden touched with the tips of his fingers the downy head.

'He is of the Faith,' said Ameera; 'for lying here in the night-watches I whispered the call to prayer and the profession of faith into his ears. And it is most marvellous that he was born upon a Friday, as I was born. Be careful of him, my life; but he can almost grip with his hands.'

Holden found one helpless little hand that closed feebly on his finger. And the clutch ran through his body till it settled about his heart. Till then his sole thought had been for Ameera. He began to realize that there was someone else in the world, but he could not feel that it was a veritable son with a soul. He sat down to think, and Ameera dozed lightly.

'Get hence, Sahib,' said her mother under her breath. 'It is not good that she should find you here on waking. She must be still.'

'I go,' said Holden submissively. 'Here be rupees. See that my *baba* gets fat and finds all that he needs.'

The chink of the silver roused Ameera. 'I am his mother, and no hireling,' she said weakly. 'Shall I look to him more or less for the sake of money? Mother, give it back. I have borne my lord a son.'

The deep sleep of weakness came upon her almost before the sentence was completed. Holden went down to the courtyard very softly with his heart at ease. Pir Khan, the old watchman, was chuckling with delight. 'This house is now complete,' he said, and without further comment thrust into Holden's hands the hilt of a sabre worn many years ago when he, Pir Khan, served the Queen in the police. The bleat of a tethered goat came from the well-kerb.

'There be two,' said Pir Khan, 'two goats of the best. I bought them, and they cost much money; and since there is no birth-party assembled their flesh will be all mine. Strike craftily, Sahib! 'Tis an ill-balanced sabre at the best. Wait till they raise their heads from cropping the marigolds.'

'And why?' said Holden, bewildered.

'For the birth-sacrifice. What else? Otherwise the child being unguarded from fate may die. The Protector of the Poor knows the fitting words to be said.'

Holden had learned them once with little thought that he would ever speak them in earnest. The touch of the cold sabre-hilt in his palm turned suddenly to the clinging grip of the child upstairs – the child that was his own son – and a dread of loss filled him.

'Strike!' said Pir Khan. 'Never life came into the world but life was paid for it. See, the goats have raised their heads. Now! With a drawing cut!'

Hardly knowing what he did Holden cut twice as he muttered the Mahomedan prayer that runs: 'Almighty! In place of this my son I offer life for life, blood for blood, head for head, bone for bone, hair for hair, skin for skin.' The waiting horse snorted and bounded in his pickets at the smell of the raw blood that spurted over Holden's riding-boots.

'Well smitten!' said Pir Khan, wiping the sabre. 'A swordsman was lost in thee. Go with a light heart, Heaven-born. I am thy servant, and the servant of thy son. May the Presence live a thousand years and . . . the flesh of the goats is all mine?' Pir Khan drew back richer by a month's pay. Holden swung himself into the saddle and rode off through the low-hanging wood-smoke of the evening. He was full of riotous exultation, alternating with a vast vague tenderness directed towards no particular object, that made him choke as he bent over the neck of his uneasy horse. 'I never felt like this in my life,' he thought. 'I'll go to the club and pull myself together.'

A game of pool was beginning, and the room was full of men. Holden entered, eager to get to the light and the company of his fellows, singing at the top of his voice –

> 'In Baltimore a-walking, a lady I did meet!'

'Did you?' said the club-secretary from his corner. 'Did she happen to tell you that your boots were wringing wet? Great goodness, man, it's blood!'

'Bosh!' said Holden, picking his cue from the rack. 'May I cut in? It's dew. I've been riding through high crops. My faith! My boots are in a mess though!

> 'And if it be a girl she shall wear a wedding-ring,
> And if it be a boy he shall fight for his king,
> With his dirk, and his cap, and his little jacket blue,
> He shall walk the quarter-deck – '

'Yellow on blue – green next player,' said the marker monotonously.

'*He shall walk the quarter-deck* – Am I green, marker? *He shall walk the quarter-deck* – eh! that's a bad shot – *As his daddy used to do!*'

'I don't see that you have anything to crow about,' said a zealous junior civilian acidly. 'The Government is not exactly pleased with your work when you relieved Sanders.'

'Does that mean a wigging from headquarters?' said Holden with an abstracted smile. 'I think I can stand it.'

The talk beat up round the ever-fresh subject of each man's work, and steadied Holden till it was time to go to his dark empty bungalow, where his butler received him as one who knew all his affairs. Holden remained awake for the greater part of the night, and his dreams were pleasant ones.

II

'How old is he now?'

'*Ya illah!* What a man's question! He is all but six weeks old; and on this night I go up to the housetop with thee, my life, to count the stars. For that is auspicious. And he was born on a Friday under the sign of the Sun, and it has been told to me that he will outlive us both and get wealth. Can we wish for aught better, beloved?'

'There is nothing better. Let us go up to the roof, and thou shalt count the stars – but a few only, for the sky is heavy with cloud.'

'The winter rains are late, and maybe they come out of season. Come, before all the stars are hid. I have put on my richest jewels.'

'Thou has forgotten the best of all.'

'*Ai!* Ours. He comes also. He has never yet seen the skies.'

Ameera climbed the narrow staircase that led to the flat roof. The child, placid and unwinking, lay in the hollow of her right arm, gorgeous in silver-fringed muslin with a small skull-cap on his head. Ameera wore all that she valued most. The diamond nose-stud that takes the place of the Western patch in drawing attention to the curve of the nostril, the gold ornament in the centre of the forehead studded with tallow-drop emeralds and flawed rubies, the heavy circlet of beaten gold that was fastened around her neck by the softness of the pure metal, and the chinking curb-patterned silver anklets hanging low over the rosy ankle-bone. She was dressed in jade-green muslin as befitted a daughter of the Faith, and from shoulder to elbow and elbow to wrist ran bracelets of silver tied with floss silk, frail glass bangles slipped over the wrist in proof of the slenderness of the hand, and certain heavy gold bracelets that had no part in her country's ornaments but, since they were Holden's gift and fastened with a cunning European snap, delighted her immensely.

They sat down by the low white parapet of the roof, overlooking the city and its lights.

'They are happy down there,' said Ameera. 'But I do not think that they are as happy as we. Nor do I think the white *mem-log* are as happy. And thou?'

'I know they are not.'

'How dost thou know?'

'They give their children over to the nurses.'

'I have never seen that,' said Ameera with a sigh, 'nor do I wish to see. *Ahi!*' she dropped her head on Holden's shoulder – 'I have counted forty stars, and I am tired. Look at the child, love of my life, he is counting too.'

The baby was staring with round eyes at the dark of the heavens. Ameera placed him in Holden's arms, and he lay there without a cry.

'What shall we call him among ourselves?' she said. 'Look! Art thou ever tired of looking? He carries thy very eyes. But the mouth – '

'Is thine, most dear. Who should know better than I?'

''Tis such a feeble mouth. Oh, so small! And yet it holds my heart between its lips. Give him to me now. He has been too long away.'

'Nay, let him lie; he has not yet begun to cry.'

'When he cries thou wilt give him back – eh? What a man of mankind thou art! If he cried he were only the dearer to me. But, my life, what little name shall we give him?'

The small body lay close to Holden's heart. It was utterly helpless and very soft. He scarcely dared to breathe for fear of crushing it. The caged green parrot that is regarded as a sort of guardian-spirit in most native households moved on its perch and fluttered a drowsy wing.

'There is the answer,' said Holden. 'Mian Mittu has spoken. He shall be the parrot. When he is ready he will talk mightily and run about. Mian Mittu is the parrot in thy – in the Mussulman tongue, is it not?'

'Why put me so far off?' said Ameera fretfully. 'Let it be like unto some English name – but not wholly. For he is mine.'

'Then call him Tota, for that is likest English.'

'Ay, Tota, and that is still the parrot. Forgive me, my lord, for a minute ago, but in truth he is too little to wear all the weight of Mian Mittu for name. He shall be Tota – our Tota to us. Hearest thou, O small one? Littlest, thou art Tota.' She touched the child's cheek, and he waking wailed, and it was necessary to return him to his mother, who soothed him with the wonderful rhyme of *Aré koko Jaré koko!* which says:

Oh crow! Go crow! Baby's sleeping sound,
And the wild plums grow in the jungle, only a penny a pound.
Only a penny a pound, *baba*, only a penny a pound.

Reassured many times as to the price of those plums, Tota cuddled himself down to sleep. The two sleek, white well-bullocks in the courtyard were steadily chewing the cud of their evening meal; old Pir Khan squatted at the head of Holden's horse, his police sabre across his knees, pulling drowsily at a big water-pipe that croaked like a bull-frog in a pond. Ameera's mother sat spinning in the lower verandah, and the wooden gate was shut and barred. The music of a marriage-procession came to the roof above the gentle hum of the city, and a string of flying-foxes crossed the face of the low moon.

'I have prayed,' said Ameera after a long pause, 'I have prayed for two things. First, that I may die in thy stead if thy death is demanded, and in the second that I may die in the place of the child. I have prayed to the Prophet and to Beebee Miriam [the Virgin Mary]. Thinkest thou either will hear?'

'From thy lips who would not hear the lightest word?'

'I asked for straight talk, and thou hast given me sweet talk. Will my prayers be heard?'

'How can I say? God is very good.'

'Of that I am not sure. Listen now. When I die, or the child dies, what is thy fate? Living, thou wilt return to the bold white *mem-log*, for kind calls to kind.'

'Not always.'

'With a woman, no; with a man it is otherwise. Thou wilt in this life, later on, go back to thine own folk. That I could almost endure, for I should be dead. But in thy very death thou wilt be taken away to a strange place and a paradise that I do not know.'

'Will it be paradise?'

'Surely, for who would harm thee? But we two – I and the child – shall be elsewhere, and we cannot come to thee, nor canst thou come to us. In the old days, before the child was born, I did not think of these things; but now I think of them always. It is very hard talk.'

'It will fall as it will fall. To-morrow we do not know,

but to-day and love we know well. Surely we are happy now.'

'So happy that it were well to make our happiness assured. And thy Beebee Miriam should listen to me; for she is also a woman. But then she would envy me! It is not seemly for men to worship a woman.'

Holden laughed aloud at Ameera's little spasm of jealousy.

'Is it not seemly? Why didst thou not turn me from worship of thee, then?'

'Thou a worshipper! And of me? My king, for all thy sweet words, well I know that I am thy servant and thy slave, and the dust under thy feet. And I would not have it otherwise. See!'

Before Holden could prevent her she stooped forward and touched his feet; recovering herself with a little laugh she hugged Tota closer to her bosom. Then, almost savagely –

'Is it true that the bold white *mem-log* live for three times the length of my life? Is it true that they make their marriages not before they are old women?'

'They marry as do others – when they are women.'

'That I know, but they wed when they are twenty-five. Is that true?'

'That is true.'

'*Ya illah!* At twenty-five! Who would of his own will take a wife even of eighteen? She is a woman – aging every hour. Twenty-five! I shall be an old woman at that age, and – Those *mem-log* remain young for ever. How I hate them!'

'What have they to do with us?'

'I cannot tell. I know only that there may now be alive on this earth a woman ten years older than I who may come to thee and take thy love ten years after I am an old woman, grey-headed, and the nurse of Tota's son. That is unjust and evil. They should die too.'

'Now, for all thy years thou art a child, and shalt be picked up and carried down the staircase.'

'Tota! Have a care for Tota, my lord! Thou at least art foolish as any babe!' Ameera tucked Tota out of harm's way in the hollow of her neck, and was carried downstairs laughing in Holden's arms, while Tota opened his eyes and smiled after the manner of the lesser angels.

He was a silent infant, and, almost before Holden could realize that he was in the world, developed into a small gold-coloured little god and unquestioned despot of the house overlooking the city. Those were months of absolute happiness to Holden and Ameera – happiness withdrawn from the world, shut in behind the wooden gate that Pir Khan guarded. By day Holden did his work with an immense pity for such as were not so fortunate as himself, and a sympathy for small children that amazed and amused many mothers at the little station-gatherings. At nightfall he returned to Ameera – Ameera, full of the wondrous doings of Tota; how he had been seen to clap his hands together and move his fingers with intention and purpose – which was manifestly a miracle – how later, he had of his own initiative crawled out of his low bedstead on to the floor and swayed on both feet for the space of three breaths.

'And they were long breaths, for my heart stood still with delight,' said Ameera.

Then Tota took the beasts into his councils – the well-bullocks, the little grey squirrels, the mongoose that lived in a hole near the well, and especially Mian Mittu, the parrot, whose tail he grievously pulled, and Mian Mittu screamed till Ameera and Holden arrived.

'O villain! Child of strength! This to thy brother on the house-top! *Tobah, tobah!* Fie! Fie! But I know a charm to make him wise as Suleiman and Aflatoun [Solomon and Plato]. Now look,' said Ameera. She drew from an embroidered bag a handful of almonds. 'See! we count seven. In the name of God!'

She placed Mian Mittu, very angry and rumpled, on the top of his cage, and seating herself between the babe and the bird she cracked and peeled an almond less white than her teeth. 'This is a true charm, my life, and do not laugh. See! I give the parrot one half and Tota the other.' Mian Mittu with careful beak took his share from between Ameera's lips, and she kissed the other half into the mouth of the child, who ate it slowly with wondering eyes. 'This I will do each day of seven, and without doubt he who is ours will be a bold speaker and wise. Eh, Tota, what wilt thou be when thou art a man and I am grey-headed?' Tota tucked his fat legs into adorable creases. He could crawl, but he was not going to waste the spring of his youth in idle speech. He wanted Mian Mittu's tail to tweak.

When he was advanced to the dignity of a silver belt – which, with a magic square engraved on silver and hung round his neck, made up the greater part of his clothing – he staggered on a perilous journey down the garden to Pir Khan and proffered him all his jewels in exchange for one little ride on Holden's horse, having seen his mother's mother chaffering with pedlars in the verandah. Pir Khan wept and set the untried feet on his own grey head in sign of fealty, and brought the bold adventurer to his mother's arms, vowing that Tota would be a leader of men ere his beard was grown.

One hot evening, while he sat on the roof between his father and mother watching the never-ending warfare of the kites that the city boys flew, he demanded a kite of his own with Pir Khan to fly it, because he had a fear of dealing with anything larger than himself, and when Holden called him a 'spark,' he rose to his feet and answered slowly in defence of his new-found individuality, '*Hum'park nahin hai. Hum admi hai* [I am no spark, but a man].'

The protest made Holden choke and devote himself very seriously to a consideration of Tota's future. He need hardly have taken the trouble. The delight of that life was too perfect to endure. Therefore it was taken away as many things are taken away in India – suddenly and without warning. The little lord of the house, as Pir Khan called him, grew sorrowful and complained of pains who had never known the meaning of pain. Ameera, wild with terror, watched him through the night, and in the dawning of the second day the life was shaken out of him by fever – the seasonal autumn fever. It seemed altogether impossible that he could die, and neither Ameera nor Holden at first believed the evidence of the little body on the bedstead. Then Ameera beat her head against the wall and would have flung herself down the well in the garden had Holden not restrained her by main force.

One mercy only was granted to Holden. He rode to his office in broad daylight and found waiting him an unusually heavy mail that demanded concentrated attention and hard work. He was not, however, alive to this kindness of the gods.

III

The first shock of a bullet is no more than a brisk pinch. The wrecked body does not send in its protest to the soul till ten or fifteen seconds later. Holden realized his pain slowly, exactly as he had realized his happiness, and with the same imperious necessity for hiding all trace of it. In the beginning he only felt that there had been a loss, and that Ameera needed comforting, where she sat with her head on her knees shivering as Mian Mittu from the house-top called, *Tota! Tota! Tota!* Later all his world and the daily life of it rose up to hurt him. It was an outrage that any one of the children at the band-stand in the evening should be alive and clamorous, when his own child lay dead. It was more than mere pain when one of them touched him, and stories told by over-fond fathers of their children's latest performances cut him to the quick. He could not declare his pain. He had neither help, comfort, nor sympathy; and Ameera at the end of each weary day would lead him through the hell of self-questioning reproach which is reserved for those who have lost a child, and believe that with a little – just a little – more care it might have been saved.

'Perhaps,' Ameera would say, 'I did not take sufficient heed. Did I, or did I not? The sun on the roof that day when he played so long alone and I was – *ahi!* braiding my hair – it may be that the sun then bred the fever. If I had warned him from the sun he might have lived. But, oh my life, say that I am guiltless! Thou knowest that I loved him as I love thee. Say that there is no blame on me, or I shall die – I shall die!'

'There is no blame – before God, none. It was written and how could we do aught to save? What has been, has been. Let it go, beloved.'

'He was all my heart to me. How can I let the thought go when my arm tells me every night that he is not here? *Ahi! Ahi!* O Tota, come back to me – come back again, and let us be all together as it was before!'

'Peace, peace! For thine own sake, and for mine also, if thou lovest me – rest.'

'By this I know thou dost not care; and how shouldst

thou? The white men have hearts of stone and souls of iron. Oh, that I had married a man of mine own people – though he beat me – and had never eaten the bread of an alien!'

'Am I an alien – mother of my son?'

'What else – Sahib? . . . Oh, forgive me – forgive! The death has driven me mad. Thou art the life of my heart, and the light of my eyes, and the breath of my life, and – and I have put thee from me, though it was but for a moment. If thou goest away, to whom shall I look for help? Do not be angry. Indeed, it was the pain that spoke and not thy slave.'

'I know, I know. We be two who were three. The greater need therefore that we should be one.'

They were sitting on the roof as of custom. The night was a warm one in early spring, and sheet-lightning was dancing on the horizon to a broken tune played by far-off thunder. Ameera settled herself in Holden's arms.

'The dry earth is lowing like a cow for the rain, and I – I am afraid. It was not like this when we counted the stars. But thou lovest me as much as before, though a bond is taken away? Answer!'

'I love more because a new bond has come out of the sorrow that we have eaten together, and that thou knowest.'

'Yea, I knew,' said Ameera in a very small whisper. 'But it is good to hear thee say so, my life, who art so strong to help. I will be a child no more, but a woman and an aid to thee. Listen! Give me my *sitar* and I will sing bravely.'

She took the light silver-studded *sitar* and began a song of the great hero Rajah Rasalu. The hand failed on the strings, the tune halted, checked, and at a low note turned off to the poor little nursery-rhyme about the wicked crow –

And the wild plums grow in the jungle, only a penny a pound.
Only a penny a pound, *baba* – only . . .

Then came the tears, and the piteous rebellion against fate till she slept, moaning a little in her sleep, with the right arm thrown clear of the body as though it protected something that was not there. It was after this night that life became a little easier for Holden. The ever-present pain of loss drove him into his work, and the work repaid him by filling up his mind for nine or ten hours a day. Ameera sat alone in the house and brooded, but grew happier when she understood that Holden was more at ease, according to the custom of women. They touched happiness again, but this time with caution.

'It was because we loved Tota that he died. The jealousy of God was upon us,' said Ameera. 'I have hung up a large black jar before our window to turn the evil eye from us, and we must make no protestations of delight, but go softly underneath the stars, lest God find us out. Is that not good talk, worthless one?'

She had shifted the accent on the word that means 'beloved,' in proof of the sincerity of her purpose. But the kiss that followed the new christening was a thing that any deity might have envied. They went about henceforward saying, 'It is naught, it is naught'; and hoping that all the Powers heard.

The Powers were busy on other things. They had allowed thirty million people four years of plenty wherein men fed well and the crops were certain, and the birthrate rose year by year; the districts reported a purely agricultural population varying from nine hundred to two thousand to the square mile of the overburdened earth; and the Member for Lower Tooting, wandering about India in pot-hat and frock-coat, talked largely of the benefits of British rule and suggested as the one thing needful the establishment of a duly qualified electoral system and a general bestowal of the franchise. His long-suffering hosts smiled and made him welcome, and when he paused to admire, with pretty picked words, the blossom of the blood-red *dhak*-tree that had flowered untimely for a sign of what was coming, they smiled more than ever.

It was the Deputy Commissioner of Kot-Kumharsen, staying at the club for a day, who lightly told a tale that made Holden's blood run cold as he overheard the end.

'He won't bother any one any more. Never saw a man so astonished in my life. By Jove, I thought he meant to ask a question in the House about it. Fellow-passenger in his ship – dined next him – bowled over by cholera and died in eighteen hours. You needn't laugh, you fellows. The Member for Lower Tooting is awfully angry about it; but he's more scared. I think he's going to take his enlightened self out of India.'

'I'd give a good deal if he were knocked over. It might keep a few vestrymen of his kidney to their own parish. But what's this about cholera? It's full early for anything of that kind,' said the warden of an unprofitable salt-lick.

'Don't know,' said the Deputy Commissioner reflectively. 'We've got locusts with us. There's sporadic cholera all along the north – at least we're calling it sporadic for decency's sake. The spring crops are short in five districts, and nobody seems to know where the rains are. It's nearly March now. I don't want to scare anybody, but it seems to me that Nature's going to audit her accounts with a big red pencil this summer.'

'Just when I wanted to leave, too!' said a voice across the room.

'There won't be much leave this year, but there ought to be a great deal of promotion. I've come in to persuade the

Government to put my pet canal on the list of famine-relief works. It's an ill-wind that blows no good. I shall get that canal finished at last.'

'Is it the old programme then,' said Holden; 'famine, fever, and cholera?'

'Oh no. Only local scarcity and an unusual prevalence of seasonal sickness. You'll find it all in the reports if you live till next year. You're a lucky chap. *You* haven't got a wife to send out of harm's way. The hill stations ought to be full of women this year.'

'I think you're inclined to exaggerate the talk in the *bazars*,' said a young civilian in the Secretariat. 'Now I have observed – '

'I daresay you have,' said the Deputy Commissioner, 'but you've a great deal more to observe, my son. In the meantime, I wish to observe to you – ' and he drew him aside to discuss the construction of the canal that was so dear to his heart. Holden went to his bungalow and began to understand that he was not alone in the world, and also that he was afraid for the sake of another – which is the most soul-satisfying fear known to man.

Two months later, as the Deputy had foretold, Nature began to audit her accounts with a red pencil. On the heels of the spring-reapings came a cry for bread, and the Government, which had decreed that no man should die of want, sent wheat. Then came the cholera from all four quarters of the compass. It struck a pilgrim-gathering of half a million at a sacred shrine. Many died at the feet of their god; the others broke down and ran over the face of the land carrying the pestilence with them. It smote a walled city and killed two hundred a day. The people crowded the trains, hanging on to the footboards and squatting on the roofs of the carriages, and the cholera followed them, for at each station they dragged out the dead and the dying. They died by the roadside, and the horses of the Englishmen shied at the corpses in the grass. The rains did not come, and the earth turned to iron lest man should escape death by hiding in her. The English sent their wives away to the hills and went about their work, coming forward as they were bidden to fill the gaps in the fighting-line. Holden, sick with fear of losing his chiefest treasure on earth, had done his best to persuade Ameera to go away with her mother to the Himalayas.

'Why should I go?' she said one evening on the roof.

'There is sickness, and people are dying, and all the white *mem-log* have gone.'

'All of them?'

'All – unless perhaps there remain some old scald-head who vexes her husband's heart by running risk of death.'

'Nay; who stays is my sister, and thou must not abuse her, for I will be a scald-head too. I am glad all the bold *mem-log* are gone.'

'Do I speak to a woman or a babe? Go to the hills and I will see to it that thou goest like a queen's daughter. Think, child. In a red-lacquered bullock-cart, veiled and curtained, with brass peacocks upon the pole and red cloth hangings. I will send two orderlies for guard, and – '

'Peace! Thou art the babe in speaking thus. What use are those toys to me? *He* would have patted the bullocks and played with the housings. For his sake, perhaps – thou hast made me very English – I might have gone. Now I will not. Let the *mem-log* run.'

'Their husbands are sending them, beloved.'

'Very good talk. Since when hast thou been my husband to tell me what to do? I have but borne thee a son. Thou art only all the desire of my soul to me. How shall I depart when I know that if evil befall thee by the breadth of so much as my littlest finger-nail – is that not small? – I should be aware of it though I were in paradise. And here, this summer thou mayest die – *ai, janee,* die! and in dying they might call to tend thee a white woman, and she would rob me in the last of thy love!'

'But love is not born in a moment or on a death-bed!'

'What dost thou know of love, stoneheart? She would take thy thanks at least and, by God and the Prophet and Beebee Miriam the mother of thy Prophet, that I will never endure. My lord and my love, let there be no more foolish talk of going away. Where thou art, I am. It is enough.' She put an arm round his neck and a hand on his mouth.

There are not many happinesses so complete as those that are snatched under the shadow of the sword. They sat together and laughed, calling each other openly by every pet name that could move the wrath of the gods. The city below them was locked up in its own torments. Sulphur fires blazed in the streets; the conches in the Hindu temples screamed and bellowed, for the gods were inattentive in those days. There was a service in the great Mahomedan shrine, and the call to prayer from the minarets was almost unceasing. They heard the wailing in the houses of the dead, and once the shriek of a mother who had lost a child and was calling for its return. In the grey dawn they saw the dead borne out through the city gates, each litter with its own little knot of mourners. Wherefore they kissed each other and shivered.

It was a red and heavy audit, for the land was very sick and needed a little breathing-space ere the torrent of cheap life should flood it anew. The children of immature fathers and undeveloped mothers made no resistance. They were cowed and sat still, waiting till the sword should be sheathed in November if it were so willed. There were gaps among the English, but the gaps were filled. The work of superintending famine-relief, cholera-sheds, medicine-distribution, and what little sanitation was possible, went forward because it was so ordered.

Holden had been told to keep himself in readiness to move to replace the next man who should fall. There were twelve hours in each day when he could not see Ameera, and she might die in three. He was considering what his pain would be if he could not see her for three months, or if she died out of his sight. He was absolutely certain that her death would be demanded – so certain that when he looked up from the telegram and saw Pir Khan breathless in the doorway, he laughed aloud. 'And?' said he –

'When there is a cry in the night and the spirit flutters into the throat, who has a charm that will restore? Come swiftly, Heaven-born! It is the black cholera.'

Holden galloped to his home. The sky was heavy with clouds, for the long-deferred rains were near and the heat was stifling. Ameera's mother met him in the courtyard, whimpering, 'She is dying. She is nursing herself into death. She is all but dead. What shall I do, Sahib?'

Ameera was lying in the room in which Tota had been born. She made no sign when Holden entered, because the human soul is a very lonely thing and, when it is getting ready to go away, hides itself in a misty borderland where the living may not follow. The black cholera does its work quietly and without explanation. Ameera was being thrust out of life as though the Angel of Death had himself put his hand upon her. The quick breathing seemed to show that she was either afraid or in pain, but neither eyes nor mouth gave any answer to Holden's kisses. There was nothing to be said or done. Holden could only wait and suffer. The first drops of the rain began to fall on the roof, and he could hear shouts of joy in the parched city.

The soul came back a little and the lips moved. Holden

bent down to listen. 'Keep nothing of mine,' said Ameera. 'Take no hair from my head. *She* would make thee burn it later on. That flame I should feel. Lower! Stoop lower! Remember only that I was thine and bore thee a son. Though thou wed a white woman to-morrow, the pleasure of receiving in thy arms thy first son is taken from thee for ever. Remember me when thy son is born – the one that shall carry thy name before all men. His misfortunes be on my head. I bear witness – I bear witness' – the lips were forming the words on his ear – 'that there is no God but – thee, beloved!'

Then she died. Holden sat still, and all thought was taken from him – till he heard Ameera's mother lift the curtain.

'Is she dead, Sahib?'

'She is dead.'

'Then I will mourn, and afterwards taken an inventory of the furniture in this house. For that will be mine. The Sahib does not mean to resume it? It is so little, so very little, Sahib, and I am an old woman. I would like to lie softly.'

'For the mercy of God be silent a while. Go out and mourn where I cannot hear.'

'Sahib, she will be buried in four hours.'

'I know the custom. I shall go ere she is taken away. That matter is in thy hands. Look to it, that the bed on which – on which she lies – '

'Aha! That beautiful red-lacquered bed. I have long desired – '

'That the bed is left here untouched for my disposal. All else in the house is thine. Hire a cart, take everything, go hence, and before sunrise let there be nothing in this house but that which I have ordered thee to respect.'

'I am an old woman. I would stay at least for the days of

mourning, and the rains have just broken. Whither shall I go?'

'What is that to me? My order is that there is a going. The house-gear is worth a thousand rupees and my orderly shall bring thee a hundred rupees to-night.'

'That is very little. Think of the cart-hire.'

'It shall be nothing unless thou goest, and with speed. O woman, get hence and leave me with my dead!'

The mother shuffled down the staircase, and in her anxiety to take stock of the house-fittings forgot to mourn. Holden stayed by Ameera's bedside and the rain roared on the roof. He could not think connectedly by reason of the noise, though he made many attempts to do so. Then four sheeted ghosts glided dripping into the room and stared at him through their veils. They were the washers of the dead. Holden left the room and went out to his horse. He had come in a dead, stifling calm through ankle-deep dust. He found the courtyard a rain-lashed pond alive with frogs; a torrent of yellow water ran under the gate, and a roaring wind drove the bolts of the rain like buckshot against the mud-walls. Pir Khan was shivering in his little hut by the gate, and the horse was stamping uneasily in the water.

'I have been told the Sahib's order,' said Pir Khan. 'It is well. This house is now desolate. I go also, for my monkey-face would be a reminder of that which has been. Concerning the bed, I will bring that to thy house yonder in the morning; but remember, Sahib, it will be to thee a knife turning in a green wound. I go upon a pilgrimage, and I will take no money. I have grown fat in the protection of the Presence whose sorrow is my sorrow. For the last time I hold his stirrup.'

He touched Holden's foot with both hands and the horse sprang out into the road, where the creaking bamboos were whipping the sky and all the frogs were chuckling. Holden could not see for the rain in his face. He put his hands before his eyes and muttered –

'Oh you brute! You utter brute!'

The news of his trouble was already in his bungalow. He read the knowledge in his butler's eyes when Ahmed Khan brought in food, and for the first and last time in his life laid a hand upon his master's shoulder, saying, 'Eat, Sahib, eat. Meat is good against sorrow. I also have known. Moreover the shadows come and go, Sahib; the shadows come and go. These be curried eggs.'

Holden could neither eat nor sleep. The heavens sent down eight inches of rain in that night and washed the earth clean. The waters tore down walls, broke roads, and scoured open the shallow graves on the Mahomedan burying-ground. All next day it rained, and Holden sat still in his house considering his sorrow. On the morning of the third day he received a telegram which said only, 'Ricketts, Myndonie. Dying. Holden relieve. Immediate.' Then he thought that before he departed he would look at the house wherein he had been master and lord. There was a break in the weather, and the rank earth steamed with vapour.

He found that the rains had torn down the mud pillars of the gateway, and the heavy wooden gate that had guarded his life hung lazily from one hinge. There was grass three inches high in the courtyard; Pir Khan's lodge was empty, and the sodden thatch sagged between the beams. A grey squirrel was in possession of the verandah, as if the house had been untenanted for thirty years instead of three days. Ameera's mother had removed everything except some mildewed matting. The *tick-tick* of the little scorpions as they hurried across the floor was the only sound in the house. Ameera's room and the other one where Tota had lived were heavy with mildew; and the narrow staircase leading to the roof was streaked and stained with rain-borne mud. Holden saw all these things, and came out again to meet in the road Durga Dass, his landlord – portly, affable, clothed in white muslin, and driving a Cee-spring buggy. He was overlooking his property to see how the roofs stood the stress of the first rains.

'I have heard,' said he, 'you will not take this place any more, Sahib?'

'What are you going to do with it?'

'Perhaps I shall let it again.'

'Then I will keep it on while I am away.'

Durga Dass was silent for some time. 'You shall not take it on, Sahib,' he said. 'When I was a young man I also – , but to-day I am a member of the Municipality. Ho! Ho! No. When the birds have gone what need to keep the nest? I will have it pulled down – the timber will sell for something always. It shall be pulled down, and the Municipality shall make a road across, as they desire, from the burning-ghat to the city wall, so that no man may say where this house stood.'

FLORA ANNIE STEEL

Lâl

Who was Lâl? What was he? This was a question I asked many times; and though it was duly answered, Lâl remained, and remains still, an unknown quantity – an abstraction, a name, and nothing more. L A L. The same backwards and forwards, self-contained, self-sufficing.

The first time I heard of Lâl was on a bright spring morning, one of those mornings when the plains of Northern India glitter with dewdrops; when a purple haze of cloud-mountain bounds the pale wheat-fields to the north, and a golden glow strikes skywards from the sand-hills in the south. I was in a tamarisk jungle on the banks of the Indus, engaged in the decorous record of all the thefts and restitutions made during the year by that most grasping and generous of rivers. For year after year, armed by the majesty of law and bucklered by foot-rules and maps, the Government of India, in the person of one of its officers, came gravely and altered the proportion of land and water on the surface of the globe, while the river gurgled and dimpled as if it were laughing in its sleeve.

Strange work, but pleasant too, with a charm of its own wrought by infinite variety and sudden surprise. Sometimes watching the stream sapping at a wheat-field, where the tender green spikes fringed the edges of each crack and fissure in the fast-drying soil. A promise of harvest, – and then, sheer down, the turbid water gnawing hungrily. Every now and again a splash, telling that another inch or two of solid earth had yielded. Sometimes standing on a mud-bank where the ever-watchful villagers had sown a trial crop of coarse vetch; thus, as it were, casting their bread on the water in hopes of finding it again some day. But when? Would it be there at harvest-time? Grey-bearded patriarchs from the village would wag their heads sagely over the problem, and younger voices protest that it was not worth while to enter such a flotsam-jetsam as a field. But the ruthless iron chain would come into requisition, and another green spot be daubed on the revenue map, for Governments ignore chance. And still the river dimpled and gurgled with inward mirth; for if it gave the vetch, had it not taken the wheat?

So from one scene of loss or gain to another, while the sun shone in the cloudless sky overhead. Past pools of shining water where red-billed cranes stood huddled up on one leg, as if they felt cold in the crisp morning air. Out on the bare stretches of sand where glittering streams and flocks of white egrets combined to form a silver embroidery on the brown expanse. Over the shallow ford where the bottle-nosed alligators slipped silently into the stream, or lay still as shadows on the sun-baked sand. Down by the big river, where the swirling water parted right and left, and where the grey-beards set their earthen pots a-swimming to decide which of the two streams would provide its strength by bearing away the greater number, – a weighty question, not lightly to be decided, since the land to the west of the big stream belonged to one village, and the land eastward to another. Back again to higher ground through thickets of tamarisk dripping with dew. The bushes sparse below with their thin brown stems, so thick above where the feathery pink-spiked branches interlaced. Riding through it, the hands had to defend the face from the sharp switch of the rosy flowers as they swung back disentangled; such tiny flowers, too, no bigger than a mustard seed, and leaving a pink powder of pollen behind them.

It was after forcing my way through one of these tamarisk jungles that I came out on an open patch of rudely ploughed land, where a mixed crop of pulse and barley grew sturdily, outlining an irregular oval with a pale green carpet glistening with dew. In the centre a shallow pool of water still testified to past floods, and from it a purple heron winged its flight, lazily craning its painted neck against the sky.

The whole *posse comitatus* of the village following me broke by twos and threes through the jungle, and gathered round me as I paused watching the bird's flight.

'Take the bridle from his honour's pony,' cried a venerable pantaloon breathlessly. 'Let the steed of the Lord of the Universe eat his fill. Is not this the field of Lâl?'

Twenty hands stretched out to do the old head-man's bidding; twenty voices re-echoed the sentiment in varying words. A minute more, and my pony's nose was well down on the wet, sweet tufts of vetch, and I was asking for the first time, 'Who is Lâl?'

Lâl, came the answer, why, Lâl was – Lâl. This was his field. Why should not the pony of the Protector of the Poor have a bellyful? Was it not more honourable than the parrot people and the squirrel people and the pig people who battened on the field of Lâl?

It was early days yet for the flocks of green parrots to frequent the crops, and the dainty squirrels were, I knew, still snugly abed waiting for the sun to dry the dew; but at my feet sundry furrows and scratches told that the pig had already been at work.

'Is Lâl here?' I asked.

A smile, such as greets a child's innocent ignorance, came to the good-humoured faces around me.

Lâl, they explained, came when the crop was ripe, when the parrot, the squirrel, and the pig people – and his honour's pony too – had had their fill. Lâl was a good man, one who walked straight, and laboured truly.

'But where is he?' I insisted.

Face looked at face half puzzled, half amused. Who could tell where Lâl was? He might be miles away, or in the next jungle. Some one had seen him at Sukkhur a week agone, but that was no reason why he should not be at Bhukkur now, for Lâl followed the river, and like it was here to-day, gone to-morrow.

Baulked in my curiosity, I took refuge in business by inquiring what revenue Lâl paid on his field. This was too much for the polite gravity of my hearers. The idea of Lâl's paying revenue was evidently irresistibly comic, and the venerable pantaloon actually choked himself between a cough and a laugh, requiring to be held up and patted on the back.

'But some one must pay the revenue,' I remarked a little testily.

Certainly! the Lord of the Universe was right. The village community paid it. It was the village which lent Lâl the field, and the bullocks, and the plough. It was the village which gave him the few handfuls of seed-grain to scatter broadcast over the roughly-tilled soil. So much they lent to Lâl. The sun and the good God gave him the rest. All, that is to say, that was not wanted for the parrot, the pig, and the squirrel people, and, of course, for the pony of the Lord of the Universe.

There are so many mysteries in Indian peasant life, safe hidden from alien eyes, that I was lazily content to let Lâl and his field slip into limbo of things not thoroughly understood, and so, ere long, I forgot all about him. Spring passed ripening the crops; summer came bringing fresh floods to the river; and autumn watched the earth once more make way against the water; but Lâl was to me as though he had not been.

It was only when another year found me once more in the strange land which lies, as the natives say, 'in the stomach of the river,' that memory awoke with the words, 'This is the field of Lâl.' There was, however, no suggestion made about loosening my pony's bridle as on the former occasion, the reason for such reticence being palpable. Lâl had either been less fortunate in his original choice of a field this year, or else the sun and the good God had been less diligent care-takers. A large portion of the land, too, bore marks of an over-recent flood in a thick deposit of fine glistening white sand. A favourite trick of the mischievous Indus, by which she disappoints hope raised by previous gifts of rich alluvial soil – a trick which has given her a bad name, the worst a woman can bear, because she gives and destroys with one hand. Here and there, in patches, the sparse crop showed green; but for the most part the ground lay bare, cracking into large fissures under the noonday sun, and peeling at the top into shiny brown scales.

'A bad look-out for Lâl,' I remarked.

Bad, they said, for the squirrel people and the parrot people, no doubt; but for Lâl – that was another matter. Lâl did not live by bread alone. The river gave, the river took away; but to Lâl at any rate it gave more than it stole.

'What does it give?' I asked.

It gave crocodiles. Of all things in the world crocodiles! Not a welcome gift to many, but Lâl, it seemed, was a hunter of crocodiles. Not a mere slayer of alligators, like the men of the half-savage tribes who frequent the river land; who array themselves in a plethora of blue beads, and live by the creeks and *jheels* on what they can catch or steal; who track the cumbersome beasts to their nightly lair in some narrow inlet, and, after barring escape by a stealthy earthwork, fall on the helpless creature at dawn with spears and arrows. Lâl was not of these; he was of another temper. He hunted the crocodile in its native element, stalked it through the quicksands, knife in hand, dived with it into the swift stream, sped like a fish to the soft belly beneath, and struck upwards with unerring hand, once, twice, thrice, while the turbid orange water glowed crimson with the spouting blood.

I heard this tale curiously, but incredulously. Why, I asked, should Lâl run such risks? What good were crocodiles to him when they were slain? There was not so much risk, after all, they replied, for it was only the bottle-nosed ones that he hunted, and though, of course, the snub-nosed ones lived in the river also – God destroy the horrid monsters! – still they did not interfere in the fight. And Lâl was careful, all the more careful because he had but two possessions to guard, his skin and his knife. As to what Lâl did with the crocodiles, why, he ate them, of course. Not all; he spared some for his friends, for those who were good to him, and gave him something in return. Had the Presence never heard that the poor ate crocodile flesh? They themselves, of course, did not touch the unclean animal; and their gifts to Lâl were purely disinterested. He was a straight-walking, a labourful man, and that was the only reason why they lent him a field. Even the Presence would acknowledge that crocodile flesh without bread would be uninteresting diet; but as a rule the pig, the parrots, the squirrels left enough for Lâl to eat with his jerked meat. The village lent him the sickle, of course, and the flail, and the mill, sometimes even the girdle on which to bake the unleavened bread; but all for love, only for love. Yet if the Presence desired it they could show him the jerked meat, some that Lâl had left for the poor. It was dry? Oh yes! Lâl cut the great beasts into strips, and laid them in the sun on the dry sand, sitting beside them to scare away the carrion birds. Sometimes there would be a crowd of vultures, and Lâl with his knife sitting in the midst. 'He will have to sell some of his jerked crocodile to pay his revenue this year,' I remarked, just to amuse them. Again the idea was comic; evidently Lâl and money were incompatible, and the very idea of his owning any caused them to chuckle unrestrainedly amongst themselves. Then, growing grave, they explained at length how Lâl had nothing in the world but his knife. All the rest – the sun, the river, the crocodiles, the field, the bullocks, the plough, and the seed-grain – were lent to him by them and the good God; lent to him and to the other people who ate of the field of Lâl.

As I rode away a brace of black partridges rose from one of the green patches, and close to the tamarisk shelter a brown rat sat balancing a half-dried stalk of barley. The river gleamed in the distance, a wedge-shaped flight of *coolin* cleft the sky. All that day, when the shadow-like crocodiles slipped into the sliding water, I thought of Lâl and his knife. Was it a crocodile, after all; or was it a man, stealthy, swift, and silent? Who could tell, when there was nothing but a shadow, a slip, and then a few air bubbles on the sliding river? Or was that Lâl yonder where the vultures ringed a sandbank far on the western side? Why not? None knew whence he came or whither he went, what he hoped, or what he feared; only his field bare witness to one human frailty – hunger; and that he shared with the pig and the parrot and the squirrel people. But though my thoughts were full of Lâl for a day or two, the memory of him passed as I left the river land, and once more spring, summer, and autumn brought forgetfulness.

There were busy times for all the revenue officers next year. The fitful river had chosen to desert its eastern bank altogether, and concentrate its force upon the western; so while yard after yard of ancestral land was giving way before the fierce stream, amidst much wringing of hands on the one side, there was joy on the other over long rich stretches ready for the plough and the red tape of measurement. In the press of work even the sight of the river land failed to awake any memory of Lâl. It was not until I was re-entering the outskirts of the village at sundown that something jogged my brain, making me turn to the *posse comitatus* behind me and ask, –

'And where, this year, is the field of Lâl?'

We were passing over an open space baked almost to whiteness by the constant sun, – a hard resonant place set round with gnarled *jhand* trees, and dotted over with innumerable little mud mounds.

'There,' wheezed the venerable pantaloon, pressing forward and pointing to one newer than the rest. 'That is the field of Lâl.'

Then I saw that we were in the village burial-ground. I looked up inquiringly.

'*Huzoor!*' repeated a younger man, 'that is Lâl's field. It is his own this time; but for all that the Sirkâr will not charge him revenue.' The grim joke, and the idea of Lâl's having six feet of earth of his own at last, once more roused their sense of humour.

'And the other people who ate of the field of Lâl?' I asked, half in earnest, for somehow my heart was sad.

'The good God will look after them, as He has after the crocodiles.'

Since then, strangely enough, the memory of Lâl has remained with me, and I often ask myself if he really existed, and if he really died. Does he still slip silently into the stream, knife in hand? Does he still come back to his field under the broad harvest moon, to glean his scanty share after the other people have had their fill? I cannot say; but whenever I see a particularly fat squirrel I say to myself, 'It has been feeding in the field of Lâl.'

FLORA ANNIE STEEL

Heera Nund

He stood in the verandah, salaaming with both hands, in each of which he held a bouquet – round-topped, compressed, prim little posies, with fat bundles of stalk bound spirally with date-fibre; altogether more like ninepins than bouquets, for the time of flowers was not yet, and only a few ill-conditioned rosebuds, suggestive of worms, and a dejected *champak* or two, showed amongst the green.

The holder was hardly more decorative than the posies. Bandy, hairy brown legs, with toes set wide open by big brass rings, – a sight bringing discomfort within one's own slippers from sheer sympathy; a squat body, tightly buttoned into a sleeveless white coat; a face of mild ugliness overshadowed by an immaculately white turban. From the coral and gold necklace round his thick throat, and the crescent-shaped ear-rings in his spreading ears, I guessed him to be of the Arain caste. He was, in fact, Heera Nund, gardener to my new landlord; therefore, for the present, my servant. Had I inquired into the matter, I should probably have found that his forebears had cultivated the surrounding land for centuries; certainly long years before masterful men from the West had jotted down their trivial boundary pillars to divide light from darkness, the black man from the white, cantonments from the rest of God's earth. One of these little white pillars stood in a corner of my garden, and beyond it lay an illimitable stretch of bare brown plain, waiting till the young wheat came to clothe its nakedness.

I did not inquire, however; few people do in India.

Perhaps they are intimidated by the extreme antiquity of all things, and dread letting loose the floodgates of garrulous memory. Be that as it may, I was content to accept the fact that Heera Nund, whether representing ancestral proprietors or not, had come to congratulate me, a stranger, on having taken, not only the house, but the garden also. The Sahibs, he said, went home so often nowadays that they had ceased to care for gardens. This one having been in a contractor's hands for years had become, as it were, a miserable low-degree native place. In fact, he had found it necessary to steep his own knowledge in oblivion in order that content should grow side by side with country vegetables. Yet he had not forgotten the golden age, when, under the aegis of some judge with a mysterious name, he, too, Heera Nund the Arain, had raised celery and beetroot, French beans and artichokes, asparagus and parsley. He reeled off the English names with a glibness and inaccuracy in which, somehow, there lurked a pathetic dignity. Then suddenly, from behind a favouring pillar, he sprung upon me the usual native offering, consisting of a flat basket decorated with a few coarse vegetables. A bunch of rank-smelling turnips, half-a-dozen blue radishes running two to the pound, various heaps of native greens, a bit off an overblown cauliflower proclaiming its bazaar origin by the turmeric powder adhering to it in patches, a leaf-cup of mint ornamented by two glowing chillies. He laid the whole at my feet with a profound obeisance. 'This dust-like offering,' he said gravely, 'is all that the good God [*Khuda*] can give to the Sahib. Let the Presence [*Huzoor*] wait a few months and see what Heera Nund can do for him.'

I shall not soon forget the ludicrous solemnity of voice and gesture, or the simple self-importance, overlaying the ugly face with the smile of a cat licking cream.

I did not see him again for some days, for accession to a

new office curtails leisure. When, however, I found time for a stroll round my new domain I discovered Heera Nund hard at work. His coatee hung on a bush; his bare, brown back glistened in the sunshine as he stooped down to deepen a watercourse with his adze-like shovel. A brake of sugar-cane, red-brown and gold, showed where the garden proper merged into the peasants' land beyond; for the well, whence the water came that flowed round Heera Nund's hidden feet as he stood in the runnel, irrigated quite a large stretch of the fields around my holding. The well-wheel creaked in recurring discords, every now and again giving out a note or two as if it were going to begin a tune. The red evening sun shone through the mango-trees, where the green parrots hung like unripe fruit. The bullocks circled round and round; the water dripped and gurgled.

'How about the seeds I sent you?' I asked, when Heera Nund drew his wet feet from the stream, and composing himself for the effort, produced an elaborate *salaam*.

He left humility behind him as he stalked over to a narrow strip of ground on the other side of the well, a long strip portioned out into squares and circles like a doll's garden, with tiny one-span walks between.

'Behold!' he said, 'his Honour will observe that the cabbage caste have life already.'

Truly enough the half-covered seeds showed gussets of white in their brown jackets. 'But where are the tickets? I sent word specially that you were to be sure and stick the labels on each bed. How am I to know which is which?'

'The Presence can see that the sticks are there,' he answered with a superior smile; 'but there are others beside the Sahibs who love tickets.'

He pointed to the tree above us, where on a branch sat a peculiarly bushy-tailed squirrel, as happy as a king over the brussels-sprouts' wrapper, which he was crumpling into a ball with deft hands and sharp teeth. How I came to know it was this particular wrapper happened thus: I threw my cap at the offender, and in his flight he dropped the paper on my bald head; it was hard, and had points.

'They are misbegotten devils,' remarked Heera cheerfully; 'but they are building nests, Sahib, and like to paper the inside. Notwithstanding, the Presence need fear no confusion; his slave has many names in his head. This is *arly walkrin* [Early Walcheren], that is *droomade* [Drumhead], yonder is *dookoyark* [Duke of York], and that, that, and that – ' He would have gone on interminably, had I not changed the subject by asking what was growing beneath a dilapidated hand-light, which stood next to a sturdy crop of broad-cast radishes. Only a few panes of glass remained intact, but the vacancies had been neatly supplied by coarse muslin. The gardener's face, always simple in expression, became quite homogeneous with pure content.

'*Huzoor!* It is the *mâlin*.'

'The *mâlin*! What on earth do you mean?'

Have you ever watched the face of a general servant when she takes the covers off the Christmas dinner? Have you ever seen a very young conjurer lift his father's hat to show you that the handkerchief (which he has palpably secreted elsewhere) is no longer in its legitimate hiding-place? Something of that mingled triumph and fear lest some accident may have befallen skill in the interim showed itself in Heera Nund's countenance as he removed the light with a flourish, thus disclosing to view a fat and remarkably black baby asleep on a bed of leaves. It was attired in a pair of silver bangles, and a Maw's feeding-bottle grew, like some new kind of root-crop, from the ground beside it.

'My daughter, *Huzoor* – little Dhropudi the *mâlin*.'

His voice thrilled even my bachelor ears as he squatted

down and began mechanically to fan the swift-gathering flies from the sleeping child.

'You seem to be very fond of her,' I remarked after a pause. 'It is only a girl after all. Have you no son?'

He shook his head.

'She is the only one, and I waited for her ten years. Ten long years; so I was glad even to get a *mâlin*. Dhropudi grows as fast as a boy, almost as fast as the *Huzoor*'s cabbages. Only the other day she was no bigger than my hand.'

'Your wife is dead, I suppose?' The question was, perhaps, a little brutal, but it was so unusual to see a man doing dry nurse to a baby girl, that I took it for granted that the mother had died months before, at the child's birth. I never saw a face change more rapidly than his; the simplicity left it, and in place thereof came a curious anxiety such as a child might show with the dawning conviction that it has lost itself.

'She is not at all dead, *Huzoor*; on the contrary she is very young. Children cry sometimes, and my house does not like crying. You see, when people are young they require more sleep; when she is old as I am she will be able to keep awake.'

His tone was argumentative, as if he were reasoning the matter out for his own edification. 'Not that Dhropudi keeps me awake often,' he added, in hasty apology to that infant's reputation; 'considering how young a person she is, her ways are very straight-walking and meek.'

'If she cries you can always stop her with the watering-pot, I suppose.'

He looked shocked at the suggestion.

'*Huzoor!* it is not difficult to stop them; such a very little thing pleases a baby. Sometimes it is the sunshine, – sometimes it is the wind in the trees, – sometimes it is the birds, or the squirrels, or the flowers. When it is tired of these there is always the milk in its stomach. Dhropudi's goat is yonder; it lives on your Honour's weeds. You are her father and mother.'

However much I might repudiate the relationship, I soon became quite accustomed to finding Dhropudi in the most unexpected places in my garden. For, soon after my first introduction to her, the claims of an early crop of lettuces to protection from the squirrels led Heera Nund to transfer the hand-light from one of his charges to another. Dhropudi, he said, could grow nicely without it now; the black ants could not carry her off, and the squirrels had quite begun to recognize that she was of the race of Adam. At first, however, he took precautions against mistakes, and many a time I have seen the sleeping child stuck round with pea-sticks, or decorated with fluttering feathers on a string, to scare away the birds. Sometimes she was blanching with the celery, and once I nearly trod on her as she lay among the toppings in a thick plantation of blossoming beans. But she never came to harm; the only misadventure being when her father would lay her to sleep in some dry water channel, and, forgetting which one it was, turn the shallow stream that way. Then there would be a momentary outcry at the cold bath; but the next, she would be pacified with a flower, and sit in the sun to dry, for to say sooth, no more good-tempered child ever existed than Dhropudi. In this, at any rate, she was like her father, though I could trace no resemblance in other ways. 'She is like my house,' he would say, when I noticed the fact. 'She is young, and I am old, – quite old.'

Indeed, as time passed I saw that Heera Nund was older than I thought at first. Before the barber came in the morning there was quite a silver stubble on his bronze cheek, and his bright, restless eyes were haggard and anxious. Despite his almost comic jauntiness and self-importance, he struck me as having a hunted look at times, especially when he came out from the mud-walled enclosure at the further end of the garden, where his 'house' lived. He went there but seldom, spending his days in tending Dhropudi and his plants with an almost extravagant devotion. His state of mind when that young lady used her new accomplishment of crawling, to the detriment of a bed of *sootullians* (Sweet Williams) in which he took special pride, was quite pathetic. I found him simply howling between regret for the plants and fear lest I should order punishment to the offender. His gratitude when I laughed was unbounded.

After this Dhropudi used to be set in a twelve-inch pot, half sunk in the ground, where she would stay contentedly for hours, drumming the sides with a carrot, while Heera weeded and dibbled.

'She grows,' he would say, snatching her up fiercely in his arms; 'she grows as all my plants grow. See my *sootullians*! They will blossom soon, and then all the Sahibs will come and say, "See the *sootullians* which Heera Nund and Dhropudi have grown for the *Huzoor*."'

Yet with all this blazoning of content the man was curiously restless – almost like a child in his desire for action and vivid interest in trivialities. 'See the misbegotten creature I have found eating the honourable *Huzoor*'s roots!' he would say, casting a wire-worm on the verandah steps, and dancing on it vindictively. 'It was in the *Huzoor*'s carnations, but by the blessing of God and Heera Nund's vigilance it is dead. Nothing escapes me. Have I not fought wire-worms since the beginning of all things, I and my fathers? We kill all creeping, crawling things, except the holy snake that brings fruit and blossom to the garden.'

One night I was disturbed by unseemly noises, coming

apparently from the servants' quarters; but my remonstrances next morning were met, by my bearer, with swift denial. 'It is Heera. He, poor man, has to beat his wife almost every night now. I wonder the Presence has not heard her before; she screams very loud.'

I stood aghast.

'He should let her go, or kill her,' continued the bearer placidly. 'She is not worth the trouble of beating; but he is a fool, because she is Dhropudi's mother. Yes, he is a fool; he beats her when he finds her lover there. He should beat her well before the man comes. That is the best way with women.'

It was an old story, it seemed, dating before Dhropudi's appearance on the scene. It occurred to me that perhaps a deeper tragedy than I had thought for was ripening in my garden among the ripening plants. I found myself watching Dhropudi and her father with an almost morbid interest, and hoping that, if my idle suspicion was right, kindly fate might hide the truth away for ever in the bottom of that well where Heera often held the child to smile at her own reflection, far down where the water showed like a huge round dewdrop.

So time went on, until the *sootullians* showed blossom buds, and Dhropudi cut her first tooth on one and the same day. Perhaps the excitement of the double event was too much for Heera's nerves; perhaps what happened was due anyhow; but as I strolled through the garden that evening at sundown I saw the most comically pathetic sight my eyes ever beheld. Heera Nund, clothed, but not in his right mind, was dancing a *can-can* among his *sootullians*, while Dhropudi shrieked with delight and beat frantically on her flower-pot. Even with the knowledge of all that came after, the remembrance provokes a smile. The rhythmic bobbing up and down of the uncouth figure, the cow-like kicks of the bandy legs, the preternaturally grave face above, the crushed *sootullians* below.

I sent him in charge of two sepoys to the Dispensary, and there he remained for two months, more or less. When he came back he was very quiet, very thin, and there were the marks of several blisters on the back of his head. He resumed work cheerfully, with many apologies for having been ill, and once more he and Dhropudi – who had been handed over meantime, under police supervision, to her mother – were to be found spending their days together in amicable companionship. His only regrets being, apparently, that the *sootullians* had blossomed and Dhropudi learnt to walk in his absence.

But for one or two little eccentricities I might have been tempted to forget that *can-can* among the flowers; indeed, I always met his inquiries as to the *sootullians* with the remark that they had done as well as could be expected in the circumstances. The eccentricities, however, if few, were striking. One was his exaggerated gratitude for the blisters on the back of his head; the last thing in the world one would have thought likely to produce an outburst of that Christian virtue. But it did, and an allusion to the all too visible scars invariably crowned the frequent recital of the benefits he had received at my hands. Another was the difficulty he had in distinguishing Dhropudi from the other fruits of his labour. On two separate occasions she formed part of the daily basket of vegetables which he brought in to me, and very quaint the little black morsel looked sitting surrounded by tomatoes and melons. But though he treated the matter as an elaborate joke when I remarked on it, there was a dazed, uncertain look in his eyes as if he were not quite sure as to the right end of the stick.

Nevertheless peace and contentment reigned apparently in his house. When I sat out in the dark, hot evenings, a glow of flickering firelight from within showed the mysterious mud-walled enclosure by the wall, decorous and conventional. The winking stars looking down into it knew more of the life within than I did, but at any rate no unseemly cries disturbed the scented night air and the *Huzoor*'s slumbers. Perhaps the police supervision had impressed the lover with the dangers of lurking house-trespass by night; perhaps the dark-browed, heavy-jowled young woman who had taken my warning so sullenly had learnt more craft; perhaps the languor which creeps over all things in May had sucked the vigour even from passion. Who could say? Those crumbling mud walls hid it all, and Heera seemed to have begun a new life with the hot-weather vegetables.

So matters stood when an old enemy laid hold of me. Ten days after I found myself racing Death with a determination to reach the sea, and feel the salt west wind on my face before he and I closed with each other. The strange hurry and eagerness of it all come back to some of us like a nightmare, years after the exile is over. The doctor's verdict, the swift packing of a trunk or two, the hope, the fear, the mad longing at least to see the dear faces once more.

They packed me and a half-hundred pillows into a *palki ghâri* one afternoon. The servants stood, white clad, in a row beside the white pillars, dazzling in the slanting sunlight. I drove through the flower garden dusty and scorched. At the gate stood Heera Nund, one arm occupied by Dhropudi, the other supporting a huge basket of vegetables. He looked uncertain which to present; finally, seeing the carriage drive on, he deliberately let the basket fall, and running to my side, thrust the child's chubby hands forward. They held just such ninepin bouquets as he had carried on our first introduction. 'Take them, Sahib!'

he cried. 'Take them for luck! and come back soon to the *mâli* and the *mâlin*.' As the *ghâri* turned sharp down the road I saw him standing amidst the ruins of the basket with Dhropudi in his arms.

Six months passed before I set foot on Indian soil again, and then fate and a restless Government sent me to a new station. When my servants arrived with my baggage from the old one, I naturally fell to asking questions. 'And how is Heera Nund?' was one. My bearer smiled benignly. '*Huzoor*, he is well, – in the month of July he was hanged.'

'Bearer!'

'Without doubt; it was in the month of July. He killed his wife with an axe. Dhropudi was bitten by a snake while she slept one day when Heera had to leave her with her mother; and that night he killed his wife as *she* slept also. It was a mistake to be so revengeful, for every one knew Dhropudi was not really his daughter.'

'Do you think that Heera knew?'

'She told him when the child died, in order to stop his grief; but it did not. She was very kind to him, – after the other one went to prison for lurking about.'

'And did no one tell about it all?'

'About what, *Huzoor*?'

'About the vegetables, and Dhropudi, and the *sootullians*, and the blisters on the back of his head! Did no one say the man was mad?'

'There was a new assistant at the Dispensary, Sahib, and her people were very rich; besides, Heera was not mad at all. He did it on purpose. He was a bad man, and the Sirkâr did right to hang him, – in July.'

But as I turned away I could think of nothing but that *can-can* among the *sootullians*, with little Dhropudi beating time with a carrot.

ALICE PERRIN

The White Tiger

He was called the White Tiger by the villagers of the district because his yellow skin was pale with age, and his stripes so faded and far apart as to be almost invisible.

Having grown too large and heavy for cattle killing with any ease, he had lately become a man-eater, and terrible were the stories told by those who had seen him, and escaped the fatal blow of his huge paw. He was described as being the size of a bull-buffalo, with a belly that reached the ground, and a white moon between his ears, true tokens of the man-eater, as every native of India knows. He was said to have the power of assuming different shapes, and to lure his prey by the imitation of a human voice, and certainly his craft and cunning were such that not even Mar Singh, the local *shikaree*, had ever been able to trap him, or obtain a shot at him with his famous match-lock gun. And Mar Singh had seen the tiger often, knew his favourite haunts and lairs, and could point out the very trees upon which he preferred to sharpen his murderous claws.

The brute continued to levy his terrible tax on the scanty population of a remote district, until the women and children were afraid to leave the village, and the men went out to work in the fields fearing for their lives. At last the increasing number of victims attracted the attention of the local authorities, and a reward of a hundred rupees was placed on the head of the White Tiger, with the result that Mar Singh, who clothed himself in khaki with a disreputable turban to match, and was regarded in his village as the wariest of hunters, redoubled his efforts to bring about the destruction of this awful scourge. Also, now that the fame of the White Tiger's misdeeds had penetrated to headquarters, it was more than likely that a party of 'sahibs' would appear on the scene with elephants and rifles, in which case, though the tiger would be doomed, the reward would be distributed amongst the mahouts and the beaters, and Mar Singh himself would only receive a share.

So night after night he perched in the branches of the trees above the favourite routes of the enemy, and from sunrise to sunset he haunted the outskirts of the jungle, and hung about the drinking pools in the bed of the shrinking river, for (unlike his cattle and game-killing brothers) the man-eater may be sought for at all hours. But to no purpose, the White Tiger seized a plump human victim once every few days, and Mar Singh's vision of the reward grew faint.

'The striped-one is surely an evil spirit, and no beast at all!' said Mar Singh, who never uttered the word tiger if he could help it, for fear of ill-luck.

He had come in weary and crestfallen from a long day's search, having actually caught a glimpse of the White Tiger, and followed the tracks of the huge, square pugs to the edge of a thorny thicket, without the chance of a shot that could have taken effect; and he was pouring out his irritation and disgust to Kowta, his half-brother, who sat at the door of the family hovel contentedly smoking a hookah.

'Without doubt,' agreed Kowta, 'and therefore would it not be wiser to let the sahib slay the Evil One if he be able?'

'What sahib?' asked Mar Singh sharply, pausing in the act of cleaning the precious match-lock gun, which was the envy and admiration of the village.

'Then thou hast not heard the news?' said Kowta,

innocently. 'A sahib has pitched his camp within one day's march of the village, and they say he has come to hunt the White Devil.'

The dreaded blow had fallen, and Mar Singh danced with rage.

'I will give him no news of the tiger. I will tell him nothing, and see, too, that thou remainest silent, Kowta, when he sends for information, else will it be the worse for thee!'

Kowta twiddled his big toe in the dust, always a sign of hesitation with a native, and Mar Singh scented trouble. He knew that Kowta was heavily in debt to the village usurer, and that sahibs often paid well for news of a tiger's movements. He was also aware that Kowta was jealous of his standing and reputation in the village, which would be increased ten-fold could he but destroy the tiger and earn the magnificent reward.

He changed his tone.

'See, brother,' he began insinuatingly, 'the utmost that the sahib would give thee might, perchance, be ten rupees, and thy share of the Government reward would scarcely be more than two. What are twelve rupees compared with forty, added to half the whiskers and claws of the Evil One, and perhaps the lucky bone as well? All this will I give thee when I slay the beast, as I most assuredly must do if the sahib doth not interfere.'

Kowta puffed stolidly at his hookah and was maddeningly silent.

'Also,' continued Mar Singh, eagerly, 'consider the trouble that a sahib's camp brings upon a village. His servants, being rascals, will order supplies in the name of the sahib, and pay us nothing for them, and the police will annoy us if we complain. We shall be forced to beat the jungle, and many will be hurt and some killed, if not by the tiger then by other wild beasts, also – '

'But,' interrupted Kowta, cautiously, 'how can I tell that thou wilt give me the forty rupees and half the claws and whiskers? Whereas, a sahib holds to his promises, as we all know.'

'I swear it!' cried Mar Singh with fervour, 'by the skin of the White Devil I swear to deal well by thee!'

So, after some further argument, Kowta reluctantly agreed to take his brother's side, and Mar Singh unfolded a scheme by which Kowta was to proceed to the tents of the unwelcome Englishman, and pose as the *shikaree* of the district possessing an intimate knowledge of the tiger's habits. Mar Singh would keep Kowta well informed as to the movements of the tiger through the medium of the postman who ran from village to village with news and letters, and the sahib, at all hazards, was to be led in the wrong directions, until he grew weary of the fruitless chase, and withdrew from the district with his camp and elephants.

Kowta, therefore, proceeded to don the khaki costume, which he had long coveted, and the next morning he started on his diplomatic errand, while Mar Singh betook himself to the jungle to watch the movements of the White Tiger, that he might warn Kowta by the evening runner as to which locality must be avoided the following day.

Kowta enjoyed himself immensely at the camp. He arrived at sundown, and was interviewed by the sahib himself, to whom he gave voluble, but entirely false, information concerning the tiger, and promised to lead him direct to the animal's lair in the morning. The sahib, being young and new to the country, retired to bed in happy anticipation, and Kowta repaired to the kitchen tent, where, surrounded by the servants, he sat smoking his hookah and relating blood-curdling tales of the doings of the White Tiger.

Natives seldom sleep till far on in the night, and therefore the gathering was at its height when the jingle of bells told of the postman's approach, and Kowta, explaining to the company that he was expecting news of his dying grandmother, went out into the moonlight to meet him. The chink-chink of the bunch of bells grew louder, and mingled with the regular grunts of the runner, and Kowta, stepping forward into the sandy path, checked the man's rapid trot.

'Oh! brother!' he saluted, 'what word from Mar Singh, *shikaree*?'

'Kowta, there is no word from the mouth of Mar Singh, thy brother, seeing that but an hour after thy departure he was slain by the White Tiger on the outskirts of the grazing plain, and Merijhan, the cow-herd, saw it happen. I bring the evil news to thee fresh from thy village.'

For a moment Kowta was paralysed by the horror of the dreadful and unexpected news. Then he asked quesions, and learned that his brother's body had been recovered by a party of villagers who had sallied forth with drums and fire-works and had driven the beast from its prey. The mangled remains now lay in the family hut, and Kowta's presence was required to make arrangements for the funeral.

Kowta slipped some coppers into the postman's willing hand, and charged him to keep silence as to the catastrophe when delivering letters in the camp. Then he collected his belongings, and left a plausible message for the sahib to say he had been summoned to his grandmother's deathbed, but would return with all haste the following day. He set out in the moonlight along the narrow jungle path, bordered by tall grass higher than his head, and walked rapidly, though the heat was overpowering, until, just as the dawn broke, he came within sight of the village. He strode through the fields of tobacco and young wheat, and saw the bright green parrots flashing to and fro in the vivid yellow light; partridges ran from beneath his feet, calling shrilly as they disappeared behind the clumps of dry grass; and he could hear the jungle fowl in the distance crowing to the rising sun. Everything was awake and glowing with life, and the dark interior of the hut, where the women were wailing and the atmosphere seemed charged with death, formed a sharp contrast to the outside world.

The mangled body of the dead man, torn and chewed by the tiger, lay on the string bedstead, surrounded by a noisy group of mourning relatives. There was nothing for Kowta to do but arrange for the remains to be taken to the burning-ground in the evening, and to attempt to pacify the wailing throng, until, as the fierce, hot noon came on they gradually dispersed, and even the widow of the dead man sought a siesta in a neighbour's hut, while Kowta sat down on the threshold of his home to think.

An idea had been slowly forming in his brain which brought with it a wave of exultation. Why should not *he* compass the destruction of the White Tiger, and so earn the whole reward? He was in debt to the money-lender, and he also greatly desired a plot of land that was for sale just outside the village, and the hundred rupees would not only free him from debt, but would also purchase the coveted little piece of ground. It was true that Mar Singh himself had never succeeded in shooting the White Tiger, but then his difficulty had always been the want of suitable bait, whereas *now*, – Kowta glanced back into the shadow of the hut and shivered, remembering the native belief that the soul of the tiger's victim becomes the servant of the slayer, and is bound to warn the master when danger threatens.

Mar Singh's spirit might or might not be in bondage to the White Tiger, but, in any case, the hundred rupees was worth some risk, and with proper precautions there should be little or no danger, seeing that the match-lock gun had been recovered uninjured. Kowta rose and looked up and down the little village street. Not a breeze stirred the giant leaves of the plantain trees, not a bird uttered a note, not a voice broke the breathless calm, every creature except himself was wrapped in slumber.

He made up his mind. He would attempt the plan, and afterwards, whether he succeeded or failed, he could deny all knowledge of the disappearance of his brother's body, and encourage the suggestion, which would naturally arise, that the sorcery of the White Tiger had spirited the corpse away. So he gathered the wreck of Mar Singh into a bundle, wrapping it in his own white cotton waist-cloth, and with the loaded match-lock over his shoulder, went swiftly through the sleeping village and out into the fields, invoking on his errand the blessing of Durga, the goddess who rides the tiger. Thence he took a narrow jungle path with tangled shrubs closing over his head, and as he emerged from this on to the bushy, broken ground leading to the river, he gathered a leaf from the nearest tree and muttered, –

'As thy life has departed, so may the striped-one die.'

He walked up the pebbly bed of the dwindling stream till he reached a pool of clear water, in the wet margin of which were printed countless tracks of animals that had drunk there during the night. Wild pig, jackal, fox, hyena, deer, all had slaked their thirst, but the White Tiger had not been of the company. A hundred yards off lay another pool, and around it Kowta found a solitary track – the big, square pugs of the beast who, by common consent of the other jungle inhabitants, had been given a wide berth, and allowed to drink alone.

The marks were not more than a few hours old, and Kowta followed them cautiously, grasping the gun, and dragging his other burden behind him along the gravelly sand. The footprints led him to some rocky boulders, on the summit of which a family of monkeys sat peacefully hunting for fleas, a sign that the tiger was not on the move, else would they have been crashing and chattering in the nearest trees, and pouring forth torrents of abuse. The pugs led on round the rocks to a shady thicket of thorn bushes in a deep ravine, and Kowta felt that he had tracked the White Tiger to his lair.

He laid his brother's body close to the edge of the thorny thicket, and then cast about for a safe retreat within easy shot, but no climbable trees were at hand, the cover consisting of low, scrubby bushes. The only suitable place of concealment seemed to be the nearest rock, behind which it would be easy to hide and yet command a good view of the bait.

The odour of the dead body tainted the air as the sun blazed full upon it, which suited Kowta's purpose well, for tigers prefer their food as carrion, and hunger would soon bring the beast forth. Kowta lay down behind the rock and waited. A hot, high wind was blowing, and the sand from the river bed, getting into his eyes, made them smart, but he paid no heed to the discomfort, and only watched the thicket intently for the least movement.

He held his breath when, presently, something rustled and crept out – merely a mangy little jackal with loosely-hanging brush, who sprang four feet into the air as he came suddenly on Mar Singh's body. Then the animal uttered the long, miserable wail known as the 'pheeaow cry,' and ran back into the thicket, causing Kowta's heart to beat high with hope, for he knew the jackal was a 'provider,' one that gives notice to the tiger when food is to be found.

Now, without doubt, the Evil One would steal forth, and nothing could then prevent a shot at such close quarters taking effect. A pea-fowl screeched wildly, and Kowta could hear the agitated flapping of its wings, that also was a token that the tiger moved. The monkeys set up a chatter and scuttled from the rocks. He was coming – the White Devil, the evil striped-one!

Kowta waited breathless, his pulses throbbing in his ears, thinking of the hundred rupees and the plot of ground that were now almost his own, and gazing fixedly over the sickening, twisted limbs of the mutilated body only a few yards from him.

The tension was terrible, and the cracking of a dry twig behind him sounded almost like the report of a gun, he felt a surging in his brain, and, as another stick snapped, some irresistible power compelled him to turn his head.

There, five yards behind him, crouched the White Tiger, that with silent steps and awful cunning had stalked him from the village. The ears were flattened to the broad head, the long white whiskers bristled and quivered, the wicked yellow eyes glared, and held the man helpless, spell-bound with horror, waiting for the spring that came with a hissing, growling roar, as the White Tiger claimed yet another victim.

ALICE PERRIN
Justice

The long day's work in field and jungle was over, the sunset meal had been prepared and eaten, and the dusty little Indian village lay quiet save for a monotonous murmur of voices, and the lowing of cattle penned into safety for the night. Light wreaths of smoke from fires that had cooked the rice and chupattis hung to the mud walls, twined among the branches of the old pipal tree, and mingled with the pungent fumes of the hookah that was being passed around the group of villagers squatted about the giant roots.

To-day this jungle hamlet, that lay far from the life of great cities and populous districts, had been stirred to intense excitement by the rare visit of an English official, whose camp now gleamed white in the mango-grove half a mile away. The head-man and elders of the village had spent busy hours in front of the great square tent wherein the magistrate had sat and received their petitions, examined accounts, listened to complaints, and administered justice.

Now the evening talk over the evening hookah on the spot that constituted the public meeting-place, club-house, and council-chamber of the village, was of the sahib and his curious habits, his strange clothing, the furniture in the tent, his judgments and decisions, and the offensiveness of his swaggering Mahomedan butler, who had demanded eggs and milk for his master's table.

Abstract questions concerning the white people were also earnestly discussed, such as how far the theory was correct that poison lay under their nails, which compelled them to eat with knives and forks instead of with their fingers like reasonable beings. Also whether the existence of 'the Momiai-walla Sahib' was an actual fact – that dreaded Government official whose reputed duty it was to obtain plump native victims for the purpose of distilling from their brains the magic essence known as 'Momiai,' which is said to heal all injuries.

'Truly the ways of the English are beyond comprehension,' said the head-man conclusively; 'did'st remark how the sahib entered his camp on foot this morning, having his horse led after him? Who but an Englishman would walk when he might ride?'

He offered the hookah politely to a very old man who sat huddled beside him, wrapped in a grimy cotton sheet, and having a mummy's withered shrunken visage, though the black eyes that twinkled deep in the shrivelled face were very much alive.

'Thou, Narain Singh,' continued the head-man to him courteously, 'hast lived longer and must therefore have seen more of the sahib-people and their customs than any of us here. What thinkest thou of their rule, and their manner of distributing justice?'

That morning Narain Singh, the patriarch, had travelled many miles across country from his village, on a pony that was little more than a foal, for the purpose of interviewing the Government representative concerning a question of land assessment that affected his little property. He had obtained audience of the sahib, attention and investigation had been promised him, and he was therefore elated in spirit, and disposed to be garrulously agreeable to his hosts. He took a bubbling pull at the hookah through his closed fist, for none of the company touched the mouth-piece directly with their lips.

'Without doubt the sahib-people mean well,' he said graciously, 'and endeavour to be just in their judgments, but "The weevil is ground up with the flour," and at times can they be stupid as owls and make big mistakes.' He paused, with effect, and the entire attention of a respectful audience became his. 'Many times have I been concerned with litigation – as witness, as defendant, as plaintiff, and again as onlooker only. And I have come to know that there is one thing which the Government with all its truth, and wisdom, and justice, can seldom understand, and that is the heart of a dark man towards an enemy!'

A murmur of interrogation went round the little circle, mingled with the gurgle of the hookah.

'Proof have I seen of this not once but often,' continued the quavering voice reminiscently. 'Dost recall the case of Mirat, son of Atchari, in my village?' turning to the head-man.

'Somewhat do I recall concerning it, though but faintly. Surely it was many years back? Was it not Mirat who slew his neighbour's mother, and so was hanged?'

The old man chuckled. 'Truly was Mirat hanged though he slew not the woman, and I alone have knowledge of the truth! Throughout the years have I kept silence, but now, brothers, if it please thee, will I tell how it came to pass that Mirat was hanged for the murder of old Bitia, mother of Mulloo, because the Sircar [Government] was unable to comprehend the feeling of the dark ones towards an enemy.'

'Speak, Father!' said the head-man, voicing the general wish.

The old man settled his back more comfortably against the trunk of the pipal tree. 'Then it happened thus. The fields of Mirat adjoined mine own fields, and I knew him well. He was young, and gay, and handsome, and thought much of himself. He found favour in the sight of the village girls – aye, and in the sight of the older women also. Many times have I beheld him coming forth early in the mornings to work on his land, driving his plough with the small white bullocks, his skin shining brown in the sun, and a yellow marigold set above his ear. And as he worked he would sing in a voice that was high, and sweet, and carried far. He was clever too with his tongue, and in the evenings when the day's work was done, and we sat beneath our village pipal tree, he would tell tales and sing songs. So the neighbours favoured him – all save one, and this was Mulloo, who hated him. And the two were enemies.

'Now Mulloo was stupid and of an evil countenance, and always had he been jealous because the village favoured Mirat, and because Mirat's fields and cattle prospered; whereas Mulloo was disliked, and season after season had his crops failed and his cattle died. Some there were who held that this bad fortune was only to be expected because Bitia, the mother of Mulloo, was a widow and, it was said, a witch also. Moreover, she had but one eye, which all know is a mark of ill-omen and will cause disaster.

'The quarrel between Mirat and Mulloo arose concerning a field that divided their dwelling-places, and which was claimed by both. First Mulloo would begin to cultivate it, and Mirat would destroy the work and commence to plough for himself. Then Mulloo would also undo the labour of Mirat and turn his cattle on to the land. Thus it went on, and nothing was permitted to flourish in the plot because of the ill-feeling between these two. When they met they would revile one another from opposite ends of the fields, but there was no fighting or beating till Mirat's best bullock fell sick, and died as though by magic. The next morning, in the village, Mirat fell upon Mulloo as one possessed of an evil spirit, and beat him sorely, crying out that Bitia, the hag, had overlooked his beast with her one eye and so caused its death – for had he not beheld her crossing his field the night before, and in an hour from then was not his bullock dead? The anger of Mirat was hot and swift, and I and others that stood by saw the fierce light of it in his eyes, and heard him swear that he would kill the old woman, and her son, and all their relations, should any of them so much as come nigh the field again. Mulloo was in fear of his life. He covered his head and ran to a place of safety, and from thence he abused his enemy with a loud voice, and took an oath to be avenged.

'But Mirat, having cooled his anger by beating Mulloo, went on his way with laughter, repeating the saying that "Though an enemy's words may be terrible, death still comes at the appointed time," and from that hour he tilled the field undisturbed in the early mornings and sowed his seed, singing of love, and battle, and riches, in his strong young voice. And Mulloo listened with a dark face behind his mud boundary wall, and whispered that his day of reckoning was yet to come. Then Mulloo brought an action against Mirat in the Civil Courts, and after many months he lost his case and was well-nigh ruined. The field was adjudged to belong to Mirat, and Mulloo hated his enemy more bitterly than before, while Mirat laughed and triumphed.

'It was at this time that I took Lachmi, the girl widow, to dwell in my house, for my wife was old, and the work of the spinning and cooking and milking was heavy. It was at the urging of Chunia, my wife, that I took to myself a younger woman to be her co-wife and helpmeet. She was a girl whose husband had died in infancy and she was young and fair, with a face like the moon at its full, and limbs that were rounded and smooth. At first was she all humility and gratitude, and she worked well and did as she was bid by my wife; and the sweetness of her warmed my heart that was growing chill, even then, with advancing years. She would laugh, and sing, and her little hands were soft to the touch, and her eyes bright and tender as a fawn's. I loved her as I had loved Chunia, my wife, in the days when she came to me as a bride.

'Ai! little did I suspect of the trick that was to be played on me by Mirat who was my neighbour – Mirat the bold, the handsome, with the ringing voice, and the fierce temper. Little did I guess of the treachery of Lachmi, when Mirat cast eyes of desire upon her; and I knew not that her caresses had grown false, or that the lips she gave me were yet hot with the kisses of her lover, until the evening when I beheld the two with mine own eyes in the mango grove, clasped in each other's arms.

'Behind the trunk of a tree did I wait and watch, and I heard their words of love, their mockery of me, the old man, and their arrangement for the next meeting, which was to be that night in the field of Mirat when all in my house should be sleeping. I waited and saw Mirat leave her with many a backward look of longing, whilst Lachmi gathered up the bundle of fodder she had been sent into the jungle to cut, and, raising it to her head, passed on alone into the open fields. I did not strike her down as she stood, I did not follow her to kill her, my wrath was no flame like that of Mirat my neighbour, but a slow, steady fire that does not die. With Lachmi I meant presently to deal as is the custom with such light women who are false to their homes. That night would I cut off her nose, so that neither Mirat nor any other man should desire to look upon her twice, and henceforth should she drudge for the household in her shame, eating the leavings of the meals, sleeping on the ground, wearing once more the coarse garments of the outcast.

'With Mirat did I plan to deal in mine own way.

And that night, when the punishment of Lachmi was accomplished, and she lay in a corner of the cow-shed bleeding and moaning, did I go forth (though somewhat weakened with the struggle, for the girl was young and strong), bearing my muzzle-loading gun, for which I held a permit from the Government so that I might protect my crops from the deer and wild pigs. The moon was rising, and in the field that had caused the enmity between Mirat and Mulloo a crop of pulse, tall and vigorous as the sower thereof, showed black and thick, save where, in the corner, a patch was left uncultivated as a refuge for the spirits. I went on to the edge of this crop where the shadow was darkest, and sat down on my heels to await the coming of Mirat, who thought to meet Lachmi in his field when all in my house should be safely sleeping. And as I sat I beheld a man who crept along the boundary wall like a wild beast that fears the hunter, bearing something in his arms. Often did he stop and look round, and I could hear his breathing. He saw me not, though he passed near to where I sat, for I was in the shadow of the pulse-crop. The man was Mulloo, and the thing that he carried in his arms was the body of old Bitia his mother, and her head hung over to one side as though she were dead.

'I watched him cross the field, stealing along the edge of the crop, and presently he stopped. I saw him push the body of Bitia, the old woman, in amongst the pulse, and then he came back like a jackal, bending low to the ground, and looking swiftly to the right and to the left. When he reached his boundary wall he climbed it as though he were pursued by a devil, and I heard his footsteps quick and short as he ran to his hut on the other side.

'I sat on, and turned over in my mind the thing that I had seen; and understanding came to me. I knew then that Mulloo had murdered his mother and placed her body in the pulse-field, that Mirat his enemy might be accused of her death and so hanged. Had we not all heard the words of Mirat when he swore he would slay Bitia, or any of the people of Mulloo who set foot upon his land? I sat and pondered, and presently, as I had expected, Mirat came forth from his dwelling-place and stood at the top of the field in the moonlight, singing softly to himself. But "Singing songs and making a bower is all unseemly without a lover": and he was waiting for Lachmi. I hid my face in my wrapper and laughed, for I knew that Lachmi was lying in the cow-shed with her beauty gone for ever, and that never more would she seek her lover in the field, or the mango-grove, or anywhere else. Whilst he stood there, singing and waiting, I crept back in the shadow of the crop to my home, knowing that I had only to keep silent for Mirat to be punished, without trouble to myself, for the injury he had wrought me, his neighbour.

'And so it happened. Old Bitia was found next morning, strangled, in the crop of pulse, and Mirat was arrested; for the field was his, and his words were remembered, and I, being called as one of the witnesses, spoke truth when I testified that Mirat had threatened to kill the old woman. Also I gave evidence that having risen on the night of the murder to scare wild pigs from my crops, had I beheld Mirat standing in the moonlight at the top of his field, near to where the body was found.

'As I spoke in the Court I met the eyes of the man who had stolen from me the love of Lachmi the widow, and he understood full well that there was more that I could tell if I would, but that I meant to keep silence: "The lizard was as wide as the snake was long!"

'His defence was that Mulloo had slain the woman and placed her body in the field to bring trouble upon him, the two being at enmity; and the district judge, who had seen much, and knew more than most *Feringhees* concerning the hearts of black people, said that it might well be. And so the case went up to the High Court, while Mirat remained in prison. The judge-sahibs of the High Court ruled that such a thing was not possible; that no man, black or white, would murder his own mother to be avenged on his neighbour, and the evidence being strong against Mirat, they sentenced him to be hanged.

'On the morning when Mirat was to die, Lachmi went forth as usual into the jungle to cut grass for the beasts, and she never returned. What became of her I know not to this day, nor did it greatly matter, for there are widows in plenty, and Chunia my wife chose another woman who was strong and faithful, but neither young nor fair.

'As for Mulloo, now that the evil influence of his mother's one eye had been removed, his crops flourished and his cattle prospered; also he purchased the field that had been Mirat's, which yielded a rich return, so that when he died, full of years, his son and his son's sons inherited wealth.

'So it is true what I have said – that there are few white men who can see into the heart of a dark man desiring to be avenged on an enemy; and that though the sahib-people mean well, and endeavour to be just and sound in their judgments, sometimes can they be stupid as owls and make mistakes. But though Mirat had not killed Bitia, the old woman, still had he tricked me, Narain Singh, his neighbour, and defiled the honour of my house; and "It is sin whether you steal oil or sugar." Therefore, to my mind, was he deservedly punished – and without further trouble or undertaking on my part. What sayest thou, O my brothers?'

A chorus of approval arose from the little crowd of listeners, and the hookah gurgled freely as it passed from hand to hand.

'It were well done,' said the head-man graciously; and at the same time he drew his wrapper closer about his shoulders. 'The night grows chilly,' he added, restraining a yawn, 'and the hour of crow-caw will soon be at hand. Come, let us sleep.'

BITHIA MARY CROKER

The Proud Girl

A SKETCH IN BLACK AND WHITE

The first time I ever saw Miss Sheene, was one Saturday afternoon at Hurlingham; it happened to be a notable occasion for *me*, – and is therefore firmly imprinted on my memory; for I had never been to the Club before, and it was my eighteenth birthday. To tell the truth, I was not yet 'out,' but merely a callow school-girl from Cheltenham, spending part of my holidays with a smart relative (who persisted in treating me, as if I were still wearing a pigtail). For this reason, I was not presented to any of the agreeable men, or merry matrons, who accosted Aunt Sophy, and stood or sat beside us, – where we were established on the edge of the polo ground. Luckily the sensation of being 'left out in the cold,' did not affect me in the smallest degree, in fact, I preferred the rôle of dummy – as it afforded me ample time to gaze about, and take in, my novel, and exciting surroundings. The racing, rushing, polo ponies – who made my heart jump when their hoofs came with a resounding bang against the low wooden partition – the shouting of their captains – the weird wild strains of the Hungarian Band, and last, but not least, the ever-moving crowd of fashionable people. As they sauntered to and fro, I amused myself with making up stories about some of them. For instance, I was most deeply interested in a certain good-looking couple; the man so erect, bronzed, and soldierly, and the girl with a face like a blush rose. Yet she was not as striking, as a tall fair sylph with a willowy figure, whose gait, as she strolled by, was grace itself; a pair of haunting blue eyes, were the chief beauty of a pale, and somewhat disdainful face, half overshadowed by glorious masses of soft light hair; and country mouse as I was, yet even *I* could discern that that delicate trailing white gown, and plumed hat, had come from Paris! Their wearer looked distinguished, a 'somebody,' and in my own mind, I labelled her 'The Proud Girl!'

'The proud girl,' was supported by a stout elderly woman, with an arrogant expression, and no neck; but a scornful head, planted on a squat trunk, loses all its terrors! The lady was attired in embroidered garments of subdued magnificence, and I felt a positive conviction, that she would have preferred to have worn the price emblazoned on her toilette; however the general effect was extremely costly. A dark, rather handsome middle-aged man, walked beside the girl; and I could see, that he was making pitiable, nay, slavish, attempts, to entertain her, and win her approval; also that the damsel barely listened to him, and received his futile efforts with an air of supercilious forbearance. By-and-by Aunt Sophy and I moved off towards the house, in order to refresh ourselves with tea and strawberries on the lawn, where we were the guest of a certain Lady Bexhill, who had assembled a party of at least twenty. Among these, to my delight, I descried 'the proud girl,' and her companions. She happened to sit beside me, and I made her acquaintance over a sugar bowl; and subsequently a common catastrophe, drew us still closer together! one of the flying waiters, upset a jug of cream, the contents of which were impartially distributed between her dress and mine. There was a little fuss and lamentation; a mopping and a wiping. I was secretly on the verge of tears – my best summer dress was ruined, – cream, leaves *such* a greasy stain, and the delicate foularde was done for! My fellow-sufferer behaved like a heroine – indeed she went farther, and treated the affair as a joke, suffering her slave to wait upon her, and receiving his sympathy, with an air of splendid condescension that filled me with awe and emulation. Should *I* ever dare to speak to a gentleman as if he were a servant? As we walked back to the polo ground together, she informed me, that this was by no means her first visit to Hurlingham, in fact, it was her third season, and she went out a great deal.

'And do you like it?' I inquired rather timidly. I felt profoundly honoured, by the notice of this beautiful haughty young princess.

'Oh yes, well enough,' she drawled. 'It's rather a grind, in the hot weather, two or three parties a night, after a day on the river or at Sandown! Auntie,' indicating the stout lady waddling in front of us, 'enjoys everything. How old are you?' she asked abruptly.

'Eighteen. Eighteen to-day.'

'And not out?'

'No' – I admitted shamefacedly – 'I'm going to my father in India. I shall come out there, next cold weather.'

'Your first visit to the gorgeous East?'

'No, I was born there.'

'So was I,' she announced with a little laugh.

'But why do you look so amazed?' she inquired with a lofty air.

'I really don't know,' I stammered, 'you are so – I can't explain – well – so English – so fair.'

'Pray did you expect me to be black because I was born in the East?' she demanded with unexpected irritation.

'No – I am not black myself,' I retorted, 'and the natives, as well as I can remember, – were pale brown, or even yellow.'

'Pale brown, or black, or even yellow! – it's all the same – I have the most invincible horror, of darkies, and black blood. You see the man, who *crawls* about after me! He is a Cuban – enormously rich! He has a tawny grandmother somewhere, – and when his hand touches me – I declare it positively makes me creep! Ah, here are some people looking for me,' and as she spoke, she came to a standstill. 'Well, I hope you'll have a good time out in India. Good-bye.' And with a faint smile, and a bow, I was alone – and my feelings were those of a humble subject who had just been dismissed from the presence of royalty.

An hour later, as my aunt and I, trudged down to Parsons Green Station, in order to catch the underground, we were rapidly overtaken by a splendid landau containing 'the proud girl,' and her relative. The former recognized me, and threw me an affable nod, from beneath her sweeping lace sunshade, whilst her carriage wheels, covered me with clouds of white dust.

'Oh, those are the people we met at tea,' exclaimed my chaperone, 'enormously rich. The girl is full of ridiculous airs and graces, and they say, that Mrs Tappadge, is looking out for a coronet for her! but *she* will only condescend to a duke. She's her adopted daughter, and naturally hated by all the old woman's relations. It was really rather hard on them, when a rich relation brought in a little stranger brat, and established her as her heiress.'

Many months had elapsed since my eighteenth birthday, and I found myself on board the *Socotra, en route* for India, carrying with me a large amount of good advice, a suitable outfit – including habits and saddle, – a quantity of parcels for the friends of friends, and the high hopes and benedictions of my relations. I was about to assume the responsible post of housekeeper, and companion to my father, – an Indian civilian of high standing.

The *Socotra* proved to be rather empty; but there were a

certain number of military and civilians, hurrying back from leave; about forty ladies, and among them to my astonishment, I caught sight of 'the proud girl.' I could scarcely credit my eyes. She looked remarkably pale, slender, and distinguished, – and was dressed in deep mourning.

'Ah,' she exclaimed, sauntering up to me, 'I see you are amazed to find *me* on this ship, and your surprise is nothing to mine. I am so glad to see one face I've met before!'

'Are you alone?' I asked in amazement.

'Yes,' she replied, 'going out in charge of the captain. And you?'

'I am in charge of Mrs Charnock, a friend of my father's. I am sorry to see you are in mourning,' I added with a glance at her black dress.

'It is for poor Mrs Tappadge, my adopted mother. Oh, by the way, you may as well know my name – it is Sheene, – Lilias Sheene. As soon as we have settled down, we must have a good talk, and I will tell you all about myself,' and with this unexpected promise, and a wave of her hand, she disappeared into an adjacent cabin. Miss Sheene's 'settling down,' was evidently a protracted operation, for we were two days at sea before I saw her again.

It was a beautiful moonlight night, and the *Socotra* was throbbing her way through a smooth still sea, when Miss Sheene suddenly appeared at my side, and appropriated my arm, and my society.

'So you are going out to your father,' she began without further ceremony.

'Yes, and I have not seen him for more than five years – ' And I sighed involuntarily.

'But why so lachrymose, my sweet child?'

'Five years is such a long time. I have grown up, and changed – and I'm afraid – '

'Of his being disappointed in your appearance!' she interrupted, with a gay laugh. 'My dear, you need not be uneasy. Your little old-fashioned phiz has never altered, since you were in pinafores! Now, I've not seen my people for twenty years – think of that! I hope they will not be disappointed in me – or,' half to herself, '*I* with them.'

'Twenty years,' I repeated blankly, 'why it will be like beginning life over again.'

'Yes, and now I will tell you all about it, for I'm in a talking mood, and I don't feel inclined to go and bore the captain! I'm full of moods, you must know! By the way, are you a good listener?'

'Yes,' I replied, 'I'd much rather listen, than *talk*!'

'*How* unique! Very well then! Years ago Mrs Tappadge was in the same little out-of-the-way up-country station, with my parents. Her husband had made an enormous fortune in indigo, and had come out, to look after his affairs, but he and her little girl both died of cholera, within a few hours of one another, and Mrs Tappadge was left quite desolate and nearly crazy. My mother took her in, in good old Indian fashion, and did her best to comfort her, but the only thing in which the poor woman found any consolation, was *myself*! I was the exact age of her infant, – and she always declared that there was an extraordinary resemblance between us – in fact, I have gathered, that she sometimes worked herself up to believe, that I was her own child. She could not endure me out of her sight, and of course it ended in her proposing to adopt me, and bring me up as her daughter.'

'Yes, and what did your father, and mother say to that?' I demanded.

'Why of course they said *Yes*, like sensible people, for I was the youngest of seven, and my father never was, or *is*, well off. I fancy my mother made some demur, as I was the youngest – the baby, and if Mrs Tappadge was to be believed, a veritable little angel! with blue, blue eyes and golden hair, a sort of Christmas card child. Well, Mrs Tappadge took me to England, and presented me to all her relations as her adopted daughter. You may imagine their enthusiasm! She petted me, and I'm afraid, spoiled me; gave me an excellent education, and every possible indulgence. Only on one subject was she harsh and stern. She would never suffer me to have the smallest intercourse with my own people – it was in the bond, she declared – unwritten, but *binding*! I never wrote to them till within the last year, when I urged, pleaded, insisted, wept, gained permission to write once at Christmas – and – and – they – wrote to me.'

Here she paused abruptly, and we continued to pace the deck in a long reflective silence; undoubtedly Miss Sheene was meditating on those letters. We had made three turns to and fro, before I ventured to speak.

'And now, that Mrs Tappadge is dead, you are coming back?' I remarked at last. 'You are returning to your own people?'

'Yes,' she assented with a little start, 'my good, kind, adopted mother, died suddenly of apoplexy – her will had not been signed. I have no legal claim, and instead of being the owner of thousands, I am rejoining my family as a mere, well-educated, useless, well-dressed, pauper. Nevertheless I am extremely happy, for after all, there is nothing like one's own flesh, and blood, is there?'

'Have you any conception of what they are like? Did they send their photographs?' I inquired.

'No, I have not the remotest idea of their appearance. Socially they are – middle – middle, class. My father has an appointment on the railway, one of my sisters is married, one is a nurse, two, live at home – so do my two brothers.

They write me most affectionate letters. – Of course,' here she gave an impatient little sigh, 'they have not had *my* advantages. I've been taken about the world – I've been to Paris and Vienna, and to nearly every "cure" in Germany. I have been presented at Court, I've had what's called "a real good time" in Europe, and now, I expect I shall have a "good time" in Asia! Somehow I'm glad to come back, – like Kipling's soldier "I can hear the East a-calling," and I feel, that I am returning home. Oh, I can't tell you *how* I am longing to see my own mother!'

'Yes, you are lucky,' I exclaimed. '*My* mother died, when I was born. How I envy you.'

'Do you indeed! And yet you will be socially a whole heaven above me. You are the daughter of a distinguished Indian official! Now my father, has no position whatever. You will walk out of a room before women old enough to be your grandmother. *I* shall be far, far away among the very last joints, of the tag-rag and bobtail! How strange it will seem,' and she laughed, as if the idea amused her a good deal.

Yes, very strange, most remarkably strange, that I – a little insignificant chit, without air, or grace, should sit aloft in high places as my father's daughter, whilst 'the proud girl,' languished below the horizon!

'I will teach my sisters, – and they shall teach me. I have a good deal to learn,' she resumed after a pause.

'What sort of things?'

'Well, to do my own hair, to sew on buttons, mend my gloves – there will be no more ladies' maids, or French dressmakers for me. Still, I believe that poverty, – the horrid cheap poverty, that has no boot-trees, or new books, is unknown in India, among our class. I'll have an ayah – she will brush my skirts, as well as hair, and mother is sure to have a carriage.'

'Oh of course,' I assented readily.

'I have heard that in India, even a sergeant's wife has a pony cart, no one walks, which is a good thing for *me*. I am so lazy – in fact, I am a lazy, penniless, encumbrance, with all the fastidious tastes, of a rich woman's spoiled child.'

'But surely Mrs Tappadge's relatives have given you money – an income?'

'Oh no – they consider, that they have behaved in a most liberal, and truly *Christian* spirit, in presenting me with my passage money, my own clothes, books, and jewellery – as well as fifty pounds, – which by the way, I have laid out in presents for my mother and sisters!'

'What are you taking them?' I inquired, guiltily conscious, that my sole offering to my father, was a pair of slippers!

'I've got mother an exquisite French tea-gown, so smart, and yet so easy to slip into, it's a perfect dream!'

'But how do you know her size? – it may not fit?' I objected.

'Oh – I think it will be all right – I have an instinct, that she and I are rather alike – in fact, that I take after *her*. At any rate I've risked the tea-gown! – it is so graceful, all lace and *crêpe de chine*. I've also picked up a perfect duck of a chatelaine, for my married sister.'

'I suppose *you* never thought of marrying anyone?' I blundered out.

'Dear me, how alarmingly, you put it!' she exclaimed. 'No, but people have thought of marrying *me*. You see, I was a notorious heiress.'

'It was not for your money I am certain,' I protested with warmth.

'Ah – one should never be certain; but I must admit, that there were one or two, who were not mercenary.'

'For instance, the dark gentleman at Hurlingham?' I ventured to suggest.

'Oh, I suppose you mean the Count de Hortos?' she answered with somewhat chilling hauteur. 'He was kind, cultivated – yes – and charming – but impossible.'

'Why impossible?' I urged audaciously.

'Simply because, he is what you have just called him – a dark gentleman. I abhor the shade – and now, that I have walked, and talked, you to death – shall we go below?'

Miss Sheene took me under her protection for the remainder of the passage, and I must confess, that I was secretly flattered by her patronage. We had much in common; we were within a year or two of the same age, we had been born in India, we were fond of music, and we had both before us, an unknown home! Although I was the daughter of a little 'Tin God' I was acutely conscious of my inferiority to 'the proud girl.' I ran all her messages. I felt miserably inferior to this beautiful, tall, graceful creature, with her exquisite clothes, her wide experience, her insolent airs, and her strong prejudices. I was small, dark and insignificant, and alas! the art of dress was a sealed book to me – I was also shy and desperately diffident. Now Miss Sheene, was possessed of absolute self-reliance, the aplomb of a diplomatist, and the courage of a Zulu warrior. I have seen her snub Mrs Charnock – my cabin companion, – a wiry little woman who had shot tigers, – snubbed her, till she withdrew, cutting a truly pitiable figure. Also, she snubbed all the would-be admiring men, – save one, – who was as cool, and exclusive as herself.

'I really wonder, what you see in that odious half-caste girl?' This remark was made to me by Mrs Charnock in the privacy of our cabin. 'I'm perfectly certain, your father would never tolerate such an intimacy. Now you are on the Indian side, you must think of your position.'

'But, Mrs Charnock, I've not the least notion of what you mean,' I protested, 'I never met a half-caste girl in all my life.'

'Yes, what about Miss Sheene?' she demanded excitedly.

'She is of English birth, and she has a morbid horror of Eurasians.'

'Morbid indeed! Why she is one herself! You have only to look at her fingers of a cold morning, and you will see how purple the skin is under her nails – a certain sign – *quite* unmistakable!'

'There are no cold mornings at present,' I replied, 'and even if your test were proved, I'm perfectly certain that Miss Sheene is a pure European.'

'Wonderfully well dressed, with an amazing amount of effrontery I grant you; also an exquisite figure, lithe as a serpent *now*, but in ten years she will resemble an enormous boa-constrictor! All these Eurasians run to flesh. My dear child, I respect you for standing up for your protégée,' (it was the other way about, did Mrs Charnock but know) 'I've been fifteen years in India for my sins, and you really must *allow* me, to recognize a half-caste when I see one! I have heard all about Miss Sheene, an adopted daughter – left out of a will – it was a shame. On the other hand, she gives herself airs of detestable superiority, talks of Wagner and Ibsen, and book-plates, and first editions, and so on. Her clothes are delicious I grant you, but these Eurasians, have a passion for dress. A girl brought up in a dainty luxurious English home, surrounded by every refinement, to be hurled back into a scrambling squalid family of poor Eurasians – oh what a hell awaits her! Her worst enemy, might *weep* at her fate.'

'Mrs Charnock,' I interrupted excitedly, 'you don't know Miss Sheene as *I* do – and if you say anything more I shall – ' here alas! I burst into tears.

I, though the daughter of a high official, in her husband's province, dared not brave Mrs Charnock, – at any rate as yet.

'Oh well, well, don't cry,' she said, patting me on the head, 'we will drop the subject, and agree to differ, but *some day*, you will find that I am right.'

With Mrs Charnock's dire announcement in my ears, I took particular notice of Miss Sheene that evening. She wore a white gown, (since the weather was now tropical,) and she looked as fair, and graceful, as her namesake the lily; in short, considering the matter quite dispassionately, I felt the humbling conviction, that *I* was far more likely to be taken for an Eurasian myself. When later, we sat together in a cool corner of the music-room, Miss Sheene murmured in a dreamy voice –

'In a few days' time, we must say goodbye. I wonder what our lives will be like? Shall we compare notes? – will you write to me, if I give you my address, – or, will you forget me in a week?'

'Never, never. I will never forget you,' I protested indignantly. 'And I will write to you every week, if you care for my letters?'

'Come, come,' she exclaimed, 'you must not make rash promises, you impulsive child; you have no idea of your father's position, and our paths in life lie far apart. I go north, you go south. I belong to a class, many rungs of the ladder below *you*.'

I laughed, and pointed significantly to our reflections in an opposite mirror.

'Oh yes,' languidly moving her great gauze fan, 'I look very superfine, and dainty, and gilt-edged! I have been pampered in the lap of luxury, and *you* are just a hardy, well-brought-up little girl, unaccustomed to the pomps and vanities of this wicked world. On Bombay Bund, we exchange rôles. There, your father will meet you, with half a dozen red and gold *chuprassis*, and several splendid carriages; but there will be no one to welcome *me* – it is a very long expensive journey up country, and I shall find my way quite easily alone – somehow it will not seem a strange land.'

'And yet you remember nothing about it?'

'Nothing but a little wooden painted toy, a figure with a yellow turban, and a red body, with gold spots. Is it not curious, how just a useless little item, sticks in a child's head! and yet she cannot recall the face of her mother.'

My father met me in Bombay. He came on board, as soon as the quarantine officer had left, and appeared sincerely glad to see me. He was a grave, reserved sort of man, whom I had always held in great awe, – the awe of the unknown; he kissed me tenderly, and welcomed me to India. There was no one, as she had predicted, to receive Miss Sheene, so I presented her to father as 'my particular friend,' and we drove her to our hotel, where she consented to share my sitting-room, until our train left that same evening. After tiffin, father went out to Malabar Hill, where he had important business with the Governor, and Miss Sheene and I, were once more tête-à-tête. I scribbled a few lines to send off by the outgoing mail, and this letter, I myself carried downstairs, in order to get stamps at the Bureau. As I stood there waiting an enormously fat old woman entered the hall. She was very dark, extremely warm, and appeared to be literally heaving, with suppressed excitement. She wore a large velvet hat covered with roses, a shapeless black costume, covered with dust; in one hand she held a pair of yellow thread gloves, and in the other, a coarse and grimy handkerchief, with which she continually mopped her face.

'Tell me, miss,' she said, accosting me eagerly, 'have you just come out from England, in the steamer *Socotra*?'

'Yes,' I admitted, 'we have just arrived.'

'Oh, then that is all right!' she resumed. She spoke with a curious foreign accent, clipping her words.

'My daughter' – she pronounced it 'datter' – 'came in the *Socotra* – you will have met her – of course.'

I shook my head with unwonted hauteur, – the recently realized dignity of the daughter of a little tin god!

'Oh but yess! – she come out first class – did you not know Miss Sheene?' and she brandished the gloves imperiously.

'*Miss Sheene!* Is she your daughter?' I gasped, and I felt as if the hotel hall, was sinking under my feet.

'Oh my yess! – why not? She was taken home to England, and brought up by a friend of mine – now she is coming back, and we are all so glad, – though we are not rich grand folks. My husband has only four hundred rupees per month, but we are a very loving familee, and there's lots of room for Lilias. Oh my! I can tell you, I am longing to see her. Oh my! when I think of my *baby*!'

Her voice had a soft plaintiveness, and hateful discovery! there was a look of Lilias in her grey eyes.

'Where is she?' Mrs Sheene continued authoritatively – unquestionably she regarded me as her daughter's keeper.

'She is upstairs, number thirty-two, but wait one moment,' I urged distractedly. Then I flew to the lift, and was instantly whirled aloft, there I tore along the corridor, and dashed open the door of our sitting-room breathless.

Miss Sheene – all unconscious of her doom – was extended at full length on the sofa, absorbed in a little book, which was daintily bound in white and gold. She too, was dressed in a delicate white gown, and wore gold bangles, rings and a pearl and gold chain, – the usual equipment of a young lady of fashion and taste. Oh what a contrast she presented to the woman who had brought her into the world, and whose heavy eager tread, was already in my wake! At all costs I must prepare Lilias, although I felt choking with pity, horror, and excitement.

'Well, what is it, you dear little cyclone?' she inquired languidly. 'What has happened? It is not possible, that you have seen a cobra?'

'No, no,' I stammered out, 'I only ran up to tell you that – that.' I paused – the announcement stuck fast. 'That – that – '

'That – that,' she repeated, mimicking my voice, 'His Excellency the Governor is below, inquiring for Miss Lathom?'

'No – it is your mother,' I panted. 'She is here – she is coming up now.'

Miss Sheene bounded to her feet, flung the book on the table. She had grown white to her lips. 'My mother here – to meet me!' and she gave a little sobbing cry.

'She is not – she is – ' I began desperately, but the heavy footsteps were now plainly audible, and an extra large shadow loomed on the threshold. – I recoiled several paces, as I caught a glimpse of a gigantic hat. '*Theese* is number thirty-two,' said a voice, and then I opened an opposite door, and fled. I trembled all over, with the awful and sickening sensation, that the room I thus quitted, was about to become a chamber of horrors. I actually felt as if I were flying from the scene of a murder. For one whole hour, I paced up and down my bedroom in a state of agitation, bordering on a serious illness. At length, I mustered up courage – I ventured forth, – went straight to the door, and rapped timidly. No answer. I turned the handle, and entered with a cautious step and a violently beating heart. But my emotions and fears, were alike wasted and unnecessary; the apartment was empty. Miss Sheene's book lay on the table, a dirty yellow cotton glove lay on the floor, there was a penetrating odour of coconut oil – and that was all!

I hurried down to the office, where I was informed, that 'the young lady and her "servant," had left the hotel about ten minutes previously – the lady had paid for half share of sitting-room, – there was no message for anyone, – and no address.'

Unfortunately we were pressed for time, and time, to an Indian magnate – who holds the threads of many fates – is of most vital importance, – only for this, I would have implored father to have remained one day – or even half a day, – in Bombay – in order to make inquiries respecting my late fellow-passenger, – but already, a splendid Government carriage, with gorgeous servants in scarlet and gold livery, was in waiting to convey us to the station – we had not a moment to lose! And from that hour to this – the period includes years – and in spite of my determined efforts, and considerable official assistance, I have never been able to discover the faintest trace, of Lilias Sheene!

LEONARD WOOLF

A Tale Told By Moonlight

Many people did not like Jessop. He had rather a brutal manner sometimes of telling brutal things – the truth, he called it. 'They don't like it,' he once said to me in a rare moment of confidence. 'But why the devil shouldn't they? They pretend these sorts of things, battle, murder, and sudden death, are so real – more real than white kid gloves and omnibuses and rose leaves – and yet when you give them the real thing, they curl up like school girls. It does them good, you know, does them a world of good.'

They didn't like it and they didn't altogether like him. He was a sturdy thick set man, very strong, a dark reserved man with black eyebrows which met over his nose. He had knocked about the world a good deal. He appealed to me in many ways; I liked to meet him. He had fished things up out of life, curious grim things, things which may have disgusted but which certainly fascinated as well.

The last time I saw him we were both staying with Alderton, the novelist. Mrs Alderton was away – recruiting after annual childbirth, I think. The other guests were Pemberton, who was recruiting after his annual book of verses, and Smith, Hanson Smith, the critic.

It was a piping hot June day, and we strolled out after dinner in the cool moonlight down the great fields which lead to the river. It was very cool, very beautiful, very romantic lying there on the grass above the river bank, watching the great trees in the moonlight and the silver water slipping along so musically to the sea. We grew silent and sentimental – at least I know I did.

Two figures came slowly along the bank, a young man with his arm round a girl's waist. They passed just under where we were lying without seeing us. We heard the murmur of his words and in the shadow of the trees they stopped and we heard the sound of their kisses.

I heard Pemberton mutter:

> A boy and girl if the good fates please
> Making love say,
> The happier they.
> Come up out of the light of the moon
> And let them pass as they will, too soon
> With the bean flowers boon
> And the blackbird's tune
> And May and June.

It loosed our tongues and we began to speak – all of us except Jessop – as men seldom speak together, of love. We were sentimental, romantic. We told stories of our first loves. We looked back with regret, with yearning to our youth and to love. We were passionate in our belief in it, love, the great passion, the real thing which had just passed us by so closely in the moonlight.

We talked like that for an hour or so, I suppose, and Jessop never opened his lips. Whenever I looked at him, he was watching the river gliding by and he was frowning. At last there was a pause; we were all silent for a minute or two and then Jessop began to speak:

'You talk as if you believed all that: it's queer, damned queer. A boy kissing a girl in the moonlight and you call it love and poetry and romance. But you know as well as I do it isn't. It's just a flicker of the body, it will be cold, dead, this time next year.'

He had stopped but nobody spoke and then he continued slowly, almost sadly: 'We're old men and middle-aged men, aren't we? We've all done that. We remember how we kissed like that in the moonlight or no light at all. It was pleasant; Lord, I'm not denying that – but some of us are married and some of us aren't. We're middle-aged – well, think of your wives, think of – ' he stopped again. I looked round. The others were moving uneasily. It was this kind of thing that people didn't like in Jessop. He spoke again.

'It's you novelists who're responsible, you know. You've made a world in which every one is always falling in love – but it's not this world. Here it's the flicker of the body.

'I don't say there isn't such a thing. There is. I've seen it, but it's rare, as rare as – as – a perfect horse, an Arab once said to me. The real thing, it's too queer to be anything but the rarest; it's the queerest thing in the world. Think of it for a moment, chucking out of your mind all this business of kisses and moonlight and marriages. A miserable tailless ape buzzed round through space on this half cold cinder of an earth, a timid bewildered ignorant savage little beast always fighting for bare existence. And suddenly it runs up against another miserable naked tailless ape and immediately everything that it has ever known dies out of its little puddle of a mind, itself, its beastly body, its puny wandering desires, the wretched fight for existence, the whole world. And instead there comes a flame of passion for something in that other naked ape, not for her body or her mind or her soul, but for something beautiful mysterious everlasting – yes that's it the everlasting passion in her which has flamed up in him. He goes buzzing on through space, but he isn't tired or bewildered or ignorant any more; he can see his way now, even among the stars.

'And that's love, the love which you novelists scatter about so freely. What does it mean? I don't understand it; it's queer beyond anything I've ever struck. It isn't animal – that's the point – or vegetable or mineral. Not one man in ten thousand feels it and not one woman in twenty thousand. How can they? It's a feeling, a passion immense, steady, enduring. But not one person in twenty thousand ever feels anything at all for more than a second, and then it's only a feeble ripple on the smooth surface of their unconsciousness.

'O yes, we've all been in love. We can all remember the kisses we gave and the kisses given to us in the moonlight. But that's the body. The body's damnably exacting. It wants to kiss and to be kissed at certain times and seasons. It isn't particular however; give it moonlight and young lips and it's soon satisfied. It's only when we don't pay for it that we call it romance and love, and the most we would ever pay is a £5 note.

'But it's not love, not the other, the real, the mysterious thing. That too exists, I've seen it, I tell you, but it's rare, Lord, it's rare. I'm middle-aged. I've seen men, thousands of them, all over the world, known them too, made it my business to know them, it interests me, a hobby like collecting stamps. And I've only known two cases of real love.

'And neither of them had anything to do with kisses and moonlight. Why should they? When it comes, it comes in strange ways and places, like most real things perversely and unreasonably. I suppose scientifically it's all right – it's what the mathematician calls the law of chances.

'I'll tell you about one of them.

'There was a man – you may have read his books, so I won't give you his name – though he's dead now – I'll call him Reynolds. He was at Rugby with me and also at Corpus. He was a thin feeble looking chap, very nervous, with a pale face and long pale hands. He was bullied a good deal at school; he was what they call a smug. I knew him rather well; there seemed to me to be something in him somewhere, some power of feeling under the nervousness and shyness. I can't say it ever came out, but he interested me.

'I went East and he stayed at home and wrote novels. I read them; very romantic they were too, the usual ideas of men and women and love. But they were clever in many ways, especially psychologically, as it was called. He was a success, he made money.

'I used to get letters from him about once in three months, so when he came travelling to the East, it was arranged that he would stay a week with me. I was in Colombo at that time, right in the passenger route. I found him one day on the deck of a P and O just the same as I'd last seen him at Oxford, except for the large sun helmet on his head and the blue glasses on his nose. And when I got back to the bungalow and began to talk with him on the broad verandah, I found that he was still just the same inside too. The years hadn't touched him anywhere, he hadn't in the ordinary sense lived at all. He had stood aside – do you see what I mean? – from shyness, nervousness, the remembrance and fear of being bullied, and watched other people living. He knew a good deal about how other people think, the little tricks and mannerisms of life and novels, but he didn't know how they felt; I expect he had never felt anything himself, except fear and shyness: he hadn't really ever known a man, and he had certainly never known a woman.

'Well, he wanted to see life, to understand it, to feel it. He had travelled 7000 miles to do so. He was very keen to begin, he wanted to see life all round, up and down, inside and out; he told me so as we looked out on the palm trees and the glimpse of the red road beyond and the unending stream of brown men and women upon it.

'I began to show him life in the East. I took him to the

clubs; the club where they play tennis and gossip, the club where they play Bridge and gossip, the club where they just sit in long chairs and gossip. I introduced him to scores of men who asked him to have a drink, and to scores of women who asked him whether he liked Colombo. He didn't get on with them at all, he said "No thank you" to the men and "Yes, very much" to the women. He was shy and felt uncomfortable, out of his element with these fat flannelled merchants, fussy civil servants, and their whining wives and daughters.

'In the evening we sat on my verandah and talked. We talked about life and his novels and romance and love even. I liked him, you know; he interested me, there was something in him which had never come out. But he had got hold of life at the wrong end somehow, he couldn't deal with it or the people in it at all. He had the novelist's view of life and – with all respect to you, Alderton – it doesn't work.

'I suppose the devil came into me that evening. Reynolds had talked so much about seeing life that at last I thought: "By Jove, I'll show him a side of life *he's* never seen before at any rate." I called the servant and told him to fetch two rickshaws.

'We bowled along the dusty roads past the lake and into the native quarter. All the smells of the East rose up and hung heavy upon the damp hot air in the narrow streets. I watched Reynolds' face in the moonlight, the scared look which always showed upon it. I very nearly repented and turned back. Even now I'm not sure whether I'm sorry that I didn't. At any rate I didn't, and at last we drew up in front of a low mean looking house standing back a little from the road.

'There was one of those queer native wooden doors made in two halves; the top half was open and through it one saw an empty whitewashed room lighted by a lamp fixed in the wall. We went in and I shut the door top and bottom behind us. At the other end were two steps leading up to another room. Suddenly there came the sound of bare feet running and giggles of laughter, and ten or twelve girls, some naked and some half clothed in bright red or bright orange cloths, rushed down the steps upon us. We were surrounded, embraced, caught up in their arms and carried into the next room. We lay upon sofas with them. There was nothing but sofas and an old piano in the room.

'They knew me well in the place, – you can imagine what it was – I often went there. Apart from anything else, it interested me. The girls were all Tamils and Sinhalese. It always reminded me somehow of the Arabian Nights; that room when you came into it so bare and empty, and then the sudden rush of laughter, the pale yellow naked women, the brilliant colours of the cloths, the white teeth, all appearing so suddenly in the doorway up there at the end of the room. And the girls themselves interested me; I used to sit and talk to them for hours in their own language; they didn't as a rule understand English. They used to tell me all about themselves, queer pathetic stories often. They came from villages almost always, little native villages hidden far away among rice fields and coconut trees, and they had drifted somehow into this hovel in the warren of filth and smells which we and our civilization had attracted about us.

'Poor Reynolds, he was very uncomfortable at first. He didn't know what to do in the least or where to look. He stammered out yes and no to the few broken English sentences which the girls repeated like parrots to him. They soon got tired of kissing him and came over to me to tell me their little troubles and ask me for advice – all of them that is, except one.

'She was called Celestinahami and was astonishingly beautiful. Her skin was the palest of pale gold with a glow in it, very rare in the fair native women. The delicate innocent beauty of a child was in her face; and her eyes, Lord, her eyes immense, deep, dark and melancholy which looked as if they knew and understood and felt everything in the world. She never wore anything coloured, just a white cloth wrapped round her waist with one end thrown over the left shoulder. She carried about her an air of slowness and depth and mystery of silence and of innocence.

'She lay full length on the sofa with her chin on her hands, looking up into Reynolds' face and smiling at him. The white cloth had slipped down and her breasts were bare. She was a Sinhalese, a cultivator's daughter, from a little village up in the hills: her place was in the green rice fields weeding, or in the little compound under the palm trees pounding rice, but she lay on the dirty sofa and asked Reynolds in her soft broken English whether he would have a drink.

'It began in him with pity. "I saw the pity of it, Jessop," he said to me afterwards, "the pity of it." He lost his shyness, he began to talk to her in his gentle cultivated voice; she didn't understand a word, but she looked up at him with her great innocent eyes and smiled at him. He even stroked her hand and her arm. She smiled at him still, and said her few soft clipped English sentences. He looked into her eyes that understood nothing but seemed to understand everything, and then it came out at last; the power to feel, the power that so few have, the flame, the passion, love, the real thing.

'It was the real thing, I tell you; I ought to know; he stayed on in my bungalow day after day, and night after night he went down to that hovel among the filth and smells. It wasn't the body, it wasn't kisses and moonlight. He wanted her of course, he wanted her body and soul; but he wanted something else: the same passion, the same fine strong thing that he felt moving in himself. She was everything to him that was beautiful and great and pure, she was what she looked, what he read in the depths of her eyes. And she might have been – why not? She might have been all that and more, there's no reason why such a thing shouldn't happen, shouldn't have happened even. One can believe that still. But the chances are all against it. She was a prostitute in a Colombo brothel, a simple soft little golden-skinned animal with nothing in the depths of the eyes at all. It was the law of chances at work as usual, you know.

'It was tragic and it was at the same time wonderfully ridiculous. At times he saw things as they were, the bare truth, the hopelessness of it. And then he was so ignorant of life, fumbling about so curiously with all the little things in it. It was too much for him; he tried to shoot himself with a revolver which he had bought at the Army and Navy Stores before he sailed; but he couldn't because he had forgotten how to put in the cartridges.

'Yes, I burst in on him sitting at a table in his room fumbling with the thing. It was one of those rotten old-fashioned things with a piece of steel that snaps down over the chamber to prevent the cartridges falling out. He hadn't discovered how to snap it back in order to get the cartridges in. The man who sold him that revolver, instead of an automatic pistol, as he ought to have done, saved his life.

'And then I talked to him seriously. I quoted his own novel to him. It was absurdly romantic, unreal, his novel, but it preached as so many of them do, that you should face facts first and then live your life out to the uttermost. I quoted it to him. Then I told him baldly brutally what the girl was – not a bit what he thought her, what his passion went out to – a nice simple soft little animal like the bitch at my feet that starved herself if I left her for a day. "It's the truth," I said to him, "as true as that you're really in love, in love with something that doesn't exist behind those great eyes. It's dangerous, damned dangerous because it's real – and that's why it's rare. But it's no good shooting yourself with that thing. You've got to get on board the next P and O, that's what you've got to do. And if you won't do that, why practise what you preach and live your life out, and take the risks."

'He asked me what I meant.

"The risks?" I said. "I can see what they are, and if you do take them, you're taking the worst odds ever offered a man. But there they are. Take the girl and see what you can make of life with her. You can buy her out of that place for fifteen rupees."

'I was wrong, I suppose. I ought to have put him in irons and shipped him off next day. But I don't know, really I don't know.

'He took the risks any way. We bought her out, it cost twenty rupees. I got them a little house down the coast on the sea shore, a little house surrounded by palm trees. The sea droned away sleepily right under the verandah. It was to be an idyll of the East; he was to live there for ever with her and write novels on the verandah.

'And, by God, he was happy – at first. I used to go down there and stay with them pretty often. He taught her English and she taught him Sinhalese. He started to write a novel about the East: it would have been a good novel I think, full of strength and happiness and sun and reality – if it had been finished. But it never was. He began to see the truth, the damned hard unpleasant truths that I had told him that night in the Colombo bungalow. And the cruelty of it was that he still had that rare power to feel, that he still felt. It was the real thing, you see, and the real thing is – didn't I say – immense, steady, enduring. It is; I believe that still. He was in love, but he knew now what she was like. He couldn't speak to her and she couldn't speak to him, she couldn't understand him. He was a civilized cultivated intelligent nervous little man and she – she was an animal, dumb and stupid and beautiful.

'I watched it happening, I had foretold it, but I cursed myself for not having stopped it, scores of times. He loved her but she tortured him. People would say, I suppose, that she got on his nerves. It's a good enough description. But the cruellest thing of all was that she had grown to love him, love him like an animal, as a bitch loves her master.' Jessop stopped. We waited for him to go on but he didn't. The leaves rustled gently in the breeze; the river murmured softly below us; up in the woods I heard a nightingale singing. 'Well, and then?' Alderton asked at last in a rather peevish voice.

'And then? Damn that nightingale!' said Jessop. 'I wish I hadn't begun this story. It happened so long ago: I thought I had forgotten to feel it, to feel that I was responsible for what happened then. There's another sort of love; it isn't the body and it isn't the flame; it's the love of dogs and women, at any rate of those slow, big-eyed women of the East. It's the love of a slave, the patient, consuming love for a master, for his kicks and his caresses, for his kisses and his blows. That was the sort of love which grew up slowly in Celestinahami for Reynolds. But it wasn't what he wanted, it was that, I expect, more than anything which got on his nerves.

'She used to follow him about the bungalow like a dog. He wanted to talk to her about his novel and she only understood how to pound and cook rice. It exasperated him, made him unkind, cruel. And when he looked into her patient, mysterious eyes he saw behind them what he had fallen in love with, what he knew didn't exist. It began to drive him mad.

'And she – she of course couldn't even understand what was the matter. She saw that he was unhappy, she thought she had done something wrong. She reasoned like a child that it was because she wasn't like the white ladies whom she used to see in Colombo. So she went and bought stays and white cotton stockings and shoes, and she squeezed herself into them. But the stays and the shoes and stockings didn't do her any good.

'It couldn't go on like that. At last I induced Reynolds to go away. He was to continue his travels but he was coming back – he said so over and over again to me and to Celestinahami. Meanwhile she was well provided for; a deed was executed: the house and the coconut trees and the little compound by the sea were to be hers – a generous settlement, a donatio inter vivos, as the lawyers call it – void, eh? – or voidable? – because for an immoral consideration. Lord! I'm nearly forgetting my law, but I believe the law holds that only future consideration of that sort can be immoral. How wise, how just, isn't it? The past cannot be immoral; it's done with, wiped out – but the future? Yes, it's only the future that counts.

'So Reynolds wiped out his past and Celestinahami by the help of a dirty Burgher lawyer and a deed of gift and a ticket issued by Thomas Cook and Son for a berth in a P and O bound for Aden. I went on board to see him off and I shook his hand and told him encouragingly that everything would be all right.

'I never saw Reynolds again but I saw Celestinahami once. It was at the inquest two days after the *Moldavia* sailed for Aden. She was lying on a dirty wooden board on trestles in the dingy mud-plastered room behind the court. Yes, I identified her: Celestinahami – I never knew her other name. She lay there in her stays and pink skirt and white stockings and white shoes. They had found her floating in the sea that lapped the foot of the convent garden below the little bungalow – bobbing up and down in her stays and pink skirt and white stockings and shoes.'

Jessop stopped. No one spoke for a minute or two. Then Hanson Smith stretched himself, yawned, and got up.

'Battle, murder, and sentimentality,' he said. 'You're as bad as the rest of them, Jessop. I'd like to hear your other case – but it's too late, I'm off to bed.'

JOHN EYTON
The Pool

Some three hundred years ago a little white temple nestled in a fold of the hills, like a mushroom in a green dell. It stood on the bank of a dark pool; wooded hills towered over it to the west, and barren hills rolled away to the east. It was a very holy place; men believed that the foot of God had touched earth here and had made a valley. So from time immemorial it had been a place of pilgrimage. Men journeyed to the hills to see it, and the steps leading down to the pool were often thronged with travellers in white garments, women in *saris* of red and blue, *sadhus* in orange and in yellow.

The water was dark – born of a deep-laid spring, which was never dry, and whose overflow ran away in a little tinkling rill into the deep woods. It was believed that the pool was bottomless – for what could resist the foot of God?

Animals came to drink quite near the temple without fear – dark, great-eyed Sambar stags – little barking deer of the colour of autumn leaves – mottled leopards. There were bright birds too about it – proud pheasants, and jays of vivid blue; big butterflies of dark green and blue, with swallow tails; and red dragon-flies haunted the reedy edges.

It was ever a place of great silence and of rest. A very holy man watched over the temple, sitting all day long, legs crossed, arms folded. He was said to be a hundred years old. His face was wizened and shrivelled and puckered in a thousand wrinkles. His head was shaven, and his forehead bore three upright lines of yellow paint. He wore but a single blanket of faded orange.

Such were the temple, and the pool, and the priest of the pool.

There came an evil day for that peaceful place. A horde of wild Mohammedan fanatics from below swept over the hills and descended like a scourge on the pool. The little old priest ran up the path towards them, his arms outstretched, adjuring them to spare the ancient holy temple. A swarthy man of great stature lifted his sharp sword and swept off the head of the little priest; others plunged their swords into the frail body, and they threw the wreck of it into the pool. They burned the temple and destroyed the peace of the place . . . Then the pestilence passed on.

Thereafter, green rushes covered the whole face of the water, save where the spring welled up in the middle. Men feared to approach the pool, where pale figures were seen at night, and where a despairing cry was sometimes heard. The peace returned; the place was left to the animals and the birds and the butterflies. But the memory of it never died.

Time passed, and the surrounding hills came into the hands of an Englishman, a retired Colonel named Brown. He was not an unkindly man, but he had a strong belief in the absolute superiority of his own race, and in the inviolability of property. He was tall, with white hair and moustache, and a face whose natural redness was enhanced by the white suits and hats which he wore. He made a pleasant estate in the hills; built a roomy bungalow; put up neat cottages; planted orchards; laid out paths everywhere; in fact, subdued the jungle with a system admirably English.

Incidentally he cleaned up the pool, which lay just beyond his boundary. The villagers refused to do the work, but he imported labour, and cleared out the rushes and dredged up the mud. In the course of the work they found a number of blackened stones and rudely carved figures, which the Colonel gave to the Lucknow Museum. Evidently there had been some sort of a temple on the spot, which lent colour to the village talk. Then the spring was analysed and found to contain good water; so the supply was utilized, pipe-lines being laid on to the gardens. The villagers resented the whole proceeding, but they always did resent innovation. Colonel Brown was justly proud of his improvements.

Then the most annoying thing happened. The Colonel was walking round the estate one afternoon when he distinctly heard the mournful chant which accompanies a funeral procession. It was the usual thing – a sentence endlessly repeated by two alternate groups, first in full tone, then faintly, like an echo. It came from the direction of the pool. When he had turned the corner he saw the awful truth – a little party of men walking swiftly down the path and bearing a stretcher on which lay a body swathed in white. Mourners trotted behind, intoning their sad chant. They were actually going to burn a dead body near the spring-head! It was monstrous. They did it too; he saw the smoke curling up from the valley, and found logs of charred wood at the fringe of the pool the next morning.

That afternoon was the beginning of the Colonel's troubles. First he put a *chowkidar* on the place, and the *chowkidar* was beaten by day and saw *bhuts* by night, and ran away. But the burning went on, in proportion to the mortality of the village. Then the Colonel summoned the head-men, who talked nonsense about the place being holy from time immemorial. He dismissed them with a purple face and a few home truths. Next, he applied to the civil authorities, who declined to interfere, since the pool was not actually on the estate of Colonel Brown, and had certainly a reputed sanctity. Lastly, he wrote to the *Pioneer* – last resource of wounded pride – and complained of 'the new spirit of pandering to the native, regardless of the position and rights of landlords,' and wondered what the Government was doing.

In spite of all, the burning continued. People refused to burn anywhere else. They believed that here was sanctity for their dead.

Then worse befell. One morning the Colonel observed through his field-glasses a little strip of red rag floating from a tree on the margin of the pool. This would not appear to be of importance; but the Colonel knew India. That red rag meant a priest, and a priest meant pilgrimage. Never was proud banner a surer challenge than was that little strip of red rag. The red rag affected the Colonel after the proverbial manner. He descended on the place, breathing unutterable things.

All he found was a solitary figure sitting under the tree which flaunted the red rag. It was a man of middle age, clad in a blanket of faded yellow; his head was clean-shaven, and his forehead bore three upright lines of yellow paint. He sat motionless, with set, staring eyes. The Colonel asked him his business . . . no answer; then he made a sort of set speech on the rights of man . . . still no answer; then he began to shout, but the priest still ignored his presence. He failed to make any impression on that holy man. Angry as he felt, he knew better than to lay hands on a priest – so he marched off, speechless with rage. They would build a temple next, he knew, if they were given a chance. So he stalked home and wrote a perfect sheaf of letters and appeals on the subject.

That evening the Colonel began a nasty attack of malaria. It is possible that he had been bitten by a mosquito on the occasion of one of his numerous visits to the pool, which was still a swampy place, hot and stuffy. However this may be, the mosquito which bit the Colonel knew his business. He was in bed a fortnight. His wife barely managed to pull him through the attack, which was unusually malignant. When he could get about again, his first walk was in the direction of the pool . . .

There, like a mushroom in a green dell, nestled a little new white temple.

With the reader's indulgence, the author begs leave to draw a picture dating some three hundred years hence . . .

Colonel Brown is long forgotten. The Englishman, and his Government, and his rights, and his laws have faded away as a ripple dies on water – as a wind stirs in the trees and is gone. But on the bank of the dark pool a little white temple still stands, and still the pilgrims come . . . for such is India.

CHRISTINE WESTON

The Devil Has the Moon

It was a summer evening and the cool air which at this hour sweeps down from the Himalayas smelled pleasant to Mr Sanderson, the Eurasian tutor, when he stepped from his room on to the gravel terrace before the house and gazed down at the lake, which lay pale and unruffled between dark-green hills. The nasal song of a Pahari on the road that skirted the lake was borne to Mr Sanderson's ears, adding to his sense of well-being. He had just finished dining with the family, his employers; now they had dispersed to their rooms and he was free for the first time today. Free, but rather lonely. He was a sociable person and would have liked to be invited by his charges, or by their parents, for a chat or a smoke before bedtime, but these little intimacies were not encouraged. The Strongs were kind to him, he was well treated and well paid, but they were English and he was Eurasian and neither he nor they could ever quite forget it. When not under the eyes of their parents, his pupils, Hilda, aged eleven, and Richard, aged eight, often took cruel advantage of him. They had early discovered his extreme sensitivity and enjoyed playing upon it, alternately exciting him to hysterical laughter and driving him to tears. Mr Sanderson was twenty years old and he would have liked to behave towards the children as an older brother, but they would not accept him. They were, he decided, incapable of finer feeling; they were not even grateful for what he did for them, striving as he did day by day to lift them out of the giddy ignorance in which they lived. He had rarely encountered children less interested in study.

Mr Strong was a retired tea planter who kept talking about going back to England to die but who never went and who seemed in no immediate danger of dying. When he had engaged Mr Sanderson as tutor for the children, he said, 'For God's sake din some education into them. I've had Hilda in school for two years and she hasn't learned a thing, not a thing, except some prayers.'

'Teach them history,' Mrs Strong had begged him. She adored her children but was not equipped to teach them anything except how to play the mandolin, which they did badly but indefatigably.

'Mathematics,' said Mr Strong, who had no head for it himself but understood its importance. 'Teach them mathematics, Sanderson. Why, Richard is eight and he can't do the simplest sum!'

Mr Sanderson had applied himself to his duties with enthusiasm; after six months the results of his perseverance were beginning to appear, and he basked in the gratitude of the parents if not in that of the children, for *they* knew that whatever knowledge they acquired was due to the merest luck; both had formidable memories for what they wished to retain and could be as fluent as parrots when in the mood. Appearances, they knew, were what actually counted – the appearance of knowledge, the appearance of good breeding. Every day, seated at the study table in the big, glassed-in balcony, they observed their tutor with sly, amused eyes.

One morning, Hilda, bored with syntax, had said, 'Ram Lal is dying. He is dying of pneumonia down there in the room above his shop.' Ram Lal was the merchant from whom the Strongs bought their groceries.

'All his relations have arrived,' said Richard. 'Listen!

You can hear them howling like jackals. In the morning Ram Lal will be dead. Will Father have to pay his bill if he dies, Mr Sanderson?'

'There is such a thing as honour,' Mr Sanderson reminded them coldly.

It had been difficult to concentrate after that, for the sound of Ram Lal's grieving relatives floated up from the bazaar into their ears.

'They'll have to cremate him,' said Hilda. 'Then we can watch it from the path behind the house.'

'You have such grisly ideas,' Richard complained sanctimoniously. 'Hasn't she, Mr Sanderson?'

'Grisly, Richard, grisly! And now let us please continue.'

Ram Lal did not die. Instead, he committed the sacrilege of recovering after the family priest had pronounced him extinct, and thereby became an outcaste. His business suffered because now only the lowest castes and the few Europeans in the place would deal with him. The tormented man sometimes trudged up the hill to the Strongs to seek advice. Mr Strong advised him to become a Christian, and when he recoiled from the idea, Mr Sanderson suggested that he embrace Islam. 'Obviously,' said the Eurasian, 'you might as well become something, since your own people won't have you, now that you're supposed to be dead.'

Ram Lal beat his forehead with his hands. 'I should have died!' he moaned. 'Yes, it would have been better for everyone if I had died.'

Discussing the situation later with his pupils, Mr Sanderson had shrugged and smiled. 'Such superstition!' he said.

'What is superstition?' asked Richard. The tutor explained as well as he could, and then, glancing at their faces, he added, 'I think one might say that prejudice is a kind of superstition also.'

'What's prejudice?'

'Oh, it might mean a number of things, like believing that one person is better than another person.' He would have enlarged on the subject, but decided not to when he saw the faint smile that passed between Hilda and Richard.

But on this cool summer evening, as he strolled on the terrace, Mr Sanderson was conscious of a rare peace of mind. The children had been unusually well behaved all day, Mrs Strong had congratulated him on his success with them, and Mr Strong had given him a raise in pay. True, no one had invited him to come in for a chat or a smoke before going to bed, but then, perhaps he was foolish to expect it. One cannot have everything, he reminded himself philosophically.

A nighthawk boomed on the hillside and the Pahari's song died away, but the tune lingered in Mr Sanderson's ears and he hummed its curious nasal melody, pitched in a minor key, until he suddenly recollected himself and stopped, casting a glance at the house, where the oil lamps had been lighted. The music of a mandolin reached him, but its tune was not that of the Pahari; it sang, instead, of mountains and fountains and dunes and moons, and at that moment Mr Sanderson remembered that tonight was the night of the moon's eclipse, and that he had promised the children to remind them of it. Earlier he had explained the phenomenon to them and they had been greatly excited, bombarding him with questions, flattering him by their earnest attention. It was on such rare occasions that Mr Sanderson achieved a self-respect that came close to a sense of superiority. For all that he was poor and of a significant darkness, still he was intelligent and sensitive; he had something to teach those who were willing to learn. So he had taken his time explaining the causes of the moon's eclipse, while Hilda perched on one arm of his chair, her golden pigtail swaying against his cheek, and Richard perched on the other arm, absent-mindedly stroking Mr Sanderson's head as if it were a dog's. Sensuous happiness welled up in the young tutor, causing his eyes to fill with tears. He remembered that moment now as he strolled on the terrace in the deepening Himalayan twilight. Night would come with a rush, then the moon would rise above the spur of the hill across the lake.

Mr Sanderson could hear Ram Lal arguing with his wife down in the bazaar, but he could not make out the words. There was a clatter of brass pots being washed and put away after the evening meal, and the crying of Ram Lal's youngest grandchild. The air thickened with darkness, and moths began to flutter among the citron trees, and Mr Sanderson observed suddenly the emerging brow of the full moon. He threw aside the stub of his cigarette and called to the children, 'Hilda! Richard!'

They appeared on the balcony of the house. 'What is it, Sandy?'

He was always secretly pleased when they addressed him by this diminutive.

'The eclipse,' he told them. 'You'll see it in a few minutes. Come down here with me.'

They joined him and all three stared at the moon's increasing radiance as it rose above the dark spur of the hill. Mr and Mrs Strong appeared on the balcony. 'I hope you remember what Mr Sanderson told you about the eclipse,' said Mr Strong to the children. 'I bet you don't!'

'Of course they do,' said Mr Sanderson. He put his hands on their shoulders as they stood on either side of him. 'Don't you, Hilda, Richard?'

They answered in unison, 'It is caused by the shadow of the earth falling on the moon's surface.'

'Hurray!' cried Mr Strong, and Mrs Strong said, 'Congratulations, Mr Sanderson!'

The valley filled with darkness. Only the lake retained light, catching it from the sky. Then the rising moon cleared the shoulder of the hill and the children stared in amazement at its face, scarred and red and unrecognizable, with what looked like an immense birthmark spreading slowly across it. A malign glance seemed to hold the world transfixed; then, from the bazaar below the hill, pandemonium broke loose, a terrific banging of pots and pans, howls, whistles, screams, and the piercing adjuration of a single voice, '*Chhor do! Chhor do! Chhor do!*'

'Why are they saying that? What do they mean?' asked Hilda.

Mr Sanderson laughed. 'They think that the devil has hold of the moon and they're shouting to him to let go. Listen!'

'*Chhor do! Chhor do! Chhor do!*'

Shrieks and groans accompanied the shouting, and a noise of drums and the bleating of trumpets. From the balcony came the laughter of Mrs Strong. 'Oh, the idiots!' she said. 'They really believe it!'

'But is it true?' demanded Richard. 'Has the devil really got hold of the moon?'

'Richard!' exclaimed Mr Sanderson, aghast. 'After what I was telling you only this afternoon!'

The boy stirred uneasily, his eyes fixed on the blemish, his ears filled with the hubbub of the mob down in the bazaar, where every voice was hurling imprecations at the sky and every pot and pan in creation seemed to be banging in unison.

'Let's go down and watch them!' cried Hilda suddenly.

'Very well,' said Mr Sanderson. 'You asked me once what was the meaning of superstition. This will be an object lesson for you. Come.'

'Better put cotton wool in your ears,' advised Mr Strong from the balcony.

'Don't let the children out of your sight, Mr Sanderson,' said Mrs Strong.

The young man held out a hand to each child. 'Come,' he said authoritatively, and a thrill went through him as their young, moist fingers clutched his. Usually, if he ventured a slight caress, he was promptly rebuffed. But tonight was different, tonight he was master of ceremonies, dispenser of favours. Holding their hands, he led them down the stony path towards the bazaar, and as they drew near, the uproar became truly deafening. 'Goodness!' said Hilda, giggling.

'Imbeciles!' said Mr Sanderson. 'Idiots!' His white-trousered legs glittered in the eerie light of the eclipse, and beside them skipped the pale, bare legs of the children; their faces were luminous on either side of him.

Just above the bazaar the path widened into a sort of rough terrace, and here they came to a halt, staring at the scene below them. The narrow street seethed with humanity – men, women, and children, all clutching bits of metal which they banged and rattled in unremitting frenzy. Their voices were lifted in screeching denunciation of the evil one who held the moon in his grip, and every eye rolled in wrath and terror towards the captive, hanging bloodily in the dark-blue sky.

'Chhor do! Chhor do! Chhor do!'

Trumpets brayed. A stone, hurled by some optimist, whizzed past Mr Sanderson's head. Richard began to laugh on a curious, helpless note. 'They're throwing stones at the devil!' he exclaimed. 'Sandy, did you see that? They're throwing stones at the devil!'

'Oh, look!' cried Hilda, pointing. They looked and saw

the slight, agile figure of Govind, the forest ranger, pushing his way forward, carrying an ancient carbine.

'Make way for Govind!' shouted someone. 'Make way, make way!'

'What will Govind do?' asked Hilda. She was clinging to Mr Sanderson's hand and he could feel the excitement running through her.

'He's probably going to take a pot shot at the devil,' said Mr Sanderson. Gently he caressed her hand.

'Look!' she cried again. 'Look, Sandy!' Govind brought the carbine to his shoulder, aiming at the moon. The mighty explosion was followed by an instant's lull and a smell of gunpowder. Govind stood with the smoking carbine in one hand, the other rubbing his shoulder, which ached from the recoil.

'He missed!' cried Richard. 'He missed the devil!' Then, in shrill Hindustani, he yelled, '*Chhor do! Chhor do!*'

It was the signal for the crowd to renew its howls, and Richard, tearing his hand free of Mr Sanderson's, plunged down the hillside towards the street, followed by Hilda, both of them shrieking blue murder.

'Children!' wailed Mr Sanderson. 'Hilda! Richard! Come back this instant! I command you! I forbid you!'

His voice was lost in the babble, and in despair he followed them down the hillside into the mob of milling, half-naked bodies. No one paid any attention to him. Sweaty limbs pummelled his immaculate clothes, bare feet tramped on his shoes. Of the children there was no sign; the mob had swallowed them. Mr Sanderson found himself standing beside Govind, the forest ranger. 'Where are the children?' the tutor demanded, his voice heavily charged with the English intonation. 'Tell me at once! Don't stand there yelling, you bloody fool!'

But Govind didn't hear him. His face pale with fright,

he was frantically trying to reload the carbine for another shot. Mr Sanderson began once more to push and claw his way through the crowd. His white suit lost its starch, sweat poured down his face, his glossy jet-black hair hung lank over his forehead. At last he caught up with his charges. They were wedged between Ram Lal and his family, who had provided them with brass pots, which they were banging together as they yelled with the others. Mr Sanderson peered at them in horror. 'Are you mad? Drop those things! Come away at once!'

Hilda paused long enough to say, 'Ram Lal told us that if we don't make the devil let go the moon, he will put out its light for ever. Then it will get pitch dark and we shall all be at his mercy.'

'What on earth are you talking about?'

'About Shaitan, the devil!' She brought two brass pots together with a sickening clang. Richard, flanked by Ram Lal's grandsons, bellowed passionately, '*Chhor do*, you beast, you fiend! *Chhor do!*'

Mr Sanderson felt strangely helpless. He was almost suffocated by the press of bodies, his ears were numb, his eyes smarted. Another shot from Govind's carbine was followed by another moment of silence, then a renewal of the yells, screams, groans. Someone thrust a pewter tray and a heavy iron ladle into Mr Sanderson's hands. Hilda stared at him, her face colourless, her eyes blazing. 'Beat it, Sandy,' she commanded hoarsely. 'Do you want us all to be killed?'

With a slight, sardonic smile, he obeyed, thumping the tray with the ladle, wincing at the added discord. The smile faded, his teeth clenched, and he beat harder and harder, the percussion sending white-hot tremors up his arms. He found himself whispering, then shouting with the others, half in mockery and half in despair. Suddenly he noticed that tears were pouring down the children's faces; between sobs Hilda cried, 'Why doesn't the devil let go? Why doesn't he? Make him let go, somebody! Sandy, make the devil let go!' She dropped her brass pots and cast herself on the ground, twisting and moaning while the crowd howled on.

Mr Sanderson saw the crumpled figure, its golden pigtail writhing in the dust. Swiftly he bent and lifted her. Then he seized Richard by an arm, and somehow, by pushing and kicking, he got the two children away from the crowd and back on to the path above the bazaar. There, for a minute, they stood with heaving chests, sobs falling away inside them, their aching eyes moving from the crowd below to the discoloured and impassive orb above.

Gradually the children's hysteria subsided. Mr Sanderson produced a handkerchief and wiped Hilda's face, then Richard's, then his own. He smoothed his hair and pulled his necktie into place. 'Hilda,' he said abruptly, 'let me see your hands.' He had noticed that she had been furtively licking them, and suspected that she might have cut them when she threw herself on the ground.

'They're all right,' she said, and put them behind her back.

'Well, see that you put iodine on them before you go to bed, unless you want to get tetanus.'

Richard asked, 'Is tetanus the same as hydrophobia?'

'No,' said Mr Sanderson. They turned and made their way slowly up the hill towards the house, where the lighted windows shone against the dark hillside. The children did not offer to take their tutor's hands, and he did not suggest that they do so. He felt utterly dispirited. Behind him the noise from the bazaar went on and on; it would, he knew, continue unabated till the shadow of the earth had passed from the moon's face, leaving it clear and unclouded once more, and he wondered briefly what charm or what logic might serve to drive away another shadow from men's minds and from their hearts.

PHILIP MASON

The Simla Thunders

Sheo Dat looked at the clock. He spent a good deal of time looking at the clock, because really no one could be expected to take any interest in lists of boots. He belonged to a comparatively unimportant part of General Headquarters, which in 1943 was in Simla because there was no room for it in Delhi, and his work was to copy out the total at the foot of each return of boots that came in from units all over India and Burma and Ceylon, and then to add up the results. He had to make fifty entries in an hour, and if he did not, the superintendent of his section would keep him back after five o'clock. It was not a difficult standard and he could do it easily if he did not spend too much time dreaming about other things or gossiping in the corridors with his friends. And it was worth doing his quota, because there was no escape from staying behind if his superintendent said he must. If he ventured on defiance, he would be put out in the street, and although sixty rupees a month was not much nowadays it was a great deal better than nothing at all. He hated staying behind, because once the door of the office closed he could hurry away to a new and exciting world that had only just opened to him, which had really brought an interest into his life. And today he was particularly anxious to get away.

He was thinking of that new world now as he looked at the clock and saw it was twenty minutes to five. He had finished thirty-seven entries already that hour, so there would be comfortable time to make thirteen more and add up the total. He could spare a moment for a glance in his mind at the stuffy little upstairs room over Gauri Shankar's food-shop in the Lakar Bazaar, where he and his friends met to conspire against the tyranny that oppressed their country and to debate on how they could strike a blow for freedom. That little room made an entrancing background to his thoughts. There was the thrill of doing something that would horrify his superiors in the office and make them shake in their shoes and there was the breathless feeling that at any moment the police might burst in upon them. Yet at the same time it was comforting to know that so far they had not actually done anything for which they could be punished, and to enjoy the conviction that their efforts were morally praiseworthy and all in the cause of patriotism. Sheo Dat for a blissful moment saw the faces of his friends, thought of the burning zeal and heroism they had so often expressed, and pictured the interest with which they would meet their new member this evening. Then he bent irritably to his work and made the thirty-eighth entry of the hour.

When he had first found that his friends Bhola Nath and Badri Parshad had ideas like his own, they had made the habit of meeting at Gauri Shankar's shop and eating their evening meal together, without any idea that their meetings would go any further or that the proprietor might eventually join them. But he must have overheard some scrap of the three young clerks' conversation, for one day when they had finished eating he came and sat down with them and ordered for each of them a big brass tumbler full of tea. He began to talk, rather cautiously at first, but he gradually revealed more and more of his mind, until at last he suggested that they should form a secret society. They agreed enthusiastically.

It was Sheo Dat's idea that they should call themselves the Simla Thunders, but it was Badri Parshad who devised most of the precautions against betrayal or discovery which gave the proceedings their peculiar fascination. The whole of the first meeting was spent on drafting a declaration of the high aims of the society and an oath, which the members must all swear and sign, to preserve perpetual secrecy and fidelity. At first Badri Parshad had intended that the whole declaration as well as the oath should be written in blood; but blood was found to be so unsatisfactory as a writing fluid that they contented themselves with ink for the declaration and blood for the oath. And of course the signatures were in blood.

Next came the question of where the documents should be kept. It was agreed after much debate that it would be unsafe for the members to take turns, as Badri Parshad had first suggested, at wearing them in a packet next to the heart, suspended by a string from the neck. No, inglorious though it might be, it was much wiser to hide them beneath a floorboard in the meeting-room, which, on payment of a reasonable rent to Gauri Shankar, had now become Bhola Nath's bedroom.

Then there had been the long discussion about the password. 'India's Freedom' had been Sheo Dat's choice and in the end this had prevailed over 'Death to Tyrants,' the runner-up. The ritual for admission had been suggested by Badri Parshad.

When all these preliminaries had been settled, the Simla Thunders were ready to conspire. But here a serious difficulty for the first time arose. For they did not know what to conspire about. They did not know how to begin. They wanted to help the enemy but they did not know anyone who could tell them what sort of help the enemy needed. It was no good Sheo Dat making his lists of boots more slowly because, quite apart from its being inglorious and unromantic, no one could seriously believe that this method would change the course of the war, while it would certainly rebound on his own head and he would find himself out of a job. And it was a job that someone else could easily be found to do. No, they could get no further by slowing down the work. And as for information, which they were constantly urged by posters to withhold from the enemy, they did not know how to get their information to the Japanese even if they had any.

'And we haven't really got anything to give them,' Sheo Dat said gloomily. 'It can't be any use sending them lists of boots. It is true the lists are marked secret, but the British mark everything secret just to deceive us. They are very cunning.'

That had been the deadlock which they had reached about ten days ago. Then Sheo Dat had his bright idea. He finished his work at five o'clock sharp that day and hurried away. He had some preliminary inquiries to make, for he was not going to present his friends with a half-baked plan with none of the details worked out. He thought he would just have time to finish his reconnaissance and get back to the meeting-place.

It took him longer than he thought, and the others had begun to eat when he arrived. He was bursting to tell them all about it, but it was a rule never to talk about the society downstairs in the eating-room, and except for a few mysterious hints he kept quiet. He gobbled his food and was finished soon after the others. It was another rule, one of Badri Parshad's, that they should leave the room one by one. Sheo Dat was the last, for Gauri Shankar had warned them he could not come that night. He was often busy about the shop.

At last Sheo Dat had finished and it was safe to move. He went quietly upstairs and tapped on the door with their secret knock, three times quickly and three times slowly.

Badri Parshad whispered a formula at the door and Sheo Dat answered with the password. He slipped in and took his place. Then at once he began to expound his plan.

'We shall need to make dummy revolvers,' he began. 'Real ones would be better but they would be very difficult to get. And we shall need masks and electric torches and a sharp knife. When the night we have chosen comes, we will creep out to the big school on the spur to the east, where the white-faced boys are trained to grow up as tyrants and oppress us. We shall cut the telephone wires. There is only one watchman, and it will be easy to threaten him with a dummy revolver and tie him up. Then we must creep into the long room where the boys sleep at night. One of us will be the guide and will hold each boy still as he lies in his sleep while another cuts his throat. It will be enough to kill six or so because by that we shall show that boys cannot be trained to be serpents with impunity and that the might of India is awake. It is better to kill the snake in the egg. Then we shall escape eastwards over the hills. We will not go down to the plains by the usual ways because they will be watching the road and the railway. When we come to the plains we will go by train to Bombay.'

They were all impressed by the splendour and daring of this plan, though probably any one of them would have wept if he had pictured the grief of his victim's mother when the plan had succeeded. But that they did not think of.

There were sixteen of them now, counting Gauri Shankar, who was away the night the plan was broached; he had introduced two more very young clerks to the society. They talked it over and portioned out the tasks of getting the masks, the dummy revolvers, and the other things that were needed. Then Badri Parshad made a very important contribution to the scheme. He said:

'But in case our plan goes wrong, we must not fall into the hands of the police, to suffer torture and humiliation. Sooner than that we must end all. We must each carry a phial of poison to be taken in case of emergency.'

Everyone agreed to this too, though none of them knew how to set about obtaining the poison. But Gauri Shankar, they thought, might be able to help over that.

They went ahead with their plans for the rest of the week and by the sixth night had collected everything except the poison. The sixth night Gauri Shankar came to the meeting; it was the first he had attended since Sheo Dat's plan was accepted. When he heard about it, he shook his head.

'No, no,' he said, 'this will not do. The boys who go to that school are never going to be high officers. They are the sons of station masters. And no one would approve of your act. It is shameful to kill children and everyone who has any right to be called an Indian would agree.'

The young men were ashamed. They saw it at once when Gauri Shankar put it to them. And of course they were disappointed that their week of effort should go for nothing. But after all, said Sheo Dat more cheerfully, dummy revolvers and masks and torches might well be useful in some other plan.

'And the poison,' said Badri Parshad eagerly, 'that we shall certainly need whatever we do.'

Gauri Shankar agreed, and said that he knew someone who, he thought, would be able to find the poison for them.

'I have been thinking for some time of bringing him into our society,' he said, 'but at first I was not quite sure of him. I had doubts that he might be a CID man. But now I am sure that he is all right. I asked him some questions last night, and I am sure he is a patriot. And he may be able to help over the poison because he was once a chemical student at Benares Hindu University. But he was expelled after a year because of his patriotism.'

They discussed this for some time and then authorized Gauri Shankar to produce the new member. He came the next day, a bird-like little man with a sallow complexion and a way of thrusting his neck forward and peering into your face. He listened to them and talked a good deal himself, fluent speeches about oppression and tyranny which assured them of his good faith. He said he was sure he could get the poison, but it would cost at least five rupees a bottle, and it might be more. In the end he collected five rupees from each of the six; Gauri Shankar said he would pay later. The new member also said that he might be able to suggest a way of helping the enemy, but he would have to make inquiries and it would take three or four days.

That was why Sheo Dat looked so eagerly at the clock at twenty to five, and turned more irritably even than usual to the entries in his list of boots. The Simla Thunders were going to get their poison tonight, and also to hear how they could strike a blow at the British by helping the Japanese. As soon as he could, he completed his totals and hurried away up the hillside to meet Badri Parshad, with whom he was going to spend the time until the meeting. A tiresome period it was, to two persons as eager and impatient as these, but at last it was over and they were sitting in the little upstairs room.

The new member produced six tiny phials of colourless liquid. He explained that this was one of the swiftest and most deadly poisons known to science.

'It looks like water,' said Sheo Dat.

'That is a great advantage,' said the new member earnestly. 'No one will suspect anything if they see it. No, I beg you! Do not undo the stopper! Even a sniff would make you ill.'

They talked about the poison for some time, and at last decided that at present it was unnecessary to carry it with them wherever they went, so the poison too joined the other properties in the hiding-place under the loose board. Then they came to the question of how they could help the enemy. The new member became very mysterious. He leaned forward and peered into each face in turn. He asked if they were each certain of the good faith of all the others, and he would not begin to talk until he had heard their protestations and looked again at the oath written in blood which they had all signed. At last he said:

'There is a German Embassy in Kabul. That is where we can sell our knowledge and strike a blow for our country.'

He explained that he knew a man who had a friend in Peshawar who traded into Afghanistan. And he would carry a letter.

They were all impressed and excited by this. It was some time before Sheo Dat said:

'But what shall we put in the letter?'

'Write first that we want to hurt the British, and then that we are clerks in General Headquarters who can get secret information. Say that we will get it if they will tell us what kind of information they want and will send money. We must ask for money because, with their low mentality, they will not believe that we are doing this for patriotism.'

They were eager to waste no time and Sheo Dat was deputed to draft the letter at once. They all had suggestions and alterations to make, but at last they were agreed and a fair copy was made and handed over to the new member. They decided not to meet again for two days and then one by one they slipped away.

The new member had stowed the letter in the inside

pocket of his coat. He waited till the last, and even when all the others had gone he stayed a few more minutes talking to Gauri Shankar. There were not many lights still showing in the house-fronts when he left the shop and went down the steep hill, turning sharp to the left at the bottom below the rickshaw works. He seemed a little uneasy, for he stopped now and then as he went and stood still as if listening; but he walked purposefully between his halts. He knew where he was going.

He reached another little tea-shop, much the same as Gauri Shankar's. It was the last to be still open and the proprietor was half asleep, but he had not closed because he still had one customer. A big man who looked like a Pathan money-lender was lolling in the corner reading a newspaper. The new member asked for tea with cardamom seeds in it, an odd order for anyone so obviously not a Tibetan. He had to speak rather loud to waken the proprietor, who went grumbling to fetch it. The Pathan lowered his newspaper and took a long look. The new member began to sip his tea; the Pathan resumed his reading, but after a few minutes threw down the paper and went out. He turned away down the hill and followed a road leading out of the bazaar.

The new member finished his tea, paid for it and went out. He too went down the hill. He stopped and listened, but moved on as if reassured. A little way beyond the shops he heard a cough from the shadow of a big cedar. He turned aside and squatted to make water. When he stood up the Pathan from the tea-shop put his hand on his shoulder. It was very dark, too dark to recognize a face. The Pathan said something in a low voice and a few seconds later went on down the hill but took the first turn up to his left, back towards the street lights and the bazaars. The new member stayed a few minutes in the shadow of the cedar and then he too moved away.

Two mornings later Sheo Dat's letter lay on the desk of an office in Delhi. The officer who was reading it seemed pleased. He said:

'This will save us a lot of trouble, and they will write much more convincing letters for us than we could ever invent ourselves. It was lucky those ham-handed policemen in Security happened to mention this instead of rounding them up straight away.'

The letter was sealed up again and went on its way. It went by the hand of an officer to Peshawar, where it was handed over to a policeman of a special kind. He did with it just what the new member of the Simla Thunders had promised. He gave it to an inconspicuous man who passed it on to a trader whose habit it was to go up and down through the passes to Afghanistan, with a string of pack animals, in the spring and autumn of every year. A few days later the trader started on his journey.

Here ill-fortune befell the letter. The last time that particular trader had been through the territory of the Pathan tribes on the Border he had made a mistake. Quite a small one, but enough to make the tribesmen wonder whether he was something else as well as the trader he seemed to be. To resolve their doubts, they went through his belongings very thoroughly. They found nothing to prove that he was spying on themselves, but they did find and read the letter from the Simla Thunders.

Now the tribesmen were not interested in the World War except to the extent it affected them. It had sent up the price of ammunition shockingly, and it had made the British rather more long-suffering than usual, that was all. They were not particularly interested in who won and certainly had no desire to help the British. But here was someone whom they suspected of spying on themselves caught in the act of plotting to help the Japanese. It was their immediate and unanimous reaction to destroy him and gain credit for themselves by betraying him to the British. So the letter went to British territory.

But the trader had followed a devious route. He had turned away westward from the Khyber, and the letter which had gone into tribal country from Peshawar came back to Malakand, where some little time was spent in sorting out the curious antecedents of that double-faced trader. Meanwhile, here was a clear case of someone trying to communicate with the enemy. The letter had invited the German Embassy to reply by the hand of the bearer to an address in Simla. Obviously the writer would not be found at that address, but it could be made the starting-point for inquiries. And it was.

The Simla Thunders had spent some time in thinking out the matter of the address. They had given a fictitious name and the address of a sweet shop whose proprietor knew none of them and had not been consulted at all. But in his employment was a friend of Badri Parshad's, who usually took the letters when the postman came, and who would certainly hear if a letter arrived for someone unknown. He believed that Badri Parshad was engaged in a love affair. If the letter was handed to him by the postman, he would say nothing about it to his employer and simply give it to Badri Parshad. There was always the danger of course that the sweetmeat-seller might meet the postman himself and refuse to accept a letter for someone he did not know, but he was inquisitive by nature and was more likely to take it and say he would make inquiries. In that case, he would probably leave it lying about and forget it and it would soon find its way to Badri Parshad. Even if he did refuse the letter, Badri Parshad's friend would hear of it and could run after the postman.

One day at lunch time, Badri Parshad's friend came to the office and sent in a note to Badri Parshad by a messenger who was sunning himself outside the building. A few minutes later Badri Parshad came out of the building and walked up to the Mall, where he met his friend and engaged in earnest conversation with him. After a few minutes' talk, he turned away and hurried back towards the office. A rickshaw coolie who had been leaning against the railings of the Mall sauntered down to the gate by which he had entered and spoke to the policeman on duty.

Badri Parshad hurried through the building to find Sheo Dat. But there was no Sheo Dat to be found; he had gone out and none of the clerks in his office knew where. Badri Parshad left a message asking him to come and see him as soon as he arrived, and meanwhile went to his own office where he sat quaking until Sheo Dat came. He led Sheo Dat outside and explained in breathless tones that the police had been making inquiries at the sweetmeat-seller's shop. So far everyone had professed ignorance and no one had been arrested. He was frightened and had no idea what to do. But Sheo Dat was made of sterner stuff. With hardly any pause for thought he said:

'We must destroy the evidence at Gauri Shankar's; you had better say you have a stomach-ache and leave office at once. Go straight there, warn Gauri Shankar and burn everything. After this we must not meet again for a long time. If we are questioned, we none of us know anything about it. I will go and warn the others.'

Sheo Dat had always been the leader, and Badri Parshad hurried off at once to do as he was told. Sheo Dat went round to tell the others. Then he went back to his lists of boots.

But he did not make any entries. He sat staring at the page, thinking how he would confront his captors, how he would refuse to speak and betray his comrades, how he would be led forth to execution. He had paused on his way to the firing-squad for a few noble words to a group of weeping relatives when the harsh voice of the superintendent pointed out that he would have to stay behind if he did not finish his quota by five o'clock. Sheo Dat bent to his work again, but a new thought struck him. Execution he could face, but not the humiliation of submitting to the police, the torture and indignities they would put upon him. He must have the poison! He had forgotten to tell Badri Parshad to bring him that.

He went quickly to the superintendent. He said he felt dizzy and ill, and he would make up the quota tomorrow. He was not a bad clerk as a rule and grudging permission to go was given. He hurried away to Gauri Shankar's shop.

He found Badri Parshad standing by the side of a smoking fire.

'The poison!' he cried. 'Give me the poison!'

'The poison? Here it is; I was just going to throw it in the fire.'

Sheo Dat seized one of the tiny phials. A chill pang assailed his stomach. Poison! Death! This was the moment, the end of all he had known. But he thought of humiliation, of rough contemptuous hands. Better death than dishonour! He uncorked the phial and drank the colourless liquid, head thrown back in a proud defiant gesture.

Nothing happened.

He waited. And waited. And waited.

J. G. HITREC

Rulers' Morning

How do I feel? Edward Parsons rose on his elbows and looked around the room. For seven years, every morning, that question encompassed all the known shades of good and bad, it possessed the uncanny power of resolving the coming day in a flash. Do I feel good? He stroked his stubble and looked at his wife. She was still asleep, only partly covered, and in that child-like peace the soft under-core of her character seemed to beam through fat and years. Or not so good?

He climbed out of bed and walked to the balcony, he scratched himself, raised the collar of his pyjama and pressed it round his neck. The sun had already disintegrated the big Circle into separate areas, bright green, brown, grey – the lawn, paths cutting it in a thoughtful pattern, the asphalt road binding it like a satin garter. Before all that brightness his eyes narrowed. If it were morning always! Morning with this dew, this nip in the air, always morning! Warmly inert, his mind registered the white-cloaked men scuttling along and across the Circle, they always carried something, when did they sleep? He scratched his head, his fingers burrowed through the hair, nearer and nearer, almost there. They tore into the itching spot pleasurably, but brought back the question. He gazed at the Circle, letting the colour take the initiative. On the sunny side the palms glittered, the long colonnaded building opposite was a huge slice of white cheese out of a wrapping. Fresh and gay, white was in the majority. I feel good, he thought, couldn't feel better.

He went into the bathroom. Somewhere in the flat a door shut gently; little Bab out for her morning walk. Every morning that door-click ushered in a little more stability. In this country children were a better idea than in most.

He rinsed his denture, gargled a few times loudly, it was time Pat woke up in the next room! and put the denture in his mouth. The flavour of the antiseptic was pungent and reviving. The sun leap-frogged from the window-pane on to the mirror; he looked at the image critically. It wasn't bad, considering, but if you looked close and long enough there were little discoveries, nothing alarming, incipient pouches seemingly there for the first time, the skin underneath mildly purple. All right, mirror, we all age! There is more silver on the temples, the mirror said impersonally, not so fast, Ed! Well, mirror, a few more years and I won't have to go fast any more. He stepped back, the image blurred and the general effect became more pleasing.

When he returned to the bedroom there was a knock on the door. He pulled the sheet over Pat; she looked at him wide-eyed, still some distance away. *Chota hazri*, he said, and one of these days you'll catch rheumatism, it's still quite cold. Come in! he said aloud. The boy came in with the tray, set it on the table at her side and went.

They sipped the hot tea; the sound of their lips and the fine fresh aroma brought complete awakening. The various sections of his brain began a lively sorting; this was speech, family, business and, between them, half-lit lanes, still drowsy, and they were being crossed by Bab, and right now by Pat, they exuded scents, colour and familiar words, and all of it geared together, smoothly, like the vitals of a delicate wrist-watch. Yep, morning is all right and I feel good. Now that the boy had gone, she had thrown off the cover and lay only in her night-gown, a pink one, my favourite colour. She looked wholesome, though soft and not-so-young, and there was something about her very white skin, forever escaping out of that gown, that was comfortable and reliable, and perhaps it was the face after all, indomitably rosy through the years of heat and dust, or the silky blonde hair that guarded her neck, like a permanent insulation, against age and erosion. But mornings were like that.

Turning over he slapped her gently, lovingly. Of the many things he had done for years some had already palled, but this was one that didn't seem to depend on time. The bed glowed with their combined smells, the disorder was an intimate one, and even the rip in the pillow-case seemed somehow a part of a greater unity.

Feeling good, Ed?

She smiled teasingly, motherly. Looking at him above the pillow, she saw him only as a man without an office, without anything to do, without clothes and a second thought. But when he tried to come nearer, she held her hand out.

The doctor said no, Ed.

Damn the doctor! Remaining poised, he thought it over. And anyway, he added, he said to use discretion.

The doctor's machines overwhelmed his other ideas, professionals always complicated simple issues. Yet, even the remembrance of the pills, the tedious treatment and the expense could not win against the fine morning. He went back to his bed and took the paper which the boy had brought. His mind worked again efficiently, now that it was allowed to. The smell of the first cigarette gave the air a crisp scent of worldliness.

He read the Public Notices page, the Trade Notices and then spent a long time on Classifieds. Someone wanted an engineer, an electrical engineer, a European, someone was being awfully optimistic – it was wartime. He went back to yesterday's deal. A good deal, I made a lot of money, wait till she hears! A few more like that and I won't have to work – the recollection made him warmly happy. A few more strokes of luck and we could pack up to the hills until the war's over. He suddenly realized that his well-being dated from yesterday, that the sleep had only furbished it, that everything was good as long as one felt safe.

Give me that part, she said.

The paper divided, both sank lazily and read. Their feet met where the beds touched. Slowly, absently, he rubbed his big toe up and down her ankle. He wondered if he should buy her a present, why shouldn't I? we can afford it now, or a nice cheque to do as she pleases, though she might go haywire, women are like that. Holding it out on her was an act of meanness. I *will* tell her, perhaps at breakfast. He poured himself another cup of tea. The sound of car-horns strayed into the room. Like all sounds from outside, always, it brought the realization of the frailty of all little worlds that happened to be inside the big ones. But, he thought, not for always. It was in the main a question of perspective.

On the front page, the fighting had run into a dust-storm. Somewhere in the bog and sludge of a tropical island men divided their time between malaria and tree-top snipers, in the hills of Arakan mortar shells blossomed in the paddy-fields; and somewhere in the open blue above Delhi a big plane, or maybe several, churned the morning freshness. He held his breath and listened, but their roar was dull, like a monsoon landslide, and it was going away. He turned the page and coughed – I ought to cut down on my tobacco. The inside page was nearer home: Seven donkeys parading the streets, each with the name of an official, that was a good one! even though it bred contempt. A nonentity of nine, ten, eleven letters, good Lord, who thinks of such names! wrote about independence, they can't think of another subject, can they? on and on, miles of it, blah, blah, blah independence. He tried to put himself in the writer's place, but gave it up. He turned to Pat and flicked the page with his fingers.

If it didn't make you sick! Where is their sense of proportion, what do they know about ruling? Do they know that you've got to rule for a hell of a long time to know something about it?

Well, who does?

She watched him and around her mouth were the beginnings of amusement. She, too, had dropped her paper and was covering her bare knees with it.

Don't be silly, Pat, *we* do of course.

Who's we? Her smile was benevolent.

All of us, what did you think? The government, all the officials, every man of status. You and me, for instance. What's funny about that?

You a ruler, Ed? She found his foot with hers and scratched it. Go on, darling.

I'm trying to talk to you seriously.

Edward Parsons Junior a ruler. Go on, I'm listening. How big is the territory?

Oh pipe down, you.

Her way of smiling hadn't changed in years and when she teased there was no sting in it. He bent over her, ruffled her hair and smacked her bare calf.

If you refuse to grow up yourself, I can't make you. Come on, we ought to be getting up.

He threw the paper at her and rose. When the tune in his head steadied, he whistled it. He went into the bathroom once more and shaved; the cream smelled of lilacs in a soft breeze, of an open landscape under a lather of clouds – it was a fine invention. Could *they* have thought of it? Could they invent the safety razor in another thousand years? And what of the electricity, the transformers, bulbs, switches and other things? Invention *was* civilization. You can't rule anybody until you're civilized yourself. You just talk your head off, bellyache about the wrong things at the wrong times, and then, finally, bellyache about the strain of your bellyaching.

The astringent set mild fire to his cheeks. He walked back into the bedroom and began to dress. He sprinkled a little talcum under his arms and a little on his feet, before pulling on socks. These things made a fine morning into a fine day, did *they* invent them?

She, too, had gone to wash. He heard the loud gushing of the big tap, there was true fastidiousness for you! He stepped into his trousers. Wonder if I should tell her, might as well combine it with a present. Being fully dressed was being fully conscious, the red tie led to the black bow-tie, are we dining out tonight? He liked dressing in the evening, one felt purged and equal to everyone else wearing the same symbols. It was a funny life and a funny country, by God, one made it bearable only by being alert.

Pat came out in a spotted blue gown. Shocked and prodded into life, she appeared even younger, he watched her in the mirror. She sat before the dressing table and combed her hair, then she buttoned the gown at the breast and rose.

I'll see about breakfast.

He felt momentarily lonely. Too long married, I suppose. He assembled the newspaper and put it under the night-table, he was finished. The traffic outside had become a regular rumble, someone was clapping hands.

The drawing and dining rooms were combined, separated only by a half-bookshelf that faced the door of the hall. Pat was already at the table. Everything shone brightly, the smell of fresh coffee made it definitive, irrevocable. He went to the desk and took the file, then sat down and propped the file against the flower vase. He buttered his toast and took the cup which she pushed towards him.

Are we dining out tonight, Pat?

Yes, with Fergussons. At the club.

I don't like Fergussons, but I suppose we'd better.

Her smile was the sublimation of the entire morning. He ate his eggs and remembered Choturam, the driver. Yesterday, Choturam was not at his post when he came out of the office. He was going to be fined eight annas. I think he knows it too.

Ed, I'm having trouble with the ayah. I think she's stealing. Bab likes her food sweet but she couldn't eat all that sugar.

If you're sure, sack her.

That's easily said. Will you try to get me another one?

Talk to her then. I subscribe to a little regulation squeeze, but stealing is quite another matter. Only you've got to be sure, Pat.

The front door clicked and Bab came in with the ayah. She kissed her parents, her cheeks were like her mother's, but she had a rash on her neck, the ointment had dried over it in white crusts. She had light blue eyes and sandy hair, she talked impetuously, four years old.

Look, Daddy, a black boy ga' me this.

She opened her hand – a dirty wooden top. Look, he played like this.

No, you don't, her father said. Give me that.

He took it away and gave it to the ayah.

Throw that away, Kanji! How many times must I tell you not to let her touch dirty things? He turned to his wife: This is your department, darling. I wish you'd do something about it.

Go and wash now, Bab, she said. I'll see you after breakfast.

Leaving the hall Bab turned around and waved.

It's getting lovelier every day, Pat said.

She imitated Bab's sing-song English and they both laughed. The idea of *babu*-English was still as droll as in the first year, and now they appreciated the finer points.

It won't be so lovely in a few years, he said, but she won't be the only one.

A few years ago the thought would have poisoned them both. Not now. We're all in the same boat, he thought, one of the things the war did to us, amongst others. Now it was merely amusing.

He opened the file, the clean copy of the contract he had prepared yesterday was on top. He clipped it to the file cover. Let me glance through it, he said to Pat. He read it again although he knew it by heart. The boy came in carrying a pot of fresh coffee, he set the tray on the table and began to pour.

Tell the ayah I want to talk to her after breakfast, Pat said to the boy.

Then, the inevitable happened.

As the boy turned to her, listening, the dark steamy spout missed the cup and splashed on the table, over the cruet, the file and the clean copy of the contract. Then it ceased just as suddenly. Both of them jumped and the boy shrank back babbling.

For God's sake! he shouted.

You fool! she said.

The servant ran for the duster and the two of them stood over the table and looked at each other. God almighty! he said through his teeth. By then blood had rushed to his head and swept everything before it. He couldn't think of a word. His hands trembled and he thrust one of them in his pocket.

Easy now, Ed! she said.

She had wiped the file with her napkin and shaken it. She took the contract copy, dabbed it and, when all the liquid had gone into the cloth, wiped the table. The boy returned and helped her. Neither looked at him standing there, still clutching the fork and gasping. When the words came, they were short and vicious but absurdly inexpressive of the tumult inside him.

You clumsy idiot –

It was unreasonable, of course, and he knew he was overdoing it, but all that was poignant and frenzied seemed to be heaved out in front. He heard the beat of his temples. Suddenly, too, the room lost its freshness and the street noise closed in. Bundled up in his wrath, in the sharp, deadly words that flitted around his mind, was this horror of the street noise coming nearer? I mustn't, he reminded himself, I mustn't, the doctor said. Better count quickly, one – two, three, four, five –

Yes, I must have been five when Mother first said: Behave or I'll call the dark Indian! It was a terrible threat. Do you know what he'll do to you, Edward? It was enough to still me for hours.

Get hold of yourself, Ed. Sit down.

She put her hand on his shoulder. The boy had again vanished. It was an unreal hand, though gentle, and its pressure forced him back into the chair, like a man uncertain of his seat. But the hand in his pocket shook as before.

Christ, they're all the same, he said with difficulty.

He thought he was beginning to control himself; he took the stained contract and put it into the file. Six, seven –

Words coalesced painfully. He closed the file and rose. I mustn't, his mind said. He walked to the drawing room and opened the desk, a little time is all I need, eight, nine, ten – He found another blue file and placed it on top of the first one.

I'll get your coat and topee, she said.

He walked to the balcony. Long, welling processions crossed the Circle in all directions, little black men dressed in white, their unremitting progress charged with a vague menace. The centipede! He recalled the newspaper article, whole lines crowded back, blah, blah, like the little bastards in the park, not stopping, face after face and all alike, always going somewhere, like some treacherous vermin. Again his temples beat louder. Fifteen, sixteen –

Martha's marriage did it finally. I was sixteen. Sister Martha who thought nothing of marrying into another race. Who thought beauty could be black and equally noble, foolish Martha.

Martha dear, it's an awful jump, believe me, not a question of prejudice.

You *are* prejudiced, Mother, why try to conceal it? Really, you talk as if he were a Zulu from darkest Africa. He's cultured and modern and, besides, I like brown men.

But, Martha, we know nothing of his background.

What difference does that make? He's lived here ever since he came to college. This is his background and home and we're going to live in London. Most important of all, I love him.

Tragic Martha who always chose the long road to wisdom. Martha whose firm, white body would be explored by black hands, shrivelled at the knuckles, bleached from inside. By those eternally purple lips, as if bruised –

Here, Ed, she said.

She held his cotton jacket and he slipped into it and

when the seams gripped his shoulders he felt a little steadier.

The car's waiting, dear. Don't think about it now, forget it. Would you like a capsule?

I'll be all right in a moment, he said.

They walked to the outer door and she held him around the waist. Her soft touch was the single communication with the warm intimacy of that earlier morning, but though reassuring it was already faint. The face, too, looked worn after the strain, the blue dots of her gown seemed mocking in comparison.

Come back early, she said. We're lunching at home today.

He bent down to kiss her cheek, stiffly. At that moment he would have liked her to smell stronger. Smells were symbolic, they had degrees, like other things in life, so much depended on them. He remembered *their* flowers. Strong-smelling and coloured, but usually dead by the evening. Smells were important.

Like the day of the flag-demonstration. The narrow street in a swirling flood of humanity, the dust and the sun beating down on them. Caught in it like a fly in a pool of oil. And terrified to the bone but afraid to show it.

We'll never get out, I said to Phil.

Philip was driving; he had spent years in the East, the sight of a large crowd, even demonstrators didn't worry him.

They're all right, Ed. A lot of noise, that's all.

What do you suppose they're shouting, Phil?

Oh something, how should I know – they always are.

How they smell!

Always do when they're excited, Philip said. But they'll be all right, don't worry.

A slow, viscous tide of hot bodies, of perspiration and acrid odour, of an overpowering imminence that made me turn yellow. Like the dank evaporation of a swamp, sweet and stomach-turning. And the flood tore at the car for a full hour, then subsided gradually, unwillingly, and left us quite alone, like a boat perched on the tallest sand-bank –

Take care of yourself, dear, she said.

As he left her he had the impression that she had grown more fragile, that standing in the open door with her hand on the gown, the murky hall framing her from behind, she was something of himself, equally helpless, equally unhappy.

Downstairs, he got into the car. The driver started.

The shops in the arcades were already open, he saw the sign JEWELLERS and remembered. I didn't tell her after all. The recollection of the present left him mutely unmoved, I'll think about it, there's no hurry, one never knows. He saw Choturam's white cap and again remembered, this time I'll do it, I'm damned if I won't, that'll teach him! it's the only kind they really understand. He watched the driver's cap and the streak of grease along its rim and then the decision in him boiled up to a fighting pitch.

As the road and the people blurred in the window he realized once more very clearly that they were all against him, that even at this moment they were plotting his doom, that there was still plenty of tough pushing ahead whether he chose to acknowledge it or ignore it.

MULK RAJ ANAND

The Tea-Party

'The Tea-Party' is from *Coolie*, first published in 1936. *Coolie* is a study in destitution. It relates a series of adventures of Munoo, a hillboy, who is forced to leave his idyllic village in the Kangra valley so that he may earn a living and see the world. The first contact with reality shatters his dreams. Arriving at the house of a bank clerk, he falls foul of his shrewish and vindictive housewife and flees. He next finds himself at a primitive pickle and jam factory, and later as one of the workers in a cotton mill in Bombay. He sweats to earn his bread in appalling working conditions. Finally, he is knocked down by the car of an Anglo-Indian woman who takes him to Simla as her servant. Here he dies of tuberculosis, watching the peaceful hills and valleys he had abandoned for the plains.

The following episode comes early in the novel, soon after Munoo has been installed as a servant in the household of Babu Nathoo Ram:

Unfortunately, however, the road to perfection is punctuated by pitfalls, and it was not long before he tripped up and brought the odium of his mistress's wrath upon himself.

It so happened that Mr W. P. England came to tea with Babu Nathoo Ram and family one afternoon.

Mr England was the chief cashier of the Sham Nagar branch of the Imperial Bank of India in whose office Babu Nathoo Ram was a sub-accountant. He was a tall Englishman with an awkward, shuffling gait, accentuated by the wooden, angular shape of his feet marching always hesitantly at an angle of forty-five degrees, and with a small, lined, expressionless face, only defined by the thick glasses on his narrow, myopic eyes. He had a rather good-natured smile on his thin lips, and it was that which led to the tea-party.

Babu Nathoo Ram had seen this smile play upon Mr England's lips every morning when the Sahib said 'Good morning' to him in response to his salute. There seemed little doubt that it was a kind smile which betokened the kindness of Mr England's heart, exactly as the frown on the face of Robert Horne, Esq., Manager of the Imperial Bank of India, Sham Nagar, betokened a vicious temperament. But then Mr England spoke so few words. The smile might just be a patronizing, put-on affair. And it was very important to Babu Nathoo Ram's purpose to know whether it was a genuine smile or an assumed one. For he wanted a recommendation from Mr England to support his application for an increase in salary and promotion to the position of the Accountant. He had aspired to this position for a long time now, but he had not been able to attain it because Babu Afzul-ul-Haq occupied it as he had occupied it for the last twenty years.

Mr England was a new officer. The Babu wanted to get him to write a recommendation before he was influenced by all the other English Officers in the Club and began to hate all Indians, before the kind smile on his lips became a smile of contempt and derision, or before it became sardonic on account of the weather. So he did not wait till he got to know Mr England better, or till Mr England got to know his work a little more, but he asked him to tea.

It had taken a great deal of courage, of course, and a lot more effort for him to ask Mr England to tea.

At first he tried several mornings to muster enough

courage to say something beyond the usual 'Good morning, Sir.' There seemed to be nothing to make the basis for an exchange of words, not even a file or letter, because they met on arrival at the office before the mail was opened. And, later in the day, there was much too much to say about files for an informal exchange of ideas. Babu Nathoo Ram began to contemplate Mr England's ever-ready smile with a certain exasperation. And he believed more than ever that these Englishmen were very slippery and confounding, because they were so reticent, just gaping at you without talking and without letting you talk.

Then someone (it was a barrister friend of Nathoo Ram's) told him that, from his experience in England, he had found that the only way of starting a conversation with an Englishman was by talking to him about the weather.

'Good morning, Sir,' said Babu Nathoo Ram respectfully every morning, without daring to use the new knowledge.

'Good morning,' mumbled Mr England, always smiling his nice smile, but rather self-conscious, because he saw that the Babu was older than he by at least twenty years, and his reverence seemed rather out of place. Besides, the Babu was a rich man. He had forty thousand rupees' worth of shares in the Allahabad Bank and was surely a trusted ally of the Government, which owned most of the Banks. He certainly was well thought of by the Manager and the Directors of the Bank. But why did he not live up to his status? Horne was right, he reflected, when he said that these Indians were embarrassingly obsequious.

Nathoo Ram walked sheepishly behind Mr England in the hall one day, and the Sahib was rather ill at ease as he stepped angularly along in the cool shade cast by the drawn blinds on the windows.

'Fine morning, Sir! Beautiful day!' announced Nathoo Ram suddenly.

Mr England shuffled his feet, hesitated and turned round as if a thunderbolt had struck him. His face was suddenly pale with peevishness. Then he controlled himself and, smiling a sardonic smile, said:

'Yes, of course, very fine! Very beautiful!'

The Babu did not understand the sarcasm implicit in the Sahib's response. He was mightily pleased with himself that he had broken the ice, although he could not muster the courage to say anything more and ask him to tea.

That he did after sitting in the office for whole days, waiting in suspense for the right moment to come. It came when Mr England, seeking to relieve the tension and to put Nathoo Ram at ease, approached the Babu's table one day before going off to lunch.

'How are you, Nathoo Ram?' he asked.

'Fine morning, Sir,' said Nathoo Ram, suddenly looking up from the ledger and springing to attention as he balanced his pen, *babu*-like, across his ear.

'Yes, a bit too fine for my taste,' replied Mr England.

'Yes, Sir,' said Nathoo Ram, wondering what to say.

There was an awkward pause in which Mr England looked at the Babu and the Babu looked at Mr England.

'Well, I am going off to lunch,' said the Sahib, 'though I can't eat much in this heat.'

'Sir,' said the Babu, jumping at his chance, 'you must eat Indian food. It's very tasty.' He couldn't utter the words fast enough.

'The *khansamah* at the Club cooks curry sometimes,' returned Mr England. 'I don't like it very much, it is too hot.'

'Sir, my wife cooks very good curries. You must come and taste one of our dishes,' ventured Nathoo Ram, tumbling over his words.

'No, I don't like curries,' said Mr England. 'Thank you

very much all the same.' And smiling his charming smile, he made to go. He had realized that he was becoming too familiar with the native, a thing his friends at the Club had warned him about.

'Will you come to see my house one day, Sir?' called Nathoo Ram eagerly and with beating heart. 'My wife would be honoured if you would condescend to favour us with the presence of your company at tea, Sir. My brother, Sir – '

Mr England had almost moved his head in negation, but he ducked it to drown his confusion.

'Yes, Sir, yes, Sir, today.'

'No,' said Mr England. 'No, perhaps some day.'

After that Nathoo Ram had positively pestered Mr England with his invitations to tea. Every time he met him, morning, noon, afternoon, he requested the favour of Mr England's gracious and benign condescension at tea.

At last Mr England agreed to come, one day, a week hence.

For a week preparations for this party went on in the Babu's household, and Munoo had more than his share of the excitement. The carpets were lifted and dusted, and, though all the paraphernalia of the Babu's household, pictures, bottles, books, utensils and children's toys and clothes, lay in their original confusion, a rag was passed over everything to make it neat and respectable.

The news of a sahib's projected visit to the Babu Nathoo Ram's house had spread all round town, and in the neighbouring houses, dirty, sackcloth curtains were hung up to guard female decorum from the intrusion of foreign eyes.

As Mr England walked up, dressed for the occasion in a warm navy-blue suit, with Nathoo Ram on the one side and Prem Chand, the Babu's doctor brother, on the other, and with Daya Ram, the *chaprasi*, in full regalia following behind, he felt hot and bothered.

Between mopping his brow with a large silk handkerchief and blushing at the Babu's reiterated gratitude and flattery, Mr England wondered what Nathoo Ram's house was going to be like. Would it be like his father's home in Brixton, a semi-detached house on the Hay Mill estate, which they had furnished on the hire-purchase system with the help of Mr Drage and where he had occupied the maid's room when he was a clerk in the Midland Bank, before he came here and suddenly became the chief cashier? Or would it be like the house of 'Abdul Kerim, the Hindoo', in that Hollywood film called *The Swami's Curse*, with fountains in the hall, around which danced the various wives of the Babu in clinging draperies and glittering ornaments?

The sight of the flat-roofed structures jutting into each other on the uprise to which the Babu pointed was rather disconcerting.

'Sahib! Sahib!' a cry went up, and there was a noise of several people rushing behind sackcloth curtains.

'The Muhammadans keep strict *purdah*, Sir,' informed Babu Nathoo Ram. 'And it is the women of the household of Babu Afzul-ul-Haq running to hide themselves.' 'Fate is favourable,' the Babu thought, for he had been able to have a dig at his Mussalman adversary.

Mr England smiled in a troubled manner as he looked aside.

'Look out!' Dr Prem Chand called. 'Your head!'

Mr England just missed hitting his forehead against the low doorway which led beyond the small verandah into the Babu's sitting-room. The pink of his face heightened to purple.

There was hardly any room to stand or to walk in the

low-ceilinged, eight foot by ten room, especially as both Nathoo Ram and Daya Ram had rushed to get a chair ready for the Sahib to sit upon.

Mr England stood looking round the junk. He felt as tall as Nelson's column in this crowded atmosphere.

He could not see much, but as he sank into a throne-like chair he faced the clay image of the elephant god, Ganesha, garlanded with a chain of faded flowers. He thought it a sinister image, something horrible, one of the heathen idols which he had been taught to hate in the Wesleyan chapel he had attended with his mother.

'The god of wisdom, worldliness and wealth, Sir,' said Babu Nathoo Ram, defining his words rather pompously, as he knew his illiterate wife was overhearing him talk English to a sahib, on an equal footing, for once in his life.

'Interesting,' mumbled Mr England.

'I hope to go to England for higher studies, Mr England,' said Dr Prem Chand, more at ease because he was an independent practitioner of medicine and not the Sahib's subordinate like his elder brother.

'Yes, really!' remarked Mr England, brightening at the suggestion of 'home,' as all Englishmen in India learn to do.

'I suppose you have a big residence there,' asked Prem Chand, 'and perhaps you could give me some advice about my course of study.'

'Yes,' said Mr England in reply, blushing to realize that though he had to pose as a big top to these natives, he had no home to speak of, the semi-detached house in Brixton being not yet paid for, and he remembered that he had never been to a university and knew nothing about 'courses of study,' except those of Pitman's Typewriting and Shorthand School in Southampton Row, which he had attended for a season before going to the Midland Bank. He felt he should make a clean breast of it all, as he was really extremely honest. But his compatriots at the Club had always exhorted him to show himself off as the son of King George himself if need be. A guilty conscience added its weight of misery to his embarrassment.

'This is a family photograph taken on the occasion of my marriage, Sir,' said Nathoo Ram, lifting a huge, heavily-framed picture off its peg and clumsily dropping two others, so that Munoo, who stood in the doorway, staring at the rare sight of the pink man, rushed in to save them.

Mr England looked up with a face not devoid of curiosity.

The Babu brought the picture along and, half apprehensive at the liberties he was taking, planted it on the Sahib's knees. Mr England held it at the sides and strained his eyes almost on to the glass to scrutinize it.

Munoo was drawn by the instinctive desire for contact, which knows no barriers between high and low, to come and stand almost at the Sahib's elbow and join in the contemplation of the picture.

'Go away, fool,' whispered the Babu, and nudged the boy with his sharp, bony elbow.

Mr England, who was almost settling down, was disturbed. He did not know who Munoo was, but he might be the Babu's son. If so, it was cruel for Nathoo Ram to drive him away like that, though he was glad that the dirtily clad urchin had not come sniffling up to him, for he might be carrying some disease of the skin. All these natives, Horne said, were disease-ridden. And from the number of lepers in the street, he seemed to be right.

'The servant boy,' said Nathoo Ram confidently to the Sahib in a contemptuous tone, to justify his rudeness to Munoo.

The Sahib assented by twisting his lips and screwing his eyes into an expression of disgust.

'This is my wife, Sir,' said Nathoo Ram, pointing to a form loaded with clothes and jewellery, which sat in the middle of the group, dangling its legs in a chair and with its face entirely covered by a double veil.

Mr England looked eagerly to scan the face in the picture and, not being able to see it, blamed his myopic eyes, as he pretended to appreciate the charm of the Babu's wife by saying, 'Nice – very nice.'

But lifting his hand he saw that it was covered with dust, which lay thickly on the back of the frame, and that his trousers were ruined. He frowned.

'My wife does not observe *purdah*, but she is very shy,' said the Babu apologetically. 'So she will not come in as is the custom with the women of your country.' In the same breath he switched on again to the picture: 'This is my humble self as the bridegroom, when I was young.'

Mr England saw the form of a heavily turbaned, feebler incarnation of Nathoo Ram, with rings in his ears, garlands round his neck and white English-Indian clothes, as he stood stiffly caressing the arm of his bride's chair with the left hand and showing a European watch to the world with the right.

Mr England's eyes scanned the wizened forms of dark men in the background of the picture. Then they rested on two boys, who lay, reclining their heads against each other and on their elbows, in the manner of the odd members of cricket teams in Victorian photographs.

'Ain – ain – wain – ain – ain – ai – an,' a throaty wail wound its way out of the trumpet of the gramophone which Dr Prem Chand had set in motion.

Munoo rushed up to the door, really to hear the voice from the box sing, but making an excuse of the message that tea was ready. Sheila, who had just returned from school, came in too.

'This is our Indian music, Sir,' said Nathoo Ram proudly; 'a ghazal, sung by Miss Janki Bai of Allahabad. My elder daughter,' he added, pointing to Sheila. Then turning to her he said, 'Come and meet the Sahib.'

The child was shy and stood obstinately in the doorway, smiling awkwardly.

Mr England's confusion knew no bounds. He was perspiring profusely. The noise and commotion created by the 'ain – ain – wain – ain' were unbearable. His ears were used at the best to the exotic zigzag of Charleston or Rumba or his native tunes 'Love Is Like a Cigarette', 'Rosemarie, I Love You' and 'I want to be Happy, but I can't be Happy till I make You Happy too.' And he felt the children staring at him.

He wished it would all be over soon. He regretted that he had let himself in for it all.

'Go and get the tea,' said Nathoo Ram to Munoo.

'*Han*, Babuji,' said Munoo as he ran back, excited and happy. He nearly knocked into his uncle Daya Ram, who was coming towards the sitting-room bearing heaps of syrupy Indian sweets and hot maize-flour dumplings which Bibiji had been frying in a deep pan of olive oil the whole afternoon.

Bibiji saw Munoo rushing and would have abused him, but she was on her best behaviour today. She gave him only a furious look as she pushed some dishes of English pastries from outside the four lines of her kitchen, commanding him to take them to the sitting-room.

Munoo was in high spirits, far too exalted by the pleasure of the Sahib's company in his master's house to be damped by Bibiji's frowns. He took the dishes over, his mouth watering at the sight of the sweets.

He placed the pastries on the huge writing-table which had been converted for use as a dinner-table. He waited to look at the Sahib. A scowl on the Babu's face sent him back to the kitchen to fetch the tea-tray.

Meanwhile Babu Nathoo Ram had begun to offer food to the Sahib.

The Babu took up two dishes in his hands and brought them up to Mr England's nose.

'Sir, this is our famous sweetmeat, gulabjaman by name,' he said, 'and this is called by the name of rasgula. Made from fresh cream, Sir. The aroma of the attar of roses has been cast over them. They were specially made to my order by the confectioner.'

The perfume of the rasgulas and gulabjamans as well as the sight of them made Mr England positively sick. He recoiled from the attack of the syrupy stuff on his senses with a murmur of 'No, thank you.'

'Oh yes, Sir, yes, Sir,' urged Babu Nathoo Ram.

If Mr England had been offered a plate and a fork, or a spoon, he might have taken one of the sweets. But he was supposed to pick them up with his hand. That was impossible to the Englishman, who had never picked up even a chicken-bone in his fingers to do full justice to it.

'Some pakoras, then?' said the Babu. 'They are a specialty of my wife. Come, Daya Ram.'

The peon brought up the dish of the maize-flour dumplings. The sharp smell of the oily dark-brown stuff was enough to turn Mr England's liver. He looked at it as if it were poison and said, 'No, no, thank you, really, I had a late lunch.'

'Well, if you don't care for Indian sweets, Sir,' said Nathoo Ram in a hurt voice, 'then please eat English-made pastry that I specially ordered from Stiffles. You must, Sir.'

The pastries, too, were thickly coated with sugar and looked forbidding.

'No, thanks, really. I can't eat in this hot weather,' said Mr England, trying to give a plausible excuse.

Now Nathoo Ram was disappointed. If the Sahib did not eat and did not become indebted to him, how could he ever get the recommendation he needed?

'Sir, Sir,' he protested, thrusting the food again under Mr England's nose. 'Do please eat something – just a little bit of a thing.'

'No, thank you very much, Nathoo Ram. Really,' said Mr England, 'I will take a cup of tea and then I must go. I am a very busy man, you know.'

'Sir,' said Nathoo Ram, his under-lip quivering with emotion, 'I had hoped that you would partake of the simple hospitality that I, your humble servant, can extend to you. But you will have tea, tea. – Tea. Oh! Munoo, bring the tea!'

Munoo was hurrying in with the tea-tray. When he heard his master's call, he scurried. The tea-tray fell from his hands. All the china lay scattered on the kitchen floor.

Mr England heard the crash and guessed that a disaster had taken place.

Babu Nathoo Ram's heart sank. He had spent ten rupees of his well-earned money on the tea-party. And it had all gone to waste.

Dr Prem Chand walked deliberately out into the kitchen and cowed Bibiji into a forced restraint, poured the remains of tea and milk into a cup and brought it on a neat saucer, saying coolly, with a facetious smile:

'Our servant, Munoo, Mr England, knows that a Japanese tea-set only costs one rupee twelve annas. So he does not care how many cups and saucers he breaks.'

Mr England was sweating with the heat. He became pale with embarrassment and fury. His small mouth contracted.

He took the cup of tea and sipped it. It was hot, it almost scalded his lips and tongue.

'I must go now,' he said, and rose from his eminent position on the throne-like chair.

'We are disappointed, Sir,' said Nathoo Ram, apologizing and humble. 'But I and my wife hope you will come again.' And he followed the Sahib sheepishly, as Mr England veered round suddenly and shuffled out on his awkward feet.

'Look out! Your head!' said Dr Prem Chand, warning the Sahib in time before he was again likely to hit the low doorway. 'Good afternoon.'

Mr England smiled, then assumed a stern expression and walked out silently, followed by Babu Nathoo Ram and Daya Ram, past groups of inquisitive men and children.

The tea-party had been a fiasco.

Dr Prem Chand went into the kitchen. He was going to enjoy the sweets. But his sister-in-law was shouting at Munoo.

'*Vay*, may you die, may you be broken, may you fade away, blind one! Do you know what you have done? May the flesh of your dead body rot in hell! With what evil star did you come to this house, that you do everything wrong? That china cost us almost as much money as you earn in a month.'

'That Englishman has no taste,' said Prem Chand, coming in; 'he did not eat a thing.'

'It is all the fault of this eater of his masters,' she cried, pointing to Munoo.

'How is he responsible for that monkey-faced man's bad taste?' asked Prem Chand, 'and how is he to blame for all this junk in your house which apparently annoyed the Sahib?'

'Don't you encourage this dead one, Prem!' said Bibiji.

'Our house used to be like the houses of the sahib-logs until this brute came from the hills and spoilt it. That lovely set of china he has broken, the brute!'

'Well now, you get a pair of sun-glasses gratis for every four annas' worth of Japanese goods that you buy in the bazaar,' mocked Prem, 'so we will all have eye-glasses, even you, Bibiji!'

Munoo did not know whether to laugh or to cry. A shock of apprehension had passed through him when he dropped the china, and seized his soul in a knot of fear. He stood dumb. The mockery of the *chota* Babu stirred the warmth on the surface of his blood. He awakened from his torpor and smiled.

Bibiji sprang from her seat near the kitchen and gave him a sharp, clean slap on the cheek.

'Spoiler of our salt!' she raved. 'You have brought bad luck to our house! Beast! And I have tried hard to correct you – '

'Oh, leave him alone,' said Prem. 'It is not his fault.' And he went towards the boy.

'Don't let me hear you wail, or I will kill you, you stupid fool!' said Babu Nathoo Ram angrily as he came in with tear-filled eyes.

It was not the first time that Munoo succumbed to sleep, stifling his sobs and his cries.

R. K. NARAYAN
A Horse and Two Goats

Of the seven hundred thousand villages dotting the map of India, in which the majority of India's five hundred million live, flourish, and die, Kritam was probably the tiniest, indicated on the district survey map by a microscopic dot, the map being meant more for the revenue official out to collect tax than for the guidance of the motorist, who in any case could not hope to reach it since it sprawled far from the highway at the end of a rough track furrowed up by the iron-hooped wheels of bullock carts. But its size did not prevent its giving itself the grandiose name Kritam, which meant in Tamil 'coronet' or 'crown' on the brow of this sub-continent. The village consisted of less than thirty houses, only one of them built with brick and cement. Painted a brilliant yellow and blue all over with gorgeous carvings of gods and gargoyles on its balustrade, it was known as the Big House. The other houses, distributed in four streets, were generally of bamboo thatch, straw, mud, and other unspecified material. Muni's was the last house in the fourth street, beyond which stretched the fields. In his prosperous days Muni had owned a flock of forty sheep and goats and sallied forth every morning driving the flock to the highway a couple of miles away. There he would sit on the pedestal of a clay statue of a horse while his cattle grazed around. He carried a crook at the end of a bamboo pole and snapped foliage from the avenue trees to feed his flock; he also gathered faggots and dry sticks, bundled them, and carried them home for fuel at sunset.

His wife lit the domestic fire at dawn, boiled water in a

mud pot, threw into it a handful of millet flour, added salt, and gave him his first nourishment for the day. When he started out, she would put in his hand a packed lunch, once again the same millet cooked into a little ball, which he could swallow with a raw onion at midday. She was old, but he was older and needed all the attention she could give him in order to be kept alive.

His fortunes had declined gradually, unnoticed. From a flock of forty which he drove into a pen at night, his stock had now come down to two goats which were not worth the rent of a half rupee a month the Big House charged for the use of the pen in their back yard. And so the two goats were tethered to the trunk of a drumstick tree which grew in front of his hut and from which occasionally Muni could shake down drumsticks. This morning he got six. He carried them in with a sense of triumph. Although no one could say precisely who owned the tree, it was his because he lived in its shadow.

She said, 'If you were content with the drumstick leaves alone, I could boil and salt some for you.'

'Oh, I am tired of eating those leaves. I have a craving to chew the drumstick out of sauce, I tell you.'

'You have only four teeth in your jaw, but your craving is for big things. All right, get the stuff for the sauce, and I will prepare it for you. After all, next year you may not be alive to ask for anything. But first get me all the stuff, including a measure of rice or millet, and I will satisfy your unholy craving. Our store is empty today. Dhal, chili, curry leaves, mustard, coriander, gingelley oil, and one large potato. Go out and get all this.' He repeated the list after her in order not to miss any item and walked off to the shop in the third street.

He sat on an upturned packing case below the platform of the shop. The shopman paid no attention to him. Muni kept clearing his throat, coughing, and sneezing until the shopman could not stand it any more and demanded, 'What ails you? You will fly off that seat into the gutter if you sneeze so hard, young man.' Muni laughed inordinately, in order to please the shopman, at being called 'young man'. The shopman softened and said, 'You have enough of the imp inside to keep a second wife busy, but for the fact the old lady is still alive.' Muni laughed appropriately again at this joke. It completely won the shopman over; he liked his sense of humour to be appreciated. Muni engaged his attention in local gossip for a few minutes, which always ended with a reference to the postman's wife, who had eloped to the city some months before.

The shopman felt most pleased to hear the worst of the postman, who had cheated him. Being an itinerant postman, he returned home to Kritam only once in ten days and every time managed to slip away again without passing the shop in the third street. By thus humouring the shopman, Muni could always ask for one or two items of food, promising repayment later. Some days the shopman was in a good mood and gave in, and sometimes he would lose his temper suddenly and bark at Muni for daring to ask for credit. This was such a day, and Muni could not progress beyond two items listed as essential components. The shopman was also displaying a remarkable memory for old facts and figures and took out an oblong ledger to support his observations. Muni felt impelled to rise and flee. But his self-respect kept him in his seat and made him listen to the worst things about himself. The shopman concluded, 'If you could find five rupees and a quarter, you would pay off an ancient debt and then could apply for admission to *swarga*. How much have you got now?'

'I will pay you everything on the first of the next month.'

'As always, and whom do you expect to rob by then?'

Muni felt caught and mumbled, 'My daughter has sent word that she will be sending me money.'

'Have you a daughter?' sneered the shopman. 'And she is sending you money! For what purpose, may I know?'

'Birthday, fiftieth birthday,' said Muni quietly.

'Birthday! How old are you?'

Muni repeated weakly, not being sure of it himself, 'Fifty.' He always calculated his age from the time of the great famine when he stood as high as the parapet around the village well, but who could calculate such things accurately nowadays with so many famines occurring? The shopman felt encouraged when other customers stood around to watch and comment. Muni thought helplessly, My poverty is exposed to everybody. But what can I do?

'More likely you are seventy,' said the shopman. 'You also forget that you mentioned a birthday five weeks ago when you wanted castor oil for your holy bath.'

'Bath! Who can dream of a bath when you have to scratch the tank-bed for a bowl of water? We would all be parched and dead but for the Big House, where they let us take a pot of water from their well.' After saying this Muni unobtrusively rose and moved off.

He told his wife, 'That scoundrel would not give me anything. So go out and sell the drumsticks for what they are worth.'

He flung himself down in a corner to recoup from the fatigue of his visit to the shop. His wife said, 'You are getting no sauce today, nor anything else. I can't find anything to give you to eat. Fast till evening, it'll do you good. Take the goats and be gone now,' she cried and added, 'Don't come back before the sun is down.' He knew that if he obeyed her she would somehow conjure up some food for him in the evening. Only he must be careful not to argue and irritate her. Her temper was undependable in the morning but improved by evening time. She was sure to go out and work – grind corn in the Big House, sweep or scrub somewhere, and earn enough to buy foodstuff and keep a dinner ready for him in the evening.

Unleashing the goats from the drumstick tree Muni started out, driving them ahead and uttering weird cries from time to time in order to urge them on. He passed through the village with his head bowed in thought. He did not want to look at anyone or be accosted. A couple of cronies lounging in the temple corridor hailed him, but he ignored their call. They had known him in the days of affluence when he lorded over a flock of fleecy sheep, not the miserable gawky goats that he had today. Of course he also used to have a few goats for those who fancied them, but real wealth lay in sheep; they bred fast and people came and bought the fleece in the shearing season; and then that famous butcher from the town came over on the weekly market days bringing him betel leaves, tobacco, and often enough some bhang, which they smoked in a hut in the coconut grove, undisturbed by wives and well-wishers. After a smoke one felt light and elated and inclined to forgive everyone including that brother-in-law of his who had once tried to set fire to his home. But all this seemed like the memoirs of a previous birth. Some pestilence afflicted his cattle (he could of course guess who had laid his animals under a curse) and even the friendly butcher would not touch one at half the price . . . and now here he was left with the two scraggy creatures. He wished someone would rid him of their company too. The shopman had said that he was seventy. At seventy, one only waited to be summoned by God. When he was dead what would his wife do? They had lived in each other's company since they were children. He was told on their day of wedding that he was ten years old and she was eight. During the wedding ceremony they had had to recite their respective ages and names. He had thrashed her only a few times in their career, and later she had the upper hand. Progeny, none. Perhaps a large progeny would have brought him the blessing of the gods. Fertility brought merit. People with fourteen sons were always so prosperous and at peace with the world and themselves. He recollected the thrill he had felt when he mentioned a daughter to that shopman; although it was not believed, what if he did not have a daughter? – his cousin in the next village had many daughters, and any one of them was as good as his; he was fond of them all and would buy them sweets if he could afford it. Still, everyone in the village whispered behind their backs that Muni and his wife were a barren couple. He avoided looking at anyone; they all professed to be so high up, and everyone else in the village had more money than he. 'I am the poorest fellow in our caste and no wonder that they spurn me, but I won't look at them either,' and so he passed on with his eyes downcast along the edge of the street, and people left him also very much alone, commenting only to the extent, 'Ah, there he goes with his two great goats; if he slits their throats, he may have more peace of mind.' 'What has he to worry about anyway? They live on nothing and have nobody to worry about.' Thus people commented when he passed through the village. Only on the outskirts did he lift his head and look up. He urged and bullied the goats until they meandered along to the foot of the horse statue on the edge of the village. He sat on its pedestal for the rest of the day. The advantage of this was that he could watch the highway and see the lorries and buses pass through to the hills, and it gave him a sense of belonging to a larger world. The pedestal of the statue was broad enough for him to move around as the sun travelled up and westward; or he could also crouch under the belly of the horse, for shade.

The horse was nearly life-size, moulded out of clay, baked, burnt, and brightly coloured, and reared its head proudly, prancing its forelegs in the air and flourishing its tail in a loop; beside the horse stood a warrior with scythe-like mustachios, bulging eyes, and aquiline nose. The old image-makers believed in indicating a man of strength by bulging out his eyes and sharpening his moustache tips, and also had decorated the man's chest with beads which looked today like blobs of mud through the ravages of sun and wind and rain (when it came), but Muni would insist that he had known the beads to sparkle like the nine gems at one time in his life. The horse itself was said to have been as white as a *dhobi*-washed sheet, and had had on its back a cover of pure brocade of red and black lace, matching the multicoloured sash around the waist of the warrior. But none in the village remembered the splendour as no one noticed its existence. Even Muni, who spent all his waking hours at its foot, never bothered to look up. It was untouched by the young vandals of the village who gashed tree trunks with knives and tried to topple off milestones and inscribed lewd designs on all the walls. This statue had been closer to the population of the village at one time, when this spot bordered the village; but when the highway was laid through (or perhaps when the tank and wells dried up completely here) the village moved a couple of miles inland.

Muni sat at the foot of the statue, watching his two goats graze in the arid soil among the cactus and lantana bushes. He looked at the sun; it had tilted westward no doubt, but it was not the time yet to go back home; if he went too early his wife would have no food for him. Also he must give her time to cool off her temper and feel sympathetic, and then she would scrounge and manage to get some food. He watched the mountain road for a time signal. When the green bus appeared around the bend he could leave, and his wife would feel pleased that he had let the goats feed long enough.

He noticed now a new sort of vehicle coming down at full speed. It looked both like a motor car and a bus. He used to be intrigued by the novelty of such spectacles, but of late work was going on at the source of the river on the mountain and an assortment of people and traffic went past him, and he took it all casually and described to his wife, later in the day, not everything as he once did, but only some things, only if he noticed anything special. Today, while he observed the yellow vehicle coming down, he was wondering how to describe it later when it sputtered and stopped in front of him. A red-faced foreigner who had been driving it got down and went round it, stooping, looking, and poking under the vehicle; then he straightened himself up, looked at the dashboard, stared in Muni's direction, and approached him. 'Excuse me, is there a gas station nearby, or do I have to wait until another car comes – ' He suddenly looked up at the clay horse and cried, 'Marvellous!' without completing his sentence. Muni felt he should get up and run away, and cursed his age. He could not really put his limbs into action; some years ago he could outrun a *cheetah*, as happened once when he went to the forest to cut fuel and it was then that two of his sheep were mauled – a sign that bad times were coming. Though he tried, he could not easily extricate himself from his seat, and then there was also the problem of the goats. He could not leave them behind.

The red-faced man wore khaki clothes – evidently a policeman or a soldier. Muni said to himself, 'He will chase or shoot if I start running. Sometimes dogs chase only those who run – O Shiva protect me. I don't know why this man should be after me.' Meanwhile the foreigner cried, 'Marvellous!' again, nodding his head. He paced around the statue with his eyes fixed on it. Muni sat frozen for a while, and then fidgeted and tried to edge away. Now the other man suddenly pressed his palms together in a salute, smiled, and said, '*Namaste!* How do you do?'

At which Muni spoke the only English expression he had learnt, 'Yes, no.' Having exhausted his English vocabulary, he started in Tamil: 'My name is Muni. These two goats are mine, and no one can gainsay it – though our village is full of slanderers these days who will not hesitate to say that what belongs to a man doesn't belong to him.' He rolled his eyes and shuddered at the thought of evil-minded men and women peopling his village.

The foreigner faithfully looked in the direction indicated by Muni's fingers, gazed for a while at the two goats and the rocks, and with a puzzled expression took out his silver cigarette-case and lit a cigarette. Suddenly remembering the courtesies of the season, he asked, 'Do you smoke?' Muni answered, 'Yes, no.' Whereupon the red-faced man took a cigarette and gave it to Muni, who received it with surprise, having had no offer of a smoke from anyone for years now. Those days when he smoked bhang were gone with his sheep and the large-hearted butcher. Nowadays he was not able to find even matches, let alone bhang. (His wife went across and borrowed a fire at dawn from a neighbour.) He had always wanted to smoke a cigarette; only once had the shopman given him one on credit, and he remembered how good it had tasted. The other flicked the lighter open and offered a light to Muni. Muni felt so confused about how to act that he blew on it and put it out. The other, puzzled but undaunted, flourished his lighter, presented it again, and lit Muni's cigarette. Muni drew a deep puff and started coughing; it was racking, no doubt, but extremely pleasant. When his cough subsided he wiped his eyes and took stock of the situation, understanding that the other man was not an inquisitor of any kind. Yet, in order to make sure, he remained wary. No need to run away from a man who gave such a potent smoke. His head was reeling from the effect of one of those strong American cigarettes made with roasted tobacco. The man said, 'I come from New York,' took out a wallet from his hip pocket, and presented his card.

Muni shrank away from the card. Perhaps he was trying to present a warrant and arrest him. Beware of khaki, one part of his mind warned. Take all the cigarettes or bhang or whatever is offered, but don't get caught. Beware of khaki. He wished he weren't seventy as the shopman had said. At seventy one didn't run, but surrendered to whatever came. He could only ward off trouble by talk. So he went on, all in the chaste Tamil for which Kritam was famous. (Even the worst detractors could not deny that the famous poetess Avvaiyar was born in this area, although no one could say whether it was in Kritam or Kuppam, the adjoining village.) Out of this heritage the Tamil language gushed through Muni in an unimpeded flow. He said, 'Before God, sir, Bhagwan, who sees everything, I tell you, sir, that we know nothing of the case. If the murder was committed, whoever did it will not escape. Bhagwan is all-seeing. Don't ask me about it. I know nothing.' A body had been found mutilated and thrown under a tamarind tree at the border betwen Kritam and Kuppam a few weeks before, giving rise to much gossip and speculation. Muni added an explanation, 'Anything is possible there. People over there will stop at nothing.' The foreigner nodded his head and listened courteously though he understood nothing.

'I am sure you know when this horse was made,' said the red man and smiled ingratiatingly.

Muni reacted to the relaxed atmosphere by smiling himself, and pleaded, 'Please go away, sir. I know nothing. I promise we will hold him for you if we see any bad character around, and we will bury him up to his neck in a coconut pit if he tries to escape; but our village has always had a clean record. Must definitely be the other village.'

Now the red man implored, 'Please, please, I will speak slowly, please try to understand me. Can't you understand even a simple word of English? Everyone in this country seems to know English. I have got along with English everywhere in this country, but you don't speak it. Have you any religious or spiritual scruples for avoiding the English speech?'

Muni made some indistinct sounds in his throat and shook his head. Encouraged, the other went on to explain at length, uttering each syllable with care and deliberation. Presently he sidled over and took a seat beside the old man, explaining, 'You see, last August, we probably had the hottest summer in history, and I was working in shirt-sleeves in my office on the fortieth floor of the Empire State Building. You must have heard of the power failure, and there I was stuck for four hours, no elevator, no air conditioning. All the way in the train I kept thinking, and the minute I reached home in Connecticut, I told my wife Ruth, "We will visit India this winter, it's time to look at other civilizations." Next day she called the travel agent first thing and told him to fix it, and so here I am. Ruth came with me but is staying back at Srinagar, and I am the one doing the rounds and joining her later.'

Muni looked reflective at the end of this long peroration and said, rather feebly, 'Yes, no,' as a concession to the other's language, and went on in Tamil, 'When I was this high,' he indicated a foot high, 'I heard my uncle say . . .'

No one can tell what he was planning to say as the other interrupted him at this stage to ask, 'Boy, what is the secret of your teeth? How old are you?'

The old man forgot what he had started to say and remarked, 'Sometimes we too lose our cattle. Jackals or *cheetahs* may carry them off, but sometimes it is just theft from over in the next village, and then we will know who has done it. Our priest at the temple can see in the camphor flame the face of the thief, and when he is caught . . .' He gestured with his hands a perfect mincing of meat.

The American watched his hands intently and said, 'I know what you mean. Chop something? Maybe I am holding you up and you want to chop wood? Where is your axe? Hand it to me and show me what to chop. I do enjoy it, you know, just a hobby. We get a lot of driftwood along the backwater near my house, and on Sundays I do nothing but chop wood for the fireplace. I really feel different when I watch the fire in the fireplace, although it may take all the sections of the Sunday *New York Times* to get a fire started,' and he smiled at this reference.

Muni felt totally confused but decided the best thing would be to make an attempt to get away from this place. He tried to edge out, saying, 'Must go home,' and turned to go. The other seized his shoulder and said desperately, 'Is there no one, absolutely no one here, to translate for me?' He looked up and down the road, which was deserted in this hot afternoon; a sudden gust of wind churned up the dust and dead leaves on the roadside into a ghostly column and propelled it towards the mountain road. The stranger almost pinioned Muni's back to the statue and asked, 'Isn't this statue yours? Why don't you sell it to me?'

The old man now understood the reference to the horse, thought for a second, and said in his own language, 'I was an urchin this high when I heard my grandfather explain this horse and warrior, and my grandfather himself was this high when he heard his grandfather, whose grandfather . . .'

The other man interrupted him with, 'I don't want to seem to have stopped here for nothing. I will offer you a good price for this,' he said, indicating the horse. He had concluded without the least doubt that Muni owned this mud horse. Perhaps he guessed by the way he sat at its pedestal, like other souvenir-sellers in this country presiding over their wares.

Muni followed the man's eyes and pointing fingers and dimly understood the subject matter and, feeling relieved that the theme of the mutilated body had been abandoned at least for the time being, said again, enthusiastically, 'I was this high when my grandfather told me about this horse and the warrior, and my grandfather was this high when he himself . . .' and he was getting into a deeper bog of remembering each time he tried to indicate the antiquity of the statue.

The Tamil that Muni spoke was stimulating even as pure sound, and the foreigner listened with fascination. 'I wish I had my tape-recorder here,' he said, assuming the pleasantest expression. 'Your language sounds wonderful. I get a kick out of every word you utter, here' – he indicated his ears – 'but you don't have to waste your breath in sales talk. I appreciate the article. You don't have to explain its points.'

'I never went to a school, in those days only *Brahmin* went to schools, but we had to go out and work in the fields morning till night, from sowing to harvest time . . . and when *Pongal* came and we had cut the harvest, my father allowed me to go out and play with others at the tank, and so I don't know the *Parangi* language you speak, even little fellows in your country probably speak the *Parangi* language, but here only learned men and officers know it. We had a postman in our village who could speak to you boldly in your language, but his wife ran away with someone and he does not speak to anyone at all nowadays. Who would if a wife did what she did? Women must be watched; otherwise they will sell themselves and the home,' and he laughed at his own quip.

The foreigner laughed heartily, took out another cigarette, and offered it to Muni, who now smoked with ease, deciding to stay on if the fellow was going to be so good as to keep up his cigarette supply. The American now stood up on the pedestal in the attitude of a demonstrative lecturer and said, running his finger along some of the carved decorations around the horse's neck, speaking slowly and uttering his words syllable by syllable, 'I could give a sales talk for this better than anyone else . . . This is a marvellous combination of yellow and indigo, though faded now . . . How do you people of this country achieve these flaming colours?'

Muni, now assured that the subject was still the horse and not the dead body, said, 'This is our guardian, it means death to our adversaries. At the end of *Kali Yuga*, this world and all other worlds will be destroyed, and the Redeemer will come in the shape of a horse called Kalki; this horse will come to life and gallop and trample down all bad men'. As he spoke of bad men the figures of his shopman and his brother-in-law assumed concrete forms in his mind, and he revelled for a moment in the predicament of the fellow under the horse's hoof: served him right for trying to set fire to his home . . .

While he was brooding on this pleasant vision, the

foreigner utilized the pause to say, 'I assure you that this will have the best home in the USA. I'll push away the bookcase, you know I love books and am a member of five book clubs, and the choice and bonus volumes really mount up to a pile in our living-room, as high as this horse itself. But they'll have to go. Ruth may disapprove, but I will convince her. The TV may have to be shifted too. We can't have everything in the living-room. Ruth will probably say what about when we have a party? I'm going to keep him right in the middle of the room. I don't see how that can interfere with the party – we'll stand around him and have our drinks.'

Muni continued his description of the end of the world. 'Our pundit discoursed at the temple once how the oceans are going to close over the earth in a huge wave and swallow us – this horse will grow bigger than the biggest wave and carry on its back only the good people and kick into the floods the evil ones – plenty of them about,' he said reflectively. 'Do you know when it is going to happen?' he asked.

The foreigner now understood by the tone of the other that a question was being asked and said, 'How am I transporting it? I can push the seat back and make room in the rear. That van can take in an elephant' – waving precisely at the back of the seat.

Muni was still hovering on visions of avatars and said again, 'I never missed our pundit's discourses at the temple in those days during every bright half of the month, although he'd go on all night, and he told us that Vishnu is the highest god. Whenever evil men trouble us, he comes down to save us. He has come many times. The first time he incarnated as a great fish, and lifted the scriptures on his back when the floods and sea-waves . . .'

'I am not a millionaire, but a modest businessman. My trade is coffee.'

Amidst all this wilderness of obscure sound Muni caught the word 'coffee' and said, 'If you want to drink "kapi", drive further up, in the next town, they have Friday market, and there they open "kapi-otels" – so I learn from passers-by. Don't think I wander about. I go nowhere and look for nothing.' His thoughts went back to the avatars. 'The first avatar was in the shape of a little fish in a bowl of water, but every hour it grew bigger and bigger and became in the end a huge whale which the seas could not contain, and on the back of the whale the holy books were supported, saved and carried.' Having launched on the first avatar it was inevitable that he should go on to the next, a wild boar on whose tusk the earth was lifted when a vicious conqueror of the earth carried it off and hid it at the bottom of the sea. After describing this avatar Muni concluded, 'God will always save us whenever we are troubled by evil beings. When we were young we staged at full moon the story of the avatars. That's how I know the stories; we played them all night until the sun rose, and sometimes the European collector would come to watch, bringing his own chair. I had a good voice and so they always taught me songs and gave me the women's roles. I was always Goddess Laxmi, and they dressed me in a brocade *sari*, loaned from the Big House . . .'

The foreigner said, 'I repeat I am not a millionaire. Ours is a modest business; after all, we can't afford to buy more than sixty minutes' TV time in a month, which works out to two minutes a day, that's all, although in the course of time we'll maybe sponsor a one-hour show regularly if our sales graph continues to go up . . .'

Muni was intoxicated by the memory of his theatrical days and was about to explain how he had painted his face and worn a wig and diamond earrings when the visitor, feeling that he had spent too much time already, said, 'Tell me, will you accept a hundred rupees or not for the horse? I'd love to take the whiskered soldier also but I've no space for him this year. I'll have to cancel my air ticket and take a boat home, I suppose. Ruth can go by air if she likes, but I will go with the horse and keep him in my cabin all the way if necessary,' and he smiled at the picture of himself voyaging across the seas hugging this horse. He added, 'I will have to pad it with straw so that it doesn't break . . .'

'When we played *Ramayana*, they dressed me as Sita,' added Muni. 'A teacher came and taught us the songs for the drama and we gave him fifty rupees. He incarnated himself as Rama, and he alone could destroy Ravana, the demon with ten heads who shook all the worlds; do you know the story of *Ramayana*?'

'I have my station wagon as you see. I can push the seat back and take the horse in if you will just lend me a hand with it.'

'Do you know *Mahabharta*? Krishna was the eighth avatar of Vishnu, incarnated to help the Five Brothers regain their kingdom. When Krishna was a baby he danced on the thousand-hooded giant serpent and trampled it to death; and then he suckled the breasts of the demoness and left them flat as a disc though when she came to him her bosoms were large, like mounds of earth on the banks of a dug-up canal.' He indicated two mounds with his hands. The stranger was completely mystified by the gesture. For the first time he said, 'I really wonder what you are saying because your answer is crucial. We have come to the point when we should be ready to talk business.'

'When the tenth avatar comes, do you know where you and I will be?' asked the old man.

'Lend me a hand and I can lift off the horse from its

pedestal after picking out the cement at the joints. We can do anything if we have a basis of understanding.'

At this stage the mutual mystification was complete, and there was no need even to carry on a guessing game at the meaning of words. The old man chattered away in a spirit of balancing off the credits and debits of conversational exchange, and said in order to be on the credit side, 'O honourable one, I hope God has blessed you with numerous progeny. I say this because you seem to be a good man, willing to stay beside an old man and talk to him, while all day I have none to talk to except when somebody stops by to ask for a piece of tobacco. But I seldom have it, tobacco is not what it used to be at one time, and I have given up chewing. I cannot afford it nowadays.' Noting the other's interest in his speech, Muni felt encouraged to ask, 'How many children have you?' with appropriate gestures with his hands. Realizing that a question was being asked, the red man replied, 'I said a hundred,' which encouraged Muni to go into details, 'How many of your children are boys and how many girls? Where are they? Is your daughter married? Is it difficult to find a son-in-law in your country also?'

In answer to these questions the red man dashed his hand into his pocket and brought forth his wallet in order to take immediate advantage of the bearish trend in the market. He flourished a hundred-rupee currency note and asked, 'Well, this is what I meant.'

The old man now realized that some financial element was entering their talk. He peered closely at the currency note, the like of which he had never seen in his life; he knew the five and ten by their colours although always in other people's hands, while his own earning at any time was in coppers and nickels. What was this man flourishing the note for? Perhaps asking for change. He laughed to himself at the notion of anyone coming to him for changing a thousand- or ten-thousand-rupee note. He said with a grin, 'Ask our village head-man, who is also a moneylender; he can change even a lakh of rupees in gold sovereigns if you prefer it that way; he thinks nobody knows, but dig the floor of his puja room and your head will reel at the sight of the hoard. The man disguises himself in rags just to mislead the public. Talk to the head-man yourself because he goes mad at the sight of me. Someone took away his pumpkins with the creeper and he, for some reason, thinks it was me and my goats . . . that's why I never let my goats be seen anywhere near the farms.' His eyes travelled to the goats nosing about, attempting to wrest nutrition from minute greenery peeping out of rock and dry earth.

The foreigner followed his look and decided that it would be a sound policy to show an interest in the old man's pets. He went up casually to them and stroked their backs with every show of courteous attention. Now the truth dawned on the old man. His dream of a lifetime was about to be realized. He understood that the red man was actually making an offer for the goats. He had reared them up in the hope of selling them some day and, with the capital, opening a small shop on this very spot. Sitting here, watching the hills, he had often dreamt how he would put up a thatched roof here, spread a gunny sack out on the ground, and display on it fried nuts, coloured sweets, and green coconut for the thirsty and famished wayfarers on the highway, which was sometimes very busy. The animals were not prize ones for a cattle show, but he had spent his occasional savings to provide them some fancy diet now and then, and they did not look too bad. While he was reflecting thus, the red man shook his hand and left on his palm one hundred rupees in tens now. 'It is all for you or you may share it if you have the partner.'

The old man pointed at the station wagon and asked, 'Are you carrying them off in that?'

'Yes, of course,' said the other, understanding the transportation part of it.

The old man said, 'This will be their first ride in a motor car. Carry them off after I get out of sight, otherwise they will never follow you, but only me even if I am travelling on the path to *Yama Loka*.' He laughed at his own joke, brought his palms together in a salute, turned round and went off, and was soon out of sight beyond a clump of thicket.

The red man looked at the goats grazing peacefully. Perched on the pedestal of the horse, as the westerly sun touched the ancient faded colours of the statue with a fresh splendour, he ruminated, 'He must be gone to fetch some help, I suppose!' and settled down to wait. When a truck came downhill, he stopped it and got the help of a couple of men to detach the horse from its pedestal and place it in his station wagon. He gave them five rupees each, and for a further payment they siphoned off gas from the truck and helped him to start his engine.

Muni hurried homeward with the cash securely tucked away at his waist in his dhoti. He shut the street door and stole up softly to his wife as she squatted before the lit oven wondering if by a miracle food would drop from the sky. Muni displayed his fortune for the day. She snatched the notes from him, counted them by the glow of the fire, and cried, 'One hundred rupees! How did you come by it? Have you been stealing?'

'I have sold our goats to a red-faced man. He was absolutely crazy to have them, gave me all this money and carried them off in his motor car!'

Hardly had these words left his lips when they heard bleating outside. She opened the door and saw the two goats at her door. 'Here they are!' she said. 'What's the meaning of all this?'

He muttered a great curse and seized one of the goats by its ears and shouted, 'Where is that man? Don't you know you are his? Why did you come back?' The goat only wriggled in his grip. He asked the same question of the other too. The goat shook itself off. His wife glared at him and declared, 'If you have thieved, the police will come tonight and break your bones. Don't involve me. I will go away to my parents . . .'

RAJA RAO

Javni

> Caste and caste and caste, you say,
> What caste, pray, has he who knows God?
> KANAKADAS

I had just arrived. My sister sat by me, talking to me about a thousand things – about my health, my studies, my future, about Mysore, about my younger sister – and I lay sipping the hot, hot coffee that seemed almost like nectar after a ten-mile cycle ride on one of those bare, dusty roads of Malkad. I half listened to her and half drowsed away, feeling comfort and freedom after nine wild months in a city. And when I finished my coffee, I asked my sister to go and get another cup; for I really felt like being alone, and also I wanted some more of that invigorating drink. When my sister was gone, I lay on the mat, flat on my face with my hands stretched at my sides. It seemed to me I was carried away by a flood of some sort, caressing, feathery and quiet. I slept. Suddenly, as if in a dream, I heard a door behind me creaking. But I did not move. The door did not open completely, and somebody seemed to be standing by the threshold afraid to come in. 'Perhaps a neighbour,' I said to myself vaguely, and in my drowsiness I muttered something, stretched out my hands, kicked my feet against the floor and slowly moved my head from one side to the other. The door creaked a little again, and the figure seemed to recede. 'Lost!' I said to myself. Perhaps I had sent a neighbour away. I was a little pained. But some deeper instinct told me that the figure was still there.

Outside the carts rumbled over the paved street, and some crows cawed across the roof. A few sunbeams stealing through the tiles fell upon my back. I felt happy.

Meanwhile my sister came in, bringing the coffee. 'Ramu,' she whispered, standing by me, 'Ramu, my child, are you awake or asleep?'

'Awake,' I said, turning my head towards the door, which creaked once more and shut itself completely.

'Sita,' I whispered, 'there was somebody at the door.'

'When?' she demanded loudly.

'Now! Only a moment ago.'

She went to the door and, opening it, looked towards the street. After a while she smiled and called, 'Javni! You monkey! Why don't you come in? Who do you think is here, Javni? My brother – my brother.' She smiled broadly, and a few tears rolled down her cheeks.

'Really, Mother!' said a timid voice. 'Really! I wanted to come in. But, seeing Ramappa fast asleep, I thought I'd better wait out here.' She spoke the peasant Kannada, drawling the vowels interminably.

'So,' I said to myself, 'she already knows my name.'

'Come in!' commanded my sister.

Javni slowly approached the threshold, but still stood outside, gazing as if I were a saint or the holy elephant.

'Don't be shy, come in,' commanded my sister again.

Javni entered and, walking as if in a temple, went and sat by a sack of rice.

My sister sat by me, proud and affectionate. I was everything to her – her strength and wealth. She touched my head and said, 'Ramu, Javni is our new servant.' I turned towards Javni. She seemed to hide her face.

She was past forty, a little wrinkled beneath the lips and with strange, rapturous eyes. Her hair was turning white, her breasts were fallen and her bare, broad forehead showed pain and widowhood. 'Come near, Javni,' I said.

'No, Ramappa,' she whispered.

'No, come along,' I insisted. She came forward a few steps and sat by the pillar.

'Oh, come nearer, Javni, and see what a beautiful brother I have,' cried Sita.

I was not flattered. Only my big, taplike nose and my thick underlip seemed more monstrous than ever.

Javni crawled along till she was a few steps nearer.

'Oh! come nearer, you monkey,' cried my sister again.

Javni advanced a few feet further and, turning her face towards the floor, sat like a bride beside the bridegroom.

'He looks like a prince, Javni!' cried my sister.

'A god!' mumbled Javni.

I laughed and drank my coffee.

'The whole town is mad about him,' whispered Javni.

'How do you know?' asked Sita.

'How! I have been standing at the market-place, the whole afternoon, to see when Ramappa would come. You told me he looked like a prince. You said he rode a bicycle. And, when I saw him come by the pipal tree where-the-fisherman-Kodi-hanged-himself-the-other-day, I ran towards the town and I observed how people gazed and gazed at him. And they asked me who it was. "Of course, the Revenue Inspector's brother-in-law," I replied. "How beautiful he is!" said fat Nanjundah of the coconut shop. "How like a prince he is!" said the concubine Chowdy. "Oh, a very god!" said my neighbour, barber Venka's wife Kenchi.'

'Well, Ramu, so you see, the whole of Malkad is dazzled with your beauty,' interrupted my sister. 'Take care, my child. They say, in this town they practise magic, and I have heard many a beautiful boy has been killed by jealousy.'

I laughed.

'Don't laugh, Ramappa. With these very eyes, with these very two eyes, I have seen the ghosts of more than a hundred young men and women – all killed by magic, by magic, Ramappa,' assured Javni, for the first time looking towards me. 'My learned Ramappa, Ramappa, never go out after sunset; for there are spirits of all sorts walking in the dark. Especially never once go by the canal after the cows are come home. It is a haunted place, Ramappa.'

'How do you know?' I asked, curious.

'How! With these very eyes, I have seen, Ramappa, I have seen it all. The potter's wife Rangi was unhappy. Poor thing! Poor thing! And one night she had such heavy, heavy sorrow, she ran and jumped into the canal. The other day, when I was coming home in the deadly dark with my little lamb, whom should I see but Rangi – Rangi in a white, broad *sari*, her hair all floating. She stood in front of me. I shivered and wept. She ran and stood by a tree, yelling in a strange voice! "Away! Away!" I cried. Then suddenly I saw her standing on the bridge, and she jumped into the canal, moaning: "My girl is gone, my child is gone, and I am gone too!"'

My sister trembled. She had a horror of devils. 'Why don't you shut up, you donkey's widow, and not pour out all your Vedantic knowledge?'

'Pardon me, Mother, pardon me,' she begged.

'I have pardoned you again and again, and yet it is the same old story. Always the same *Ramayana*. Why don't you fall into the well like Rangi and turn devil?' My sister was furious.

Javni smiled and hid her face between her knees, timidly.

'How beautiful your brother is!' she murmured after a moment, ecstatic.

'Did I not say he was like a prince! Who knows what incarnation of a god he may be? Who knows?' my sister whispered, patting me, proudly, religiously.

'Sita!' I replied, and touched her lap with tenderness.

'Without Javni I could never have lived in this damned place!' said my sister after a moment's silence.

'And without you, I could not have lived either, Mother!' Her voice was so calm and rich that she seemed to sing.

'In this damned place everything is so difficult,' cursed Sita. '*He* is always struggling with the collections. The villages are few, but placed at great distances from one another. Sometimes he has been away for more than a week, and I should have died of fright had not Javni been with me. And,' she whispered, a little sadly, 'Javni, I am sure, understands my fears, my beliefs. Men, Ramu, can never understand us.'

'Why?' I asked.

'Why? I cannot say. You are too practical and too irreligious. To us everything is mysterious. Our gods are not your gods, your gods not our gods. It is a simple affair.' She seemed sadder still.

'But yet, I have always tried to understand you,' I managed to whisper.

'Of course! of course!' cried my sister, reassured.

'Mother,' muttered Javni, trembling, 'Mother! will you permit me to say one thing?' She seemed to plead.

'Yes!' answered my sister.

'Ramappa, your sister loves you,' said Javni. 'She loves you as though you were her own child. Oh! I wish I had seen her two children! They must have been angels! Perhaps they are in Heaven now – in Heaven! Children go to Heaven! But, Ramappa, what I wanted to say was this.

Your sister loves you, talks of you all the time, and says, "If my brother did not live, I should have died long ago".'

'How long have you been with Sita?' I asked Javni, trying to change the subject.

'How long? How long have I been with this family? What do I know? But let me see. The harvest was over and we were husking the grains when they came.'

'How did you happen to find her?' I asked my sister.

'Why, Ramappa,' cried Javni, proud for the first time, 'there is nobody who can work for a Revenue Inspector's family as I. You can go and ask everybody in the town, including every pariah if you like, and they will tell you, "Javni, she is good like a cow," and they will also add that there is no one who can serve a big man like the Revenue Inspector as Javni – as I.' She beat her breast with satisfaction.

'So you are the most faithful servant among the servants here!' I added a little awkwardly.

'Of course!' she cried proudly, her hands folded upon her knees. 'Of course!'

'How many Revenue Inspectors have you served?'

'How many? Now let me see.' Here she counted upon her fingers, one by one, remembering them by how many children they had, what sort of views they had, their caste, their native place, or even how good they had been in giving her two *saris*, a four-anna tip or a sack of rice.

'Javni,' I said, trying to be a little bit humorous, 'suppose I came here one day, say after ten or fifteen or twenty years, and I am not a Revenue Inspector, and I ask you to serve me. Will you or will you not?'

She looked perplexed, laughed and turned towards my sister for help.

'Answer him!' commanded my sister affectionately.

'But Ramappa,' she cried out, full of happiness, as if she

had discovered a solution, 'you cannot but be a big man like our Master, the Revenue Inspector. With your learning and your beauty you cannot be anything else. And, when you come here, of course I will be your servant.'

'But if I am not a Revenue Inspector,' I insisted.

'You must be – you must be!' she cried, as if I were insulting myself.

'All right, I shall be a Revenue Inspector in order to have you,' I joked.

'As if it were not enough that I should bleed myself to death in being one,' added my brother-in-law, as he entered through the back door, dust-covered and breathless.

Javni rose up and ran away as if in holy fear. It was the Master.

'She is a sweet thing,' I said to my sister.

'Almost a mother!' she added, and smiled.

In the byre Javni was talking to the calf.

My brother-in-law was out touring two or three days in the week. On these days Javni usually came to sleep at our house; for my sister had a terror of being alone. And, since it had become a habit, Javni came as usual even when I was there. One evening, I cannot remember why, we had dined early, and unrolling our beds, we lay down when it was hardly sunset. Javni came, peeped from the window and called in a whisper, 'Mother, Mother!'

'Come in, you monkey,' answered my sister.

Javni opened the door and stepped in. She had a sheet in her hand, and, throwing it on the floor, she went straight into the byre where her food was usually kept. I could not bear that. Time and again I had quarrelled with my sister about it all. But she would not argue with me. 'They are of the lower class, and you cannot ask them to sit and eat with you,' she would say.

'Of course!' I said. 'After all, why not? Are they not like

us, like any of us? Only the other day you said you loved her as if she were your elder sister or mother.'

'Yes!' she grunted angrily. 'But affection does not ask you to be irreligious.'

'And what, pray, is being irreligious?' I continued, furious.

'Irreligious. Irreligious. Well, eating with a woman of a lower caste is irreligious. And, Ramu,' she cried desperately, 'I have enough of quarrelling all the time. In the name of our holy mother can't you leave me alone!' There, tears!

'You are inhuman!' I spat, disgusted.

'Go and show your humanity!' she grumbled, and, hiding her face beneath the blanket, she wept harder.

I was really much too ashamed and too angry to stay in my bed. I rose and went into the byre. Javni sat in the dark, swallowing mouthfuls of rice that sounded like a cow chewing the cud. She thought I had come to go into the garden, but I remained beside her, leaning against the wall. She stopped eating and looked deeply embarrassed.

'Javni,' I said tenderly.

'Ramappa!' she answered, confused.

'Why not light a lantern when you eat, Javni?'

'What use?' she replied, and began to chew the cud.

'But you cannot see what you are eating,' I explained.

'I cannot. But there is no necessity to see what you eat.' She laughed as if amused.

'But you must!' I was angry.

'No, Ramappa. I know where my rice is, and I can feel where the pickle is, and that is enough.'

Just at that moment, the cow threw a heapful of dung, which splashed across the cobbled floor.

'Suppose you come with me into the hall,' I cried. I knew I could never convince her.

'No, Ramappa. I am quite well here. I do not want to dirty the floor of the hall.'

'If it is dirty, I will clean it,' I cried, exasperated.

She was silent. In the darkness I saw the shadow of Javni near me, thrown by the faint starlight that came from the garden door. In the corner the cow was breathing hard, and the calf was nibbling at the wisps of hay. It was a terrible moment. The whole misery of the world seemed to be weighing all about and above me. And yet – and yet – the suffering – one seemed to laugh at it all.

'Javni,' I said affectionately, 'do you eat at home like this?'

'Yes, Ramappa.' Her tone was sad.

'And why?'

'The oil is too expensive, Ramappa.'

'But surely you can buy it?' I continued.

'No, Ramappa. It costs an anna a bottle, and it lasts only a week.'

'But an anna is nothing,' I said.

'Nothing! Nothing!' She spoke as if frightened. 'Why, my learned Ramappa, it is what I earn in two days.'

'In two days!' I had rarely been more surprised.

'Yes, Ramappa, I earn one rupee each month.' She seemed content.

I heard an owl hoot somewhere, and far, far away, somewhere too far and too distant for my rude ears to hear, the world wept its silent suffering plaints. Had not the Lord said: 'Whenever there is misery and ignorance, I come'? Oh, when will that day come, and when will the Conch of Knowledge blow?

I had nothing to say. My heart beat fast. And, closing my eyes, I sank into the primal flood, the moving fount of Being. Man, I love you.

Javni sat and ate. The mechanical mastication of the rice seemed to represent her life, her cycle of existence.

'Javni,' I inquired, breaking the silence, 'what do you do with the one rupee?'

'I never take it,' she answered laughing.

'Why don't you take it, Javni?'

'Mother keeps it for me. Now and again she says I work well and adds an anna or two to my funds, and one day I shall have enough to buy a *sari*.'

'And the rest?' I asked.

'The rest? Why, I will buy something for my brother's child.'

'Is your brother poor, Javni?'

'No. But, Ramappa, I love the child.' She smiled.

'Suppose I asked you to give it to me?' I laughed, since I could not weep.

'Oh, you will never ask me, Ramappa, never. But, Ramappa, if you should, I would give it to you.' She laughed too, content and amused.

'You are a wonderful thing!' I murmured.

'At your feet, Ramappa!' She had finished eating, and she went into the bathroom to wash her hands.

I walked out into the garden and stood looking at the sparkling heavens. There was companionship in their shining. The small and the great clustered together in the heart of the quiet limpid sky. God, knew they caste? Far away a cartman chanted forth:

> The night is dark;
> Come to me, mother.
> The night is quiet;
> Come to me, friend.

The winds sighed.

On the nights when Javni came to sleep with us, we

gossiped a great deal about village affairs. She had always news to tell us. One day it would be about the postman Subba's wife, who had run away with the Mohammedan of the mango shop. On another day, it would be about the miraculous cure of Sata Venkanna's wife, Kanthi, during her recent pilgrimage to the Biligiri temple. My sister always took an interest in those things, and Javni made it her affair to find out everything about everybody. She gossiped the whole evening till we both fell asleep. My sister usually lay by the window, I near the door, and Javni at our feet. She slept on a bare wattle-mat, with a cotton sheet for a cover, and she seemed never to suffer from cold. On one of these nights when we were gossiping, I pleaded with Javni to tell me just a little about her own life. At first she waved aside my idea; but, after a moment when my sister howled at her, she accepted it, still rather unhappily. I was all ears, but my sister was soon snoring comfortably.

Javni was born in the neighbouring village of Kotehalli, where her father cultivated the fields in the winter and washed clothes in the summer. Her mother had always work to do, since there were childbirths almost every day in one village or the other, and, being a hereditary midwife, she was always sent for. Javni had four sisters and two brothers, of whom only her brother Bhima remained. She loved her parents, and they loved her too; and, when she was eighteen, she was duly married to a boy whom they had chosen from Malkad. The boy was good and affectionate, and he never once beat her. He too was a washerman, and 'What do you think?' asked Javni proudly, 'he washed clothes for the Maharaja, when he came here.'

'Really!' I exclaimed.

And she continued. Her husband was, as I have said, a good man, and he really cared for her. He never made her work too much, and he always cooked for her when she fell sick. One day, however, as the gods decided it, a snake bit him while he was washing clothes by the river, and, in spite of all the magic that the barber Subba applied, he died that very evening, crying to the last, 'Javni, Javni, my Javni.' (I should have expected her to weep here. But she continued without any exclamations or sighs.) Then came all the misfortunes one after the other, and yet she knew they were nothing, for, above all, she said, Goddess Talakamma moved and reigned.

Her husband belonged to a family of three brothers and two sisters. The elder brother was a wicked fellow, who played cards and got drunk two days out of three. The second was her husband, and the third was a haughty young fellow, who had already, it was known, made friends with the concubine Siddi, the former mistress of the priest Rangappa. He treated his wife as if she were an ox and once he actually beat her till she was bleeding and unconscious. There were many children in the family, and since one of the sisters-in-law also lived in the same village, her children too came to play in the house. So Javni lived on happily, working at home as usual and doing her little to earn for the family funds.

She never knew, she said, how it all happened, but one day a policeman came, frightened everybody, and took away her elder brother-in-law for some reason that nobody understood. The women were all terrified and everybody wept. The people in the town began to spit at them as they passed by, and left cattle to graze away all the crops in the fields to show their hatred and their revenge. Shame, poverty and quarrels, these followed one another. And because the elder brother-in-law was in prison and the younger with his mistress, the women at home made her life miserable. '"You dirty widow!" they would say and spit on me. I wept and sobbed and often wanted to go and fall into the river. But I knew Goddess Talakamma would be angry with me, and I stopped each time I wanted to kill myself. One day, however, my elder sister-in-law became so evil-mouthed that I ran away from the house. I did not know to whom to go, since I knew nobody and my brother hated me – he always hated me. But anyway, Ramappa,' she said, 'anyway, a sister is a sister. You cannot deny that the same mother has suckled you both.'

'Of course not!' I said.

'But he never treated me as you treat your sister.'

'So, you are jealous, you ill-boding widow!' swore my sister, waking up. She always thought people hated or envied her.

'No, Mother, no,' Javni pleaded.

'Go on!' I said.

'I went to my brother,' she continued. 'As soon as his wife saw me she swore and spat and took away her child that was playing on the verandah, saying it would be bewitched. After a moment my brother came out.

'"Why have you come?" he asked me.

'"I am without a home," I said.

'"You dirty widow, how can you find a house to live in, when you carry misfortune wherever you set your foot?"

'I simply wept.

'"Weep, weep!" he cried, "weep till your tears flood the Cauvery. But you will not get a morsel of rice from me. No, not a morsel!"

'"No," I said. "I do not want a morsel of rice. I want only a palm-width of shelter to put myself under."

'He seemed less angry. He looked this side and that and roared: "Do you promise me never to quarrel with anyone?"

'"Yes!" I answered, still weeping.

'"Then, for the peace of the spirit of my father, I will give you the little hut by the garden door. You can sit, weep, eat, shit, die – do what you like there," he said. I trembled. In the meantime my sister-in-law came back. She frowned and thumped the floor, swearing at me and calling me a prostitute, a donkey, a witch. Ramappa, I never saw a woman like that. She makes my life a life of tears.'

'How?' I asked.

'How! I cannot say. It is ten years or twenty since I set foot in their house. And every day I wake up with "donkey's wife" or "prostitute" in my ears.'

'But you don't have anything to do with her?' I said.

'I don't. But the child sometimes comes to me because I love it and then my sister-in-law rushes out, roaring like a tigress, and says she will flay me to death if I touch the child again.'

'You should not touch it,' I said.

'Of course I would not if I had my own child. But, Ramappa, that little boy loves me.'

'And why don't they want you to touch him?'

'Because they say I am a witch and an evil spirit.' She wept.

'Who says it?'

'They. Both of them say it. But still, Ramappa' – here she suddenly turned gay – 'I always keep mangoes and cakes that Mother gives me and save them all for the little boy. So he runs away from his mother each time the door is open. He is such a sweet, sweet thing.' She was happy.

'How old is he?' I asked.

'Four.'

'Is he their only child?'

'No. They have four more – all grown up. One is already a boy as big as you.'

'And the others, do they love you?'

'No. They all hate me, they all hate me – except that child.'

'Why don't you adopt a child?'

'No, Ramappa. I have a lamb, and that is enough.'

'You have a lamb too!' I said, surprised.

'Yes, a lamb for the child to play with now, and, when the next Durga festival comes, I will offer it to Goddess Talakamma.'

'Offer it to the Goddess! Why, Javni? Why not let it live?'

'Don't speak sacrilege, Ramappa. I owe a lamb every three years to the Goddess.'

'And what does she give in return?'

'What do you say! What!' She was angry. 'All! Everything! Should I live if that Goddess did not protect me? Would that child come to me if the Goddess did not help me? Would Mother be so good to me if the Goddess did not bless me? Why, Ramappa, everything is hers. O Great Goddess Talakamma, give everybody good health and long life and all progeny! Protect me, Mother!' She was praying.

'What will she give me if I offer a lamb?' I asked.

'Everything, Ramappa. You will grow learned; you will become a big man; you will marry a rich wife. Ramappa,' she said, growing affectionate all of a sudden, 'I have already been praying for you. When Mother said she had a brother, I said to the Goddess, "Goddess, keep that boy strong and virtuous and give him all the eight riches of Heaven and earth."'

'Do you love me more or less than your brother's child?' I asked, to change the subject.

She was silent for a moment.

'You don't know?' I said.

'No, Ramappa. I have been thinking. I offer the lamb to

the Goddess for the sake of the child. I have not offered a lamb for you. So how can I say whom I love more?'

'The child!' I said.

'No, no, I love you as much, Ramappa.'

'Will you adopt me?' No, I was not joking.

She broke into fits of laughter which woke up my sister.

'Oh, shut up!' cried Sita.

'Do you know Javni is going to adopt me?'

'Adopt you! Why does she not go and fall into the river?' she roared, and went to sleep again.

'If you adopt me, Javni, I will work for you and give you food to eat.'

'No, learned Ramappa. A *Brahmin* is not meant to work. You are the "chosen ones".'

Chosen ones, indeed! 'No, we are not!' I murmured.

'You are. You are. The sacred books are yours. The Vedas are yours. You are all, you are all, you are the twice-born. We are your servants, Ramappa – your slaves.'

'I am not a *Brahmin*,' I said half-jokingly, half-seriously.

'You are. You are. You want to make fun of me.'

'No, Javni, suppose you adopt me?'

She laughed again.

'If you do not adopt me, I shall die now and grow into a lamb in my next life and you will buy it. What will you do then?'

She did not say anything. It was too perplexing.

'Now,' I said, feeling sleepy, 'now, Javni, go to sleep and think again tomorrow morning whether you will adopt me or not.'

'Adopt you! You are a god, Ramappa, a god! I cannot adopt you.'

I dozed away. Only in the stillness I heard Javni saying: 'Goddess, Great Goddess, as I vowed, I will offer thee my lamb. Protect the child, protect Mother, protect her brother, protect Master, O Goddess! Protect me!'

The Goddess stood silent, in the little temple by the Cauvery, amidst the whisper of the woods.

A July morning, two summers later. Our cart rumbled over the boulders of the street, and we were soon at the village square. Javni was running behind the cart, with tears rolling down her cheeks. For one full week I had seen her weeping all the time, all the time dreading the day when we should leave her and she would see us no more. She was breathless. But she walked fast, keeping pace with the bullocks. I was with my sister in the back of the cart, and my brother-in-law sat in front, beside the cartman. My sister too was sad. In her heart she knew she was leaving a friend. Yes. Javni had been her friend, her only friend. Now and again they gazed at each other, and I could see Javni suddenly sobbing like a child.

'Mother, Mother,' she would say approaching the cart, 'don't forget me.'

'I will not. No, I assure you, I will not.'

Now my sister too was in tears.

'Even if she should, I will not,' I added. I myself should have wept had I not been so civilized.

When we touched the river, it was already broad morning. Now, in the summer, there was so little water that the ferry was not plying and we were going to wade through. The cartman said he would rest the bullocks for a moment, and I got out partly to breathe the fresh air and more to speak to Javni.

'Don't weep,' I said to her.

'Ramappa, how can I help but weep? Shall I ever see again a family of gods like yours? Mother was kind to me, kind like a veritable goddess. You were so, so good to me, and Master – ' Here she broke again into sobs.

'No, Javni. In contact with a heart like yours, who will not bloom into a god?'

But she simply wept. My words meant nothing to her. She was nervous, and she trembled over and over again. 'Mother, Mother,' she would say between her sobs, 'O Mother!'

The cartman asked me to get in. I got into the cart with a heavy heart. I was leaving a most wonderful soul. I was in. The cartman cried, 'Hoy, hoyee!' And the bulls stepped into the river.

Till we were on the other bank, I could see Javni sitting on a rock, and looking towards us. In my heart I seemed still to hear her sobs. A huge pipal rose behind her, and, across the blue waters of the river and the vast, vast sky above her, she seemed so small, just a spot in space, recedingly real. Who was she?

ATTIA HOSAIN

A Woman and a Child

After five empty weeks of waiting she decided to go to the city. Her husband raised no objection; he never did. He had been hag-ridden by his mother:

'Marry again, my son. Marry again. She has brought us nothing but barren death.'

He did not obey, for his wife's passionate conviction that she could and would bear him a child, her tears, her tempers, her accusations, were stronger than his mother's bullying and pleading.

Utterly worn out, he sought refuge in God. Those remnants of his will which he could salvage, he offered to Him. His body submitted to the importunate demands of his wife, but his spirit unwound itself. He accompanied her on her many pilgrimages, but when she cried and implored, 'Oh Great One, have mercy on me! Fill my empty life!' he prayed, 'Lord, let my life be empty of all but Thee!'

She said, 'There is a new lady-doctor at the zenana hospital.'

He stopped counting his beads: 'There is a Saint's tomb there also.'

She answered in impatient anger: 'You know I have been there twice already. I have sacrificed goats, I have offered *chadars* of the finest muslin. What have I left undone?'

'We go to so many places that I get confused. Ah well, I shall make the arrangements.'

She had dragged herself from shrine to shrine. 'I am a

sinner, but, *Pirji*, if you pray for me Allah will not refuse you.'

While she humbled her spirit, she pampered her body. She dressed as a young bride, imagining that from the illusion she would wring the fulfilment of her desire. The bright colours of her *dupatta* cast kind shadows on her ageing face, and the folds of her clothes hid the hard outlines of her body.

On the train she squeezed her way through struggling, nagging women into the corner nearest the mother who nursed her child. Her eyes slipped mechanically over the others, and returned again and again to the suckling child. The mother drew her veiling *dupatta* over the child's head; it pulled the thin cloth aside with a dimpled hand, and drew its mouth away from her wet breast. She buttoned her *kurta*, and the smile on her lips was reflected in her eyes. The child pulled at the black cord knotted around its wrist to thwart the evil eye, then slowly reached up to touch the spots of light that shone brightly in the dark eyes looking down.

'Oh light of my eyes,' the mother laughed. 'Would you blind me?'

She caught the exploring finger between her teeth, and the child gurgled with laughter.

'You are blessed with a beautiful child.'

The startled mother looked up at the staring stranger, and, clasping the child more closely in her protecting arms, said, 'Allah keep her from the evil eye. My life, my love . . .'

'*Masha-alla*, may those who wish her evil never prosper! Come, my little one, come to me. See what I will give you.'

She held out her hand, and the bells of her bracelet jingled, the glass bangles caught sparkling gleams of light. The child stared curiously with eyes as black as the *tika* between its brows, then hid its face in the mother's breast. The mother rocked gently, smiling: 'My little *Rani*, why are you afraid? No one will hurt you while I am here.' Her eyes shone as she sang softly, 'Sleep, my precious one, star of my eyes . . .'

When the child was asleep the mother asked, 'How many children have you?'

'I have none.'

'Poor soul! Did you lose them too?'

'I never had any.'

'Allah's ways are strange; He seems to have given you wealth, but denied you the richest of all gifts.'

The simple kindliness of the woman robbed the words of their sting. She did not feel resentment, and that was strange. Her own people made her feel unwanted, as if there were a curse on her. They also asked, 'You have no children?' but with no sympathy. First they were curious, then contemptuous, and finally resentful of her useless existence.

She remembered one instance particularly. It was her brother's wedding. The women crowded round the scented red bundle that was the bride; custom's licence unfettered their tongues. One of the bride's companions said, 'Enough of this! The girl is tired,' and she joked, 'She must feel the weight within her of her night-old child.' Her mother-in-law said scornfully, 'How would you know who never felt it?' and someone cut in, 'May the evil eye be far from the bride, and may she blossom and flower!'

The mother interrupted her thoughts: 'Do not look so unhappy.'

'I was thinking . . . why did you say, "Did you lose them *too*?"'

'Because I lost mine, four of them – all sons. Two died

of fever and one was born dead.' The mother's voice held no trace of bitterness in its resignation.

'How did the fourth die?'

'Opium. I gave it to him – a little at a time – when I had too much work to do. That was when there was a strike in the printing press where my husband works. I had to take in sewing and embroidery, and the child would disturb me, so I gave him opium. I must have left some lying about, and he took it unknowing, child-like . . .' The mother, reaching back through memory, stopped, then continued: 'It was God's will. He took away what He had given to me.'

'To some He gives nothing.'

'You must not say that. You are not ill, you are not old. My aunt told me about a woman of fifty who had her first baby after carrying it a year or more. Never despair of God's goodness.'

'I have prayed; I have been to every shrine. I have tried wearing holy amulets, and drinking holy water. Sometimes I think that all the holy water my husband has drunk has thinned his blood.'

'There is a *fakir* in my village whose amulets have great power. I shall send for one for you. Where shall I find you?'

'I have tried everything; I have even been to *hakims* and doctors. I am now going to see the lady-doctor who has just come to the City Hospital. You will find me in Nawabganj in the Lane of *Attar*-makers.'

'Fate must have brought us together. I live there too, just above the shop of Ahmad Husain Muhammad Husain, the cloth merchants. I shall bring you the amulet myself . . . The train is stopping. I hope my husband comes to help me with the luggage. I do not wish to wake the child.'

'I can have no such hope. My husband must be counting his beads, busy preparing for his arrival in heaven. I suppose I'll have to go and look for him. It is he who ought to wear the *burqa* . . .'

She wasted little time in getting to the hospital.

The doctor croaked like a bird of ill-omen. 'You cannot have a child. I can operate, if you wish, but I promise nothing . . .'

In panic of the knife she thought of the promised amulet, and sought out the woman she had met on the train. Until it was brought to her she existed in a suffocating darkness vibrant with doubts and fears. She wore it, and drank the holy water in which it was washed. The weeks of waiting that followed were as empty as her womb.

She returned to the hospital.

During clinical examinations her body had accepted the tearing of veils of prudery; now it was ready to accept a tearing of its very tissues unto the death that concealed itself within her and made barren the seed of life. For ten days she lay in the hospital, and was surrounded by the sounds of motherhood. She could hear the cries of women in labour, and was bitterly envious of their fruitful agony. She could hear the sounds of babies crying in hunger, and her dry breasts ached. She could hear them cry fretfully, and her empty arms longed to hold and soothe them. Then in bitterness and despair she wished them dead, all the sounds of life hushed, all fertility struck arid.

During visiting hours she picked out the rapid, eager footsteps of children in the passage. Sometimes curious ones peeped into the room, then scampered off. Not one of them came in.

Two days before she was to leave her friend came to see her, but without the child.

'Forgive me, sister, I could not come to see you for the little one was ill, and you know how frightened that makes me.'

'Where have you left her now?'

'She is with the doctor. You told me that the lady-doctor was clever, so I brought her here. I'll bring her to see you when they have finished examining her.'

'You must take great care of her; she is very precious.'

'How well I know it! I know that I can have no more children. I wished for a son, but God has willed it otherwise. Now you will have a son, and I shall share your happiness.'

The day she was leaving hospital the sweeper-woman came to her for the old clothes she took as her due. She threw them on the floor, careful not to touch this hag made impure by the filth and excrement she was ordained by birth to clean. She hated the woman, her ugliness, her pitying references to the operation. She disliked the secretive manner with which she came near and whispered, 'I can tell you something of interest to you.'

'What do you mean? I want nothing from you.'

'So many come here like you hoping to have children. So few have them. I can help you if the doctor cannot.'

'I do not want your help.'

'You never can tell. If you ever need me, you can send for me.'

She put on her *burqa* and followed her waiting husband to the curtained tonga.

The familiar empty pattern of waiting days and weeks followed. In the midst of his prayers and meditations her husband grew restless.

'Soon the pilgrims will start for Mecca . . .'

'You and your pilgrimage! God knows you'll never be too old for that.'

The bond of life's expectancy that held them together grew strained. She became increasingly conscious of her dislike and contempt for this weak, meek man. Her affections shrank and drew themselves into a focus of intensity. All the love that she stored for her unborn, she lavished on the child she had seen on the train. It became the only reason for continued existence while she waited for life to begin within her. She dressed the little one like a doll. She delighted in the child's pleasure in each new gift. She prepared special food and sweets for her. The waiting days lost their blankness.

The simple mother was drawn to her by the common bond of their love, glad the child was given all those things which she herself could not afford but longed to give. One day the mother laughed and said, 'She is more your child than mine. She will not rest when she is away from you.'

'She will never be away from me. Will you, my love?'

The child ran on unsteady feet, clung to her and called her '*Amma!*'

From that day a sense of possession grew in her. She became jealous of the mother, grudged her the time the child was alone with her. Her fevered imagination made herself the mother.

Two months after her return from the hospital she sent for the sweeper-woman.

'You said you could help me. What can you do for me?'

'If you eat the cord of a first-born baby you will have a child. I can get it for you from the hospital as I have done for others.'

'Get out of my sight, you ill-fated witch!' She shuddered with horror and loathing.

The day came when in desperation and anguish she sent for the hated woman again. It was not long before the woman returned with a bottle wrapped in a dirty newspaper, took a rupee in payment, gave gratuitous advice, and went away triumphant.

The day that followed was one of exhaustion. Each time she retched she felt as if the death within her would be forced out of her womb, take the shape of a monstrous jinn and possess her completely.

When the child came to see her, after what seemed an unlimited stretch of time, she was still in bed. She stroked its hair with trembling hands, and her caressing voice was weak. The child played for a while near her, then, disappointed when no new toy was given, no new games played, went home. The mother came in the evening.

'What is wrong? I understood from the child's chatter that something had happened to you, and I came as soon as I could get away from my work.'

'Nothing is seriously wrong; my stomach is upset.'

'It must be this horrible food one gets now. It would not surprise me if these wretched butchers fed us on dog's meat or human flesh.'

'How can you talk like that? Give me that bowl; I feel sick.'

'Poor, poor thing! Why don't you send for a *hakim*?'

'I hate them; I hate all of them.'

Surprised by the venomous bitterness in her voice the mother said, 'Please don't be angry. I merely suggested it because you look so ill.'

Again for some time the child stayed away and the house was unbearably silent. Her longing for the child's presence became an obsession. At last she sent a desperate message, and the mother brought the child that very evening. She thought the mother an alien presence.

'My little darling, why did you stay away from me?'

She strained the child to her until it gasped for breath and struggled away from her arms.

'I was busy,' explained the mother, 'and she would not come without me. I think she was frightened that day when you were ill.'

'Frightened of me? Nonsense!' Then she added suspiciously, 'What kept you so busy?'

'I have a lot of preparations to make before I go away to the wedding . . .'

'Wedding? What wedding? You are keeping secrets from me. You are hiding what is really in your mind. You want to take her away from me because you are jealous of me.'

The mother was bewildered: 'What do you mean? Why should I be jealous of you? I've always been grateful for the love and happiness you have given my child. I had not expected the marriage to take place so soon, and was quite unprepared. That is why I had so many things to do all at once.'

'Whose wedding is it?'

'My brother-in-law's. I shall be gone only a month or two . . .'

'A month or two! Leave the child with me, please. You know I will look after her well enough. Will you stay with me, my little one?'

The mother laughed and added, 'Or will you stay with me?'

The child ran to its mother and put its arms round her neck.

'Come to me, my love. I will give you sweets and toys and pretty clothes.'

The child ran to the other merrily. The mother teased, 'You greedy little pretender!'

That night she felt the house a shell. It held no laughter, no prattle, no unsteadily swift footsteps. Emptiness was around her and within her. If she screamed her voice would be lost in it and no one would hear her. Just as God did not hear; the Saints did not hear. If she was to live in silence why should others not share it with her? Why should another have what was hers by all the rights of desire and longing and sacrifice? Would it be easy to say 'God's will be done' when His will left no hope?

Her head was heavy and throbbed with pain. She knocked it against the wall again and again. She felt the softness of cloth against her aching forehead, and through tear-blinded eyes she saw her husband's *kurta* hanging on the wall. A flame of fury and hate burned through her. She sprang up and wrenched the flimsy muslin garment off the peg and tore it in shreds. Her impatient teeth bit and strained at each resisting seam. The frenzy burned in a focus of sizzling green.

The next day the child came without its mother. She dressed her in new clothes that shone like shoots of grass rain-washed. 'My pretty one, your mother could not give you these.' She gave her a doll that opened and shut its eyes and said *ma-ma* and made the child clap its hands and laugh. 'Your mother cannot give you this. What can she give you? Not even love – not love like mine. You are mine, my precious one, my own!'

The child stopped laughing, clutched its doll and puckered up its face with fear of the tear-splashed twisted face so near. It tried to run away and cried out, '*Amma! Amma!*'

'I am your *amma*. Don't run away from me.' She caught the child and crushed it to her breast. It struggled and whimpered, '*Amma! Amma!*'

'Sh! Sh! Sh! Don't call her. If she hears you she will come and take you away.' She pressed her harder against herself to smother its cry, '*Amma! Amma! Amma!*' The child struggled desperately . . .

The doll fell to the ground. Its china head cracked against the hard uncovered floor. The child's struggles ceased.

She held the still form tight, and swaying from side to side cried, 'You are mine. You are mine!'

KHUSHWANT SINGH

The Riot

The town lay etherized under the fresh spring twilight. The shops were closed and house-doors barred from the inside. Street lamps dimly lit the deserted roads. Only a few policemen walked about with steel helmets on their heads and rifles slung behind their backs. The sound of their hobnailed boots was all that broke the stillness of the town.

The twilight sank into darkness. A crescent moon lit the quiet streets. A soft breeze blew bits of newspaper from the pavements on to the road and back again. It was cool and smelled of the freshness of spring. Some dogs emerged from a dark lane and gathered round a lamp-post. A couple of policemen strolled past them smiling. One of them mumbled something vulgar. The other pretended to pick up a stone and hurl it at the dogs. The dogs ran down the street in the opposite direction and resumed their courtship at a safer distance.

Rāni was a pariah bitch whose litter populated the lanes and by-lanes of the town. She was a thin, scraggy specimen, typical of the pariahs of the town. Her white coat was mangy, showing patches of raw flesh. Her dried-up udders hung loosely from her ribs. Her tail was always tucked between her hind legs as she slunk about in fear and abject servility.

Rāni would have died of starvation with her first litter of eight had it not been for the generosity of the Hindu shopkeeper, Rām Jawāyā, in the corner of whose courtyard she had unloaded her womb. The shopkeeper's family fed her and played with her pups till they were told enough to run about the streets and steal food for themselves. The shopkeeper's generosity had put Rāni in the habit of sponging. Every year when spring came she would find excuse to loiter around the stall of Ramzān, the Moslem greengrocer. Beneath the wooden platform on which groceries were displayed lived the big, burly Moti. Early autumn, she presented the shopkeeper's household with half-a-dozen or more of Moti's offspring.

Moti was a cross between a Newfoundland and a spaniel. His shaggy coat and sullen look was Ramzān's pride. Ramzān had lopped off Moti's tail and ears. He fed him till Moti grew big and strong and became the master of the town's canine population. Rāni had many rivals. But year after year, with the advent of spring, Rāni's fancy lightly turned to thoughts of Moti and she sauntered across to Ramzān's stall.

This time spring had come but the town was paralysed with fear of communal riots and curfews. In the daytime people hung about the street corners in groups of tens and twenties, talking in whispers. No shops opened and long before curfew hours the streets were deserted, with only pariah dogs and policemen about.

Tonight even Moti was missing. In fact, ever since the curfew Ramzān had kept him indoors tied to a cot. He was far more useful guarding Ramzān's house than loitering about the streets. Rāni came to Ramzān's stall and sniffed about. Moti could not have been there for some days. She was disappointed. But spring came only once a year – and hardly ever did it come at a time when one could have the city to oneself with no curious children looking on – and no scandalized parents hurling stones at her. So Rāni gave up Moti and ambled down the road towards Rām Jawāyā's house. A train of suitors followed her.

Rāni faced her many suitors in front of Rām Jawāyā's doorstep. They snarled and snapped and fought with each other. Rāni stood impassively, waiting for the decision. In a few minutes a lanky black dog, one of Rāni's own progeny, won the honours. The others slunk away.

In Ramzān's house, Moti sat pensively eyeing his master from underneath his *charpoy*. For some days the spring air had made him restive. He heard the snarling in the street and smelled Rāni in the air. But Ramzān would not let him go. He tugged at the rope – then gave it up and began to whine. Ramzān's heavy hand struck him. A little later he began to whine again. Ramzān had had several sleepless nights watching and was heavy with sleep. He began to snore. Moti whined louder and then sent up a pitiful howl to his unfaithful mistress. He tugged and strained at the leash and began to bark. Ramzān got up angrily from his *charpoy* to beat him. Moti made a dash towards the door dragging the lightened string cot behind him. He nosed open the door and rushed out. The *charpoy* stuck in the doorway and the rope tightened round his neck. He made a savage wrench, the rope gave way, and he leapt across the road. Ramzān ran back to his room, slipped a knife under his shirt, and went after Moti.

Outside Rām Jawāyā's house, the illicit liaison of Rāni and the black pariah was being consummated. Suddenly the burly form of Moti came into view. With an angry growl Moti leapt at Rāni's lover. Other dogs joined the mêlée, tearing and snapping wildly.

Rām Jawāyā had also spent several sleepless nights keeping watch and yelling back war cries to the Moslems. At last fatigue and sleep overcame his newly-acquired martial spirit. He slept soundly with a heap of stones under his *charpoy* and an imposing array of soda water bottles filled with acid close at hand. The noise outside woke him.

The shopkeeper picked up a big stone and opened the door. With a loud oath he sent the missile flying at the dogs. Suddenly a human being emerged from the corner and the stone caught him squarely in the solar plexus.

The stone did not cause much damage to Ramzān but the suddenness of the assault took him aback. He yelled 'Murder!' and produced his knife from under his shirt. The shopkeeper and the grocer eyed each other for a brief moment and then ran back to their houses shouting. The petrified town came to life. There was more shouting. The drum at the Sikh temple beat a loud tattoo – the air was rent with war cries.

Men emerged from their houses making hasty enquiries. A Moslem or a Hindu, it was said, had been attacked. Someone had been kidnapped and was being butchered. A party of *goondas* were going to attack, but the dogs had started barking. They had actually assaulted a woman and killed her children. There must be resistance. There was. Groups of five joined others of ten. Tens joined twenties till a few hundred, armed with knives, spears, hatchets, and kerosene oil cans proceeded to Rām Jawāyā's house. They were met with a fusillade of stones, soda water bottles, and acid. They hit back blindly. Tins of kerosene oil were emptied indiscriminately and lighted. Flames shot up in the sky enveloping Rām Jawāyā's home and the entire neighbourhood, Hindu, Moslem and Sikh alike.

The police rushed to the scene and opened fire. Fire engines clanged their way in and sent jets of water flying into the sky. But fires had been started in other parts of the town and there were not enough fire engines to go round.

All night and all the next day the fires burnt – and houses fell and people were killed. Rām Jawāyā's home was burnt and he barely escaped with his life. For several days smoke rose from the ruins. What had once been a busy town was a heap of charred masonry.

Some months later when peace was restored, Rām Jawāyā came to inspect the site of his old home. It was all in shambles with the bricks lying in a mountainous pile. In the corner of what had once been his courtyard there was a little clearing. There lay Rāni with her litter nuzzling into her dried udders. Beside her stood Moti guarding his bastard brood.

RUTH PRAWER JHABVALA

An Experience of India

Today Ramu left. He came to ask for money and I gave him as much as I could. He counted it and asked for more, but I didn't have it to give him. He said some insulting things, which I pretended not to hear. Really I couldn't blame him. I knew he was anxious and afraid, not having another job to go to. But I also couldn't help contrasting the way he spoke now with what he had been like in the past : so polite always, and eager to please, and always smiling, saying 'Yes sir,' 'Yes madam please.' He used to look very different too, very spruce in his white uniform and his white canvas shoes. When guests came, he put on a special white coat he had made us buy him. He was always happy when there were guests – serving, mixing drinks, emptying ashtrays – and I think he was disappointed that more didn't come. The Ford Foundation people next door had a round of buffet suppers and Sunday brunches, and perhaps Ramu suffered in status before their servants because we didn't have much of that. Actually, coming to think of it, perhaps he suffered in status anyhow because we weren't like the others. I mean, I wasn't. I didn't look like a proper memsahib or dress like one – I wore Indian clothes right from the start – or ever behave like one. I think perhaps Ramu didn't care for that. I think servants want their employers to be conventional and put up a good front so that other people's servants can respect them. Some of the nasty things Ramu told me this morning were about how everyone said I was just someone from a very low sweeper caste in my own country and how sorry they were for him that he had to serve such a person.

He also said it was no wonder Sahib had run away from me. Henry didn't actually run away, but it's true that things had changed between us. I suppose India made us see how fundamentally different we were from each other. Though when we first came, we both came we thought with the same ideas. We were both happy that Henry's paper had sent him out to India. We both thought it was a marvellous opportunity not only for him professionally but for both of us spiritually. Here was our escape from that Western materialism with which we were both so terribly fed up. But once he got here and the first enthusiasm had worn off, Henry seemed not to mind going back to just the sort of life we'd run away from. He even didn't seem to care about meeting Indians any more, though in the beginning he had made a great point of doing so; now it seemed to him all right to go only to parties given by other foreign correspondents and sit around there and eat and drink and talk just the way they would at home. After a while, I couldn't stand going with him any more, so we'd have a fight and then he'd go off by himself. That was a relief. I didn't want to be with any of those people and talk about inane things in their tastefully appointed airconditioned apartments.

I had come to India to *be* in India. I wanted to be changed. Henry didn't – he wanted a change, that's all, but not to be changed. After a while because of that he was a stranger to me and I felt I was alone, the way I'm really alone now. Henry had to travel a lot around the country to write his pieces, and in the beginning I used to go with him. But I didn't like the way he travelled, always by plane and staying in expensive hotels and drinking in the bar with the other correspondents. So I would leave him and go off by myself. I travelled the way everyone travels in India, just with a bundle and a roll of bedding which I could spread out anywhere and go to sleep. I went in third-class railway carriages and in those old lumbering buses that go from one small dusty town to another and are loaded with too many people inside and with too much scruffy baggage on top. At the end of my journeys, I emerged soaked in perspiration, soot, and dirt. I ate anything anywhere and always like everyone else with my fingers (I became good at that) – thick, half-raw chapattis from wayside stalls and little messes of lentils and vegetables served on a leaf, all the food the poor eat; sometimes if I didn't have anything, other people would share with me from out of their bundles. Henry, who had the usual phobia about bugs, said I would kill myself eating that way. But nothing ever happened. Once, in a desert fort in Rajasthan, I got very thirsty and asked the old caretaker to pull some water out of an ancient disused well for me. It was brown and sort of foul-smelling, and maybe there was a corpse in the well, who knows. But I was thirsty so I drank it, and still nothing happened.

People always speak to you in India, in buses and trains and on the streets, they want to know all about you and ask you a lot of personal questions. I didn't speak much Hindi, but somehow we always managed, and I didn't mind answering all those questions when I could. Women quite often used to touch me, run their hands over my skin just to feel what it was like I suppose, and they specially liked to touch my hair which is long and blonde. Sometimes I had several of them lifting up strands of it at the same time, one pulling this way and another that way and they would exchange excited comments and laugh and scream a lot; but in a nice way, so I couldn't help but laugh and scream with them. And people in India are so hospitable.

They're always saying 'Please come and stay in my house,' perfect strangers that happen to be sitting near you on the train. Sometimes, if I didn't have any plans or if it sounded as if they might be living in an interesting place, I'd say, 'All right thanks,' and I'd go along with them. I had some interesting adventures that way.

I might as well say straight off that many of these adventures were sexual. Indian men are very, very keen to sleep with foreign girls. Of course men in other countries are also keen to sleep with girls, but there's something specially frenzied about Indian men when they approach you. Frenzied and at the same time shy. You'd think that with all those ancient traditions they have – like the Kama Sutra, and the sculptures showing couples in every kind of position – you'd think that with all that behind them they'd be very highly skilled, but they're not. Just the opposite. Middle-aged men get as excited as a fifteen-year-old boy, and then of course they can't wait, they *jump* and before you know where you are, in a great rush, it's all over. And when it's over, it's over, there's nothing left. Then they're only concerned with getting away as soon as possible before anyone can find them out (they're always scared of being found out). There's no tenderness, no interest at all in the other person as a person; only the same kind of curiosity that there is on the buses and the same sort of questions are asked, like are you married, any children, why no children, do you like wearing our Indian dress . . . There's one question though that's not asked on the buses but that always inevitably comes up during sex, so that you learn to wait for it : always, at the moment of mounting excitement, they ask 'How many men have you slept with?' and it's repeated over and over 'How many? How many?' and then they shout 'Aren't you ashamed?' and 'Bitch!' – always that one word which seems to excite them more than any other, to call you that is the height of their love-making, it's the last frenzy, the final outrage : 'Bitch!' Sometimes I couldn't stop myself but had to burst out laughing.

I didn't like sleeping with all these people, but I felt I had to. I felt I was doing good, though I don't know why, I couldn't explain it to myself. Only one of all those men ever spoke to me : I mean the way people having sex together are supposed to speak, coming near each other not only physically but also wanting to show each other what's deep inside them. He was a middle-aged man, a fellow-passenger on a bus, and we got talking at one of the stops the bus made at a wayside tea-stall. When he found I was on my way to X—— and didn't have anywhere to stay, he said, as so many have said before him, 'Please come and stay in my house.' And I said, as I had often said before, 'All right.' Only when we got there he didn't take me to his house but to a hotel. It was a very poky place in the bazaar and we had to grope our way up a steep smelly stone staircase and then there was a tiny room with just one string-cot and an earthenware water jug in it. He made a joke about there being only one bed. I was too tired to care much about anything. I only wanted to get it over with quickly and to go sleep. But afterwards I found it wasn't possible to go to sleep because there was a lot of noise coming up from the street where all the shops were still open though it was nearly midnight. People seemed to be having a good time and there was even a phonograph playing some cracked old love-song. My companion also couldn't get to sleep : he left the bed and sat down on the floor by the window and smoked one cigarette after the other. His face was lit up by the light coming in from the street outside and I saw he was looking sort of thoughtful and sad, sitting there smoking. He had rather a good face, strong bones but quite a feminine mouth and of course those feminine suffering eyes that most Indians have.

I went and sat next to him. The window was an arch reaching down to the floor so that I could see out into the bazaar. It was quite gay down there with all the lights; the phonograph was playing from the cold-drink shop and a lot of people were standing around there having highly-coloured pop-drinks out of bottles; next to it was a shop with pink and blue brassieres strung up on a pole. On top of the shop were wrought-iron balconies on which sat girls dressed up in tatty georgette and waving peacock fans to keep themselves cool. Sometimes men looked up to talk and laugh with them and they talked and laughed back. I realized we were in the brothel area; probably the hotel we were in was a brothel too.

I asked 'Why did you bring me here?'

He answered 'Why did you come?'

That was a good question. He was right. But I wasn't sorry I came. Why should I be? I said 'It's all right. I like it.'

He said 'She likes it', and he laughed. A bit later he started talking : about how he had just been to visit his daughter who had been married a few months before. She wasn't happy in her in-laws' house, and when he said goodbye to her she clung to him and begged him to take her home. The more he reasoned with her, the more she cried, the more she clung to him. In the end he had had to use force to free himself from her so that he could get away and not miss his bus. He felt very sorry for her, but what else was there for him to do. If he took her away, her in-laws might refuse to have her back again and then her life would be ruined. And she would get used to it, they always did; for some it took longer and was harder, but they all got used to it in the end. His wife too had cried a lot during the first year of marriage.

I asked him whether he thought it was good to arrange marriages that way, and he looked at me and asked how else would you do it. I said something about love and it made him laugh and he said that was only for the films. I didn't want to defend my point of view; in fact, I felt rather childish and as if he knew a lot more about things than I did. He began to get amorous again, and this time it was much better because he wasn't so frenzied and I liked him better by now too. Afterwards he told me how when he was first married, he and his wife had shared a room with the whole family (parents and younger brothers and sisters), and whatever they wanted to do, they had to do very quickly and quietly for fear of anyone waking up. I had a strange sensation then, as if I wanted to strip off all my clothes and parade up and down the room naked. I thought of all the men's eyes that follow one in the street, and for the first time it struck me that the expression in them was like that in the eyes of prisoners looking through their bars at the world outside; and then I thought maybe I'm that world outside for them – the way I go here and there and talk and laugh with everyone and do what I like – maybe I'm the river and trees they can't have where they are. Oh, I felt so sorry, I wanted to do so much. And to make a start, I flung myself on my companion and kissed and hugged him hard, I lay on top of him, I smothered him, I spread my hair over his face because I wanted to make him forget everything that wasn't me – this room, his daughter, his wife, the women in georgette sitting on the balconies – I wanted everything to be new for him and as beautiful as I could make it. He liked it for a while but got tired quite quickly, probably because he wasn't all that young any more.

It was shortly after this encounter that I met Ahmed. He was eighteen years old and a musician. His family had been musicians as long as anyone could remember and the alley they lived in was full of other musicians, so that when you walked down it, it was like walking through a magic forest all lit up with music and sounds. Only there wasn't anything magic about the place itself which was very cramped and dirty; the houses were so old that, whenever there were heavy rains, one or two of them came tumbling down. I was never inside Ahmed's house or met his family – they'd have died of shock if they had got to know about me – but I knew they were very poor and scraped a living by playing at weddings and functions. Ahmed never had any money, just sometimes if he was lucky he had a few coins to buy his betel with. But he was cheerful and happy and enjoyed everything that came his way. He was married, but his wife was too young to stay with him and after the ceremony she had been sent back to live with her father who was a musician in another town.

When I first met Ahmed, I was staying in a hostel attached to a temple which was free of charge for pilgrims; but afterwards he and I wanted a place for us to go to, so I wired Henry to send me some more money. Henry sent me the money, together with a long complaining letter which I didn't read all the way through, and I took a room in a hotel. It was on the outskirts of town which was mostly waste land except for a few houses and some of these had never been finished. Our hotel wasn't finished either because the proprietor had run out of money, and now it probably never would be for the place had turned out to be a poor proposition, it was too far out of town and no one ever came to stay there. But it suited us fine. We had this one room, painted bright pink and quite bare except for two pieces of furniture – a bed and a dressing-table, both of them very shiny and new. Ahmed loved it, he had never stayed in such a grand room before; he bounced up and down on the bed which had a mattress and stood looking at himself from all sides in the mirror of the dressing-table.

I never in all my life was so gay with anyone the way I was with Ahmed. I'm not saying I never had a good time at home; I did. I had a lot of friends before I married Henry and we had parties and danced and drank and I enjoyed it. But it wasn't like with Ahmed because no one was ever as *carefree* as he was, as light and easy and just ready to play and live. At home we always had our problems, personal ones of course, but on top of those there were universal problems – social, and economic, and moral, we really cared about what was happening in the world around us and in our own minds, we felt a responsibility towards being here alive at this point in time and wanted to do our best. Ahmed had no thoughts like that at all; there wasn't a shadow on him. He had his personal problems from time to time, and when he had them, he was very downcast and sometimes he even cried. But they weren't anything really very serious – usually some family quarrel, or his father was angry with him – and they passed away, blew away like a breeze over a lake and left him sunny and sparkling again. He enjoyed everything so much : not only our room, and the bed and the dressing-table, and making love, but so many other things like drinking Coca-Cola and spraying scent and combing my hair and my combing his; and he made up games for us to play like indoor cricket with a slipper for a bat and one of Henry's letters rolled up for a ball. He taught me how to crack his toes, which is such a great Indian delicacy, and yelled with pleasure when I got it right; but when he did it to me, I yelled with pain so he stopped at once and was terribly sorry. He was very considerate and tender. No one I've ever known was sensitive to my feelings as he was. It was like an instinct with him, as if he could feel right down into my heart and know what was going on there; and without ever having to ask anything or my ever having to explain anything, he could sense each change of mood and adapt himself to it and feel with it. Henry would always have to ask me 'Now what's up? What's the matter with you?' and when we were still all right with each other, he would make a sincere effort to understand. But Ahmed never had to make an effort, and maybe if he'd had to he wouldn't have succeeded because it wasn't ever with his mind that he understood anything, it was always with his feelings. Perhaps that was so because he was a musician and in music everything is beyond words and explanations anyway; and from what he told me about Indian music, I could see it was very, very subtle, there are effects that you can hardly perceive they're so subtle and your sensibilities have to be kept tuned all the time to the finest, finest point; and perhaps because of that the whole of Ahmed was always at that point and he could play me and listen to me as if I was his sarod.

After some time we ran out of money and Henry wouldn't send any more, so we had to think what to do. I certainly couldn't bear to part with Ahmed, and in the end I suggested he'd better come back to Delhi with me and we'd try and straighten things out with Henry. Ahmed was terribly excited by the idea; he'd never been to Delhi and was wild to go. Only it meant he had to run away from home because his family would never have allowed him to go, so one night he stole out of the house with his sarod and his little bundle of clothes and met me at the railway station. We reached Delhi the next night, tired and dirty and covered with soot the way you always get in trains here. When we arrived home, Henry was giving a party; not a big party, just a small informal group sitting around chatting. I'll never forget the expression on everyone's faces when Ahmed and I came staggering in with our bundles and bedding. My blouse had got torn in the train all the way down the side, and I didn't have a safety-pin so it kept flapping open and unfortunately I didn't have anything underneath. Henry's guests were all looking very nice, the men in smart bush-shirts and their wives in little silk cocktail dresses; and although after the first shock they all behaved very well and carried on as if nothing unusual had happened, still it was an awkward situation for everyone concerned.

Ahmed never really got over it. I can see now how awful it must have been for him, coming into that room full of strange white people and all of them turning round to stare at us. And the room itself must have been a shock to him, he can never have seen anything like it. Actually, it was quite a shock to me too. I'd forgotten that that was the way Henry and I lived. When we first came, we had gone to a lot of trouble doing up the apartment, buying furniture and pictures and stuff, and had succeeded in making it look just like the apartment we have at home except for some elegant Indian touches. To Ahmed it was all very strange. He stayed there with us for some time, and he couldn't get used to it. I think it bothered him to have so many *things* around, rugs and lamps and objets d'art; he couldn't see why they had to be there. Now that I had travelled and lived the way I had, I couldn't see why either; as a matter of fact I felt as if these things were a hindrance and cluttered up not only your room but your mind and your soul as well, hanging on them like weights.

We had some quite bad scenes in the apartment during those days. I told Henry that I was in love with Ahmed, and naturally that upset him, though what upset him most was the fact that he had to keep us both in the apartment. I also realized that this was an undesirable situation, but I couldn't see any way out of it because where else could Ahmed and I go? We didn't have any money, only Henry had, so we had to stay with him. He kept saying that he would turn both of us out into the streets but I knew he wouldn't. He wasn't the type to do a violent thing like that, and besides he himself was so frightened of the streets that he'd have died to think of anyone connected with him being out there. I wouldn't have minded all that much if he *had* turned us out : it was warm enough to sleep in the open and people always give you food if you don't have any. I would have preferred it really because it was so unpleasant with Henry; but I knew Ahmed would never have been able to stand it. He was quite a pampered boy, and though his family were poor, they looked after and protected each other very carefully; he never had to miss a meal or go dressed in anything but fine muslin clothes, nicely washed and starched by female relatives.

Ahmed bitterly repented having come. He was very miserable, feeling so uncomfortable in the apartment and with Henry making rows all the time. Ramu, the servant, didn't improve anything by the way he behaved, absolutely refusing to serve Ahmed and never losing an opportunity to make him feel inferior. Everything went out of Ahmed; he crumpled up as if he were a paper flower. He didn't want to play his sarod and he didn't want to make love to me, he just sat around with his head and his hands hanging down, and there were times when I saw tears rolling down his face and he didn't even bother to wipe them off. Although he was so unhappy in the apartment, he never left it and so he never saw any of the places he had been so eager to come to Delhi for, like the Juma Masjid and Nizamuddin's tomb. Most of the time he was thinking about his family. He wrote long letters to them in Urdu, which I posted, telling them where he was and imploring their pardon for running away; and long letters came back again and he read and read them, soaking them in tears and kisses. One night he got so bad he jumped out of bed and, rushing into Henry's bedroom, fell to his knees by the side of Henry's bed and begged to be sent back home again. And Henry, sitting up in bed in his pyjamas, said all right, in rather a lordly way I thought. So next day I took Ahmed to the station and put him on the train, and through the bars of the railway carriage he kissed my hands and looked into my eyes with all his old ardour and tenderness, so at the last moment I wanted to go with him but it was too late and the train pulled away out of the station and all that was left to me of Ahmed was a memory, very beautiful and delicate like a flavour or a perfume or one of those melodies he played on his sarod.

I became very depressed. I didn't feel like going travelling any more but stayed home with Henry and went with him to his diplomatic and other parties. He was quite glad to have me go with him again; he liked having someone in the car on the way home to talk to about all the people who'd been at the party and compare their chances of future success with his own. I didn't mind going with him, there wasn't anything else I wanted to do. I felt as if I'd failed at something. It wasn't only Ahmed. I didn't really miss him all that much and was glad to think of him back with his family in that alley full of music where he was happy. For myself I didn't know what to do next though I felt that something still awaited me. Our apartment led to an open terrace and I often went up there to look at the view which was marvellous. The house we lived in and all the ones around were white and pink and very modern, with picture windows and little lawns in front, but from up here you could look beyond them to the city and the big mosque and the fort. In between there were stretches of waste land, empty and barren except for an occasional crumbly old tomb growing there. What always impressed me the most was the sky because it was so immensely big and so unchanging in colour, and it made everything underneath it – all the buildings, even the great fort, the whole city, not to speak of all the people living in it – seem terribly small and trivial and passing somehow. But at the same time as it made me feel small, it also made me feel immense and eternal. I don't know, I can't explain, perhaps because it was itself like that and this thought – that there *was* something like that – made me feel that I had a part in it, I too was part of being immense and eternal. It was all very vague really and nothing I could ever speak about to anyone; but because of it I thought well maybe there is something more for me here after all. That was a relief because it meant I wouldn't have to go home and be the way I was before and nothing different or gained. For all the time, ever since I'd come and even before, I'd had this idea that there was something in India for me to *gain*, and even though for the time being I'd failed, I could try longer and at last perhaps I would succeed.

I'd met people on and off who had come here on a spiritual quest, but it wasn't the sort of thing I wanted for myself. I thought anything I wanted to find, I could find by myself travelling around the way I had done. But now that this had failed, I became interested in the other thing. I began to go to a few prayer-meetings and I liked the atmosphere very much. The meeting was usually conducted by a swami in a saffron robe who had renounced the world, and he gave an address about love and God and everyone sang hymns also about love and God. The people who came to these meetings were mostly middle-aged and quite poor. I had already met many like them on my travels, for they were the sort of people who sat waiting on station platforms and bus depots, absolutely patient and uncomplaining even when conductors and other officials pushed them around. They were gentle people and very clean though there was always some slight smell about them as of people who find it difficult to keep clean because they live in crowded and unsanitary places where there isn't much running water and the drainage system isn't good. I loved the expression that came into their faces when they sang hymns. I wanted to be like them, so I began to dress in plain white *saris* and I tied up my hair in a plain knot and the only ornament I wore was a string of beads not for decoration but to say the names of God on. I became a vegetarian and did my best to cast out all the undesirable human passions, such as anger and lust. When Henry was in an irritable or quarrelsome mood, I never answered him back but was very kind and patient with him. However, far from having a good effect, this seemed to make him worse. Altogether he didn't like the new personality I was trying to achieve but sneered a lot at the way I dressed and looked and the simple food I ate. Actually, I didn't enjoy this food very much and found it quite a trial eating nothing but boiled rice and lentils with him sitting opposite me having his cutlets and chops.

The peace and satisfaction that I saw on the faces of the other hymn-singers didn't come to me. As a matter of fact, I grew rather bored. There didn't seem much to be learned from singing hymns and eating vegetables. Fortunately just about this time someone took me to see a holy woman who lived on the roof of an old overcrowded house near the river. People treated her like a holy woman but she didn't set up to be one. She didn't set up to be anything really, but only stayed in her room on the roof and talked to people who came to see her. She liked telling stories and she could hold everyone spellbound listening to her, even though she was only telling the old mythological stories they had known all their lives long, about Krishna, and the Pandavas, and Rama and Sita. But she got terribly excited while she was telling them, as if it wasn't something that had happened millions of years ago but as if it was all real and going on exactly now. Once she was telling about Krishna's mother who made him open his mouth to see whether he had stolen and was eating up her butter. What did she see then, inside his mouth?

'Worlds!' the holy woman cried. 'Not just this world, not just one world with its mountains and rivers and seas, no, but world upon world, all spinning in one great eternal cycle in this child's mouth, moon upon moon, sun upon sun!'

She clapped her hands and laughed and laughed, and then she burst out singing in her thin old voice, some hymn all about how great God was and how lucky for her that she was his beloved. She was dancing with joy in front of all the people. And she was just a little shrivelled old woman, very ugly with her teeth gone and a growth on her chin : but the way she carried on it was as if she had all the looks and glamour anyone ever had in the world and was in love a million times over. I thought well whatever it was she had, obviously it was the one thing worth having and I had better try for it.

I went to stay with a *guru* in a holy city. He had a house on the river in which he lived with his disciples. They lived in a nice way : they meditated a lot and went out for boat rides on the river and in the evenings they all sat around in the *guru*'s room and had a good time. There were quite a few foreigners among the disciples, and it was the *guru*'s greatest wish to go abroad and spread his message there and bring back more disciples. When he heard that Henry was a journalist, he became specially interested in me. He talked to me about the importance of introducing the leaven of Indian spirituality into the lump of Western materialism. To achieve this end, his own presence in the West was urgently required, and to ensure the widest dissemination of his message he would also need the full support of the mass media. He said that since we live in the modern age, we must avail ourselves of all its resources. He was very keen for me to bring Henry into the ashram, and when I was vague in my answers – I certainly didn't want Henry here nor would he in the least want to come – he became very pressing and even quite annoyed and kept returning to the subject.

He didn't seem a very spiritual type of person to me. He was a hefty man with big shoulders and a big head. He wore his hair long but his jaw was clean-shaven and stuck out very large and prominent and gave him a powerful look like a bull. All he ever wore was a saffron robe and this left a good part of his body bare so that it could be seen at once how strong his legs and shoulders were. He had huge eyes which he used constantly and apparently to tremendous effect, fixing people with them and penetrating them with a steady beam. He used them on me when he wanted Henry to come, but they never did anything to me. But the other disciples were very strongly affected by them. There was one girl, Jean, who said they were like the sun, so strong that if she tried to look back at them something terrible would happen to her like being blinded or burned up completely.

Jean had made herself everything an Indian *guru* expects his disciples to be. She was absolutely humble and submissive. She touched the *guru*'s feet when she came into or went out of his presence, she ran eagerly on any errand he sent her on. She said she gloried in being nothing in herself and living only by his will. And she looked like nothing too, sort of drained of everything she might once have been. At home her cheeks were probably pink but now she was quite white, waxen, and her hair too was completely faded and colourless. She always wore a plain white cotton *sari* and that made her look paler than ever, and thinner too, it seemed to bring out the fact that she had no hips and was utterly flat-chested. But she was happy – at least she said she was – she said she had never known such happiness and hadn't thought it was possible for human beings to feel like that. And when she said that, there was a sort of sparkle in her pale eyes, and at such moments I envied her because she seemed to have found what I was looking for. But at the same time I wondered whether she really had found what she thought she had, or whether it wasn't something else and she was cheating herself, and one day she'd wake up to that fact and then she'd feel terrible.

She was shocked by my attitude to the *guru* – not touching his feet or anything, and talking back to him as if he was just an ordinary person. Sometimes I thought perhaps there was something wrong with me because everyone else, all the other disciples and people from outside too who came to see him, they all treated him with this great reverence and their faces lit up in his presence as if there really was something special. Only I couldn't see it. But all the same I was quite happy there – not because of him, but because I liked the atmosphere of the place and the way they all lived. Everyone seemed very contented and as if they were living for something high and beautiful. I thought perhaps if I waited and was patient, I'd also come to be like that. I tried to meditate the way they all did, sitting crosslegged in one spot and concentrating on the holy word that had been given to me. I wasn't ever very successful and kept thinking of other things. But there were times when I went up to sit on the roof and looked out over the river, the way it stretched so calm and broad to the opposite bank and the boats going up and down it and the light changing and being reflected back on the water : and then, though I wasn't trying to meditate or come to any higher thoughts, I did feel very peaceful and was glad to be there.

The *guru* was patient with me for a long time, explaining about the importance of his mission and how Henry ought to come here and write about it for his paper. But as the days passed and Henry didn't show up, his attitude changed and he began to ask me questions. Why hadn't Henry come? Hadn't I written to him? Wasn't I going to write to him? Didn't I think what was being done in the ashram would interest him? Didn't I agree that it deserved to be brought to the notice of the world and that to this end no stone should be left unturned? While he said all this, he fixed me with his great eyes and I squirmed – not because of the way he was looking at me, but because I was embarrassed and didn't know what to answer. Then he became very gentle and said never mind, he didn't want to force me, that was not his way, he wanted people slowly to turn towards him of their own accord, to open up to him as a flower opens up and unfurls its petals and its leaves to the sun. But next day he would start again, asking the same questions, urging me, forcing me, and when this had gone on for some time and we weren't getting anywhere, he even got angry once or twice and shouted to me that I was obstinate and closed and had fenced in my heart with seven hoops of iron. When he shouted, everyone in the ashram trembled and afterwards they looked at me in a strange way. But an hour later the *guru* always had me called back to his room and then he was very gentle with me again and made me sit near him and insisted that it should be I who handed him his glass of milk in preference to one of the others, all of whom were a lot keener to be selected for this honour than I was.

Jean often came to talk to me. At night I spread my bedding in a tiny cubby-hole which was a disused store-room, and just as I was falling asleep, she would come in and lie down beside me and talk to me very softly and intimately. I didn't like it much, to have her so close to me and whispering in a voice that wasn't more than a breath and which I could feel, slightly warm, on my neck; sometimes she touched me, putting her hand on mine ever so gently so that she hardly was touching me but all the same I could feel that her hand was a bit moist and it gave me an unpleasant sensation down my spine. She spoke about the beauty of surrender, of not having a will and not having thoughts of your own. She said she too had been like me once, stubborn and ego-centred, but now she had learned the joy of yielding, and if she could only give me some inkling of the infinite bliss to be tasted in this process – here her breath would give out for a moment and she couldn't speak for ecstasy. I would take the opportunity to pretend to fall asleep, even snoring a bit to make it more convincing; after calling my name a few times in the hope of waking me up again, she crept away disappointed. But next night she'd be back again, and during the day too she would attach herself to me as much as possible and continue talking in the same way.

It got so that even when she wasn't there, I could still hear her voice and feel her breath on my neck. I no longer enjoyed anything, not even going on the river or looking out over it from the top of the house. Although they hadn't bothered me before, I kept thinking of the funeral pyres burning on the bank, and it seemed to me that the smoke they gave out was spreading all over the sky and the river and covering them with a dirty yellowish haze. I realized that nothing good could come to me from this place now. But when I told the *guru* that I was leaving, he got into a great fury. His head and neck swelled out and his eyes became two coal-black demons rolling around in rage. In a voice like drums and cymbals, he *forbade* me to go. I didn't say anything but I made up my mind to leave next morning. I went to pack my things. The whole ashram was silent and stricken, no one dared speak. No one dared come near me either till late at night when Jean came as usual to lie next to me. She lay there completely still and crying to herself. I didn't know she was crying at first because she didn't make a sound but slowly her tears seeped into her side of the pillow and a sensation of dampness came creeping over to my side of it. I pretended not to notice anything.

Suddenly the *guru* stood in the doorway. The room faced an open courtyard and this was full of moonlight which illuminated him and made him look enormous and eerie. Jean and I sat up. I felt scared, my heart beat fast. After looking at us in silence for a while, he ordered Jean to go away. She got up to do so at once. I said 'No, stay,' and clung to her hand but she disengaged herself from me and, touching the *guru*'s feet in reverence, she went away. She seemed to dissolve in the moonlight outside, leaving no trace. The *guru* sat beside me on my bedding spread on the floor. He said I was under a delusion, that I didn't really want to leave; my inmost nature was craving to stay by him – he knew, he could hear it calling out to him. But because I was afraid, I was attempting to smother this craving and to run away. 'Look how you're trembling,' he said. 'See how afraid you are.' It was true, I was trembling and cowering against the wall as far away from him as I could get. Only it was impossible to get very far because he was so huge and seemed to spread and fill the tiny closet. I could feel him close against me, and his pungent male smell, spiced with garlic, overpowered me.

'You're right to be afraid,' he said : because it was his intention, he said, to batter and beat me, to smash my ego till it broke and flew apart into a million pieces and was scattered into the dust. Yes, it would be a painful process and I would often cry out and plead for mercy, but in the end – ah, with what joy I would step out of the prison of my own self, remade and reborn! I would fling myself to the ground and bathe his feet in tears of gratitude. Then I would be truly his. As he spoke, I became more and more afraid because I felt, so huge and close and strong he was, that perhaps he really had the power to do to me all that he said and that in the end he would make me like Jean.

I now lay completely flattened against the wall, and he had moved up and was squashing me against it. One great hand travelled up and down my stomach, but its activity seemed apart from the rest of him and from what he was saying. His voice became lower and lower, more and more intense. He said he would teach me to obey, to submit myself completely, that would be the first step and a very necessary one. For he knew what we were like, all of us who came from Western countries : we were self-willed, obstinate, *licentious*. On the last word his voice cracked with emotion, his hand went further and deeper. *Licentious*, he repeated, and then, rolling himself across the bed so that he now lay completely pressed against me, he asked 'How many men have you slept with?' He took my hand and made me hold him : how huge and hot he was! He pushed hard against me. 'How many? Answer me!' he commanded, urgent and dangerous. But I was no longer afraid : now he was not an unknown quantity nor was the situation any longer new or strange. 'Answer me, answer me!' he cried, riding on top of me, and then he cried 'Bitch!' and I laughed in relief.

I quite liked being back in Delhi with Henry. I had lots of baths in our marble bathroom, soaking in the tub for hours and making myself smell nice with bath salts. I stopped wearing Indian clothes and took out all the dresses I'd brought with me. We entertained quite a bit, and Ramu scurried around in his white coat, emptying ashtrays. It wasn't a bad time. I stayed around all day in the apartment with the airconditioner on and the curtains drawn to keep out the glare. At night we drove over to other people's apartments for buffet suppers of boiled ham and potato salad; we sat around drinking in their living rooms, which were done up more or less like ours, and talked about things like the price of whisky, what was the best hill station to go to in the summer, and servants. This last subject often led to other related ones like how unreliable Indians were and how it was impossible ever to get anything done. Usually this subject was treated in a humorous way, with lots of funny anecdotes to illustrate, but occasionally someone got quite passionate; this happened usually if they were a bit drunk, and then they went off into a long thing about how dirty India was and backward, riddled with vile superstitions – evil, they said – corrupt – corrupting.

Henry never spoke like that – maybe because he never got drunk enough – but I know he didn't disagree with it. He disliked the place very much and was in fact thinking of asking for an assignment elsewhere. When I asked where, he said the cleanest place he could think of. He asked how would I like to go to Geneva. I knew I wouldn't like it one bit, but I said all right. I didn't really care where

I was. I didn't care much about anything these days. The only positive feeling I had was for Henry. He was so sweet and good to me. I had a lot of bad dreams nowadays and was afraid of sleeping alone, so he let me come into his bed even though he dislikes having his sheets disarranged and I always kick and toss about a lot. I lay close beside him, clinging to him, and for the first time I was glad that he had never been all that keen on sex. On Sundays we stayed in bed all day reading the papers and Ramu brought us nice English meals on trays. Sometimes we put on a record and danced together in our pyjamas. I kissed Henry's cheeks which were always smooth – he didn't need to shave very often – and sometimes his lips which tasted of toothpaste.

Then I got jaundice. It's funny, all that time I spent travelling about and eating anything anywhere, nothing happened to me, and now that I was living such a clean life with boiled food and boiled water, I got sick. Henry was horrified. He immediately segregated all his and my things, and anything that I touched had to be sterilized a hundred times over. He was for ever running into the kitchen to check up whether Ramu was doing this properly. He said jaundice was the most catching thing there was, and though he went in for a whole course of precautionary inoculations that had to be specially flown in from the States, he still remained in a very nervous state. He tried to be sympathetic to me, but couldn't help sounding reproachful most of the time. He had sealed himself off so carefully, and now I had let this in. I knew how he felt, but I was too ill and miserable to care. I don't remember ever feeling so *ill*. I didn't have any high temperature or anything, but all the time there was this terrible nausea. First my eyes went yellow, then the rest of me as if I'd been dyed in the colour of nausea, inside and out. The whole world went yellow and sick. I couldn't bear anything : any noise, any person near me, worst of all any smell. They couldn't cook in the kitchen any more because the smell of cooking made me scream. Henry had to live on boiled eggs and bread. I begged him not to let Ramu into my bedroom for, although Ramu always wore nicely laundered clothes, he gave out a smell of perspiration which was both sweetish and foul and filled me with disgust. I was convinced that under his clean shirt he wore a cotton vest, black with sweat and dirt, which he never took off but slept in at night in the one-room servant quarter where he lived crowded together with all his family in a dense smell of cheap food and bad drains and unclean bodies.

I knew these smells so well – I thought of them as the smells of India, and had never minded them; but now I couldn't get rid of them, they were like some evil flood soaking through the walls of my airconditioned bedroom. And other things I hadn't minded, had hardly bothered to think about, now came back to me in a terrible way so that waking and sleeping I saw them. What I remembered most often was the disused well in the Rajasthan fort out of which I had drunk water. I was sure now that there had been a corpse at the bottom of it, and I saw this corpse with the flesh swollen and blown but the eyes intact : they were like the *guru*'s eyes and they stared, glazed and jellied, into the darkness of the well. And worse than seeing this corpse, I could taste it in the water that I had drunk – that I was still drinking – yes, it was now, at this very moment, that I was raising my cupped hands to my mouth and feeling the dank water lap around my tongue. I screamed out loud at the taste of the dead man and I called to Henry and clutched his hand and begged him to get us sent to Geneva quickly, quickly. He disengaged his hand – he didn't like me to touch him at this time – but he promised.

Then I grew calmer, I shut my eyes and tried to think of Geneva and of washing out my mouth with Swiss milk.

I got better, but I was very weak. When I looked at myself in the mirror, I started to cry. My face had a yellow tint, my hair was limp and faded; I didn't look old but I didn't look young any more either. There was no flesh left, and no colour. I was drained, hollowed out. I was wearing a white night-dress and that increased the impression. Actually, I reminded myself of Jean. I thought so this is what it does to you (I didn't quite know at that time what I meant by it – jaundice in my case, a *guru* in hers; but it seemed to come to the same). When Henry told me that his new assignment had come through, I burst into tears again; only now it was with relief. I said let's go now, let's go quickly. I became quite hysterical so Henry said all right; he too was impatient to get away before any more of those bugs he dreaded so much caught up with us. The only thing that bothered him was that the rent had been paid for three months and the landlord refused to refund. Henry had a fight with him about it but the landlord won. Henry was furious but I said never mind, let's just get away and forget all about all of them. We packed up some of our belongings and sold the rest; the last few days we lived in an empty apartment with only a couple of kitchen chairs and a bed. Ramu was very worried about finding a new job.

Just before we were to leave for the airport and were waiting for the car to pick us up, I went on the terrace. I don't know why I did that, there was no reason. There was nothing I wanted to say goodbye to, and no last glimpses I wanted to catch. My thoughts were all concentrated on the coming journey and whether to take air-sickness pills or not. The sky from up on the terrace looked as immense as ever, the city as small. It was evening and the light was just fading and the sky wasn't any definite colour now : it was sort of translucent like a pearl but not an earthly pearl. I thought of the story the little saintly old woman had told about Krishna's mother and how she saw the sun and the moon and world upon world in his mouth. I liked that phrase so much – world upon world – I imagined them spinning around each other like glass balls in eternity and everything as shining and translucent as the sky I saw above me. I went down and told Henry I wasn't going with him. When he realized – and this took some time – that I was serious, he knew I was mad. At first he was very patient and gentle with me, then he got in a frenzy. The car had already arrived to take us. Henry yelled at me, he grabbed my arm and began to pull me to the door. I resisted with all my strength and sat down on one of the kitchen chairs. Henry continued to pull and now he was pulling me along with the chair as if on a sleigh. I clung to it as hard as I could but I felt terribly weak and was afraid I would let myself be pulled away. I begged him to leave me. I cried and wept with fear – fear that he would take me, fear that he would leave me.

Ramu came to my aid. He said it's all right Sahib, I'll look after her. He told Henry that I was too weak to travel after my illness but later, when I was better, he would take me to the airport and put me on a plane. Henry hesitated. It was getting very late; and if he didn't go, he too would miss the plane. Ramu assured him that all would be well and Henry need not worry at all. At last Henry took my papers and ticket out of his inner pocket. He gave me instructions how I was to go to the air company and make a new booking. He hesitated a moment longer – how sweet he looked all dressed up in a suit and tie ready for travelling, just like the day we got married – but the car was hooting furiously downstairs and he had to go. I held on hard to the chair. I was afraid if I didn't I might get up and run after him. So I clung to the chair, trembling and crying. Ramu was quite happily dusting the remaining chair. He said we would have to get some more furniture. I think he was glad that I had stayed and he still had somewhere to work and live and didn't have to go tramping around looking for another place. He had quite a big family to support.

I sold the ticket Henry left with me but I didn't buy any new furniture with it. I stayed in the empty rooms by myself and very rarely went out. When Ramu cooked anything for me, I ate it, but sometimes he forgot or didn't have time because he was busy looking for another job. I didn't like living like that but I didn't know what else to do. I was afraid to go out : everything I had once liked so much – people, places, crowds, smells – I now feared and hated. I would go running back to be by myself in the empty apartment. I felt people looked at me in a strange way in the streets; and perhaps I was strange now from the way I was living and not caring about what I looked like any more; I think I talked aloud to myself sometimes – once or twice I heard myself doing it. I spent a lot of the money I got from the air ticket on books. I went to the bookshops and came hurrying back carrying armfuls of them. Many of them I never read, and even those I did read, I didn't understand very much. I hadn't had much experience in reading these sort of books – like the Upanishads and the Vedanta Sutras – but I liked the sound of the words and I liked the feeling they gave out. It was as if I were all by myself on an immensely high plateau breathing in great lungfuls of very sharp, pure air. Sometimes the landlord came to see what I was doing. He went round all the rooms, peering suspiciously into corners, testing the fittings. He kept asking how much longer I was going to stay; I said till the three months' rent was up. He brought prospective tenants to see the apartment, but when they saw me squatting on the floor in the empty rooms, sometimes with a bowl of half-eaten food which Ramu had neglected to clear away, they got nervous and went away again rather quickly. After a time the electricity got cut off because I hadn't paid the bill. It was very hot without the fan and I filled the tub with cold water and sat in it all day. But then the water got cut off too. The landlord came up twice, three times a day now. He said if I didn't clear out the day the rent was finished he would call the police to evict me. I said it's all right, don't worry, I shall go. Like the landlord, I too was counting the days still left to me. I was afraid what would happen to me.

Today the landlord evicted Ramu out of the servant quarter. That was when Ramu came up to ask for money and said all those things. Afterwards I went up on the terrace to watch him leave. It was such a sad procession. Each member of the family carried some part of their wretched household stock, none of which looked worth taking. Ramu had a bed with tattered strings balanced on his head. In two days' time I too will have to go with my bundle and my bedding. I've done this so often before – travelled here and there without any real destination – and been so happy doing it; but now it's different. That time I had a great sense of freedom and adventure. Now I feel compelled, that I *have* to do this whether I want to or not. And partly I don't want to, I feel afraid. Yet it's still like an adventure, and that's why besides being afraid I'm also excited, and most of the time I don't know why my heart is beating fast, is it in fear or in excitement, wondering what will happen to me now that I'm going travelling again.

RUSKIN BOND

A Prospect of Flowers

Fern Hill, The Oaks, Hunter's Lodge, The Parsonage, The Pines, Dumbarnie, Mackinnon's Hall and Windermere. These are the names of some of the old houses that still stand on the outskirts of one of the smaller Indian hill stations. Most of them have fallen into decay and ruin. They are very old, of course – built over a hundred years ago by Britishers who sought relief from the searing heat of the plains. Today's visitors to the hill stations prefer to live near the markets and cinemas and many of the old houses, set amidst oak and maple and deodar, are inhabited by wild cats, bandicoots, owls, goats, and the occasional charcoal-burner or mule-driver.

But amongst these neglected mansions stands a neat, whitewashed cottage called Mulberry Lodge. And in it, up to a short time ago, lived an elderly English spinster named Miss Mackenzie.

In years Miss Mackenzie was more than 'elderly,' being well over eighty. But no one would have guessed it. She was clean, sprightly, and wore old-fashioned but well-preserved dresses. Once a week, she walked the two miles to town to buy butter and jam and soap and sometimes a small bottle of *eau-de-Cologne*.

She had lived in the hill station since she had been a girl in her teens, and that had been before the First World War. Though she had never married, she had experienced a few love affairs and was far from being the typical frustrated spinster of fiction. Her parents had been dead thirty years; her brother and sister were also dead. She had no relatives in India, and she lived on a small pension of forty rupees a month and the gift parcels that were sent out to her from New Zealand by a friend of her youth.

Like other lonely old people, she kept a pet, a large black cat with bright yellow eyes. In her small garden she grew dahlias, chrysanthemums, gladioli and a few rare orchids. She knew a great deal about plants, and about wild flowers, trees, birds and insects. She had never made a serious study of these things, but, having lived with them for so many years, had developed an intimacy with all that grew and flourished around her.

She had few visitors. Occasionally the padre from the local church called on her, and once a month the postman came with a letter from New Zealand or her pension papers. The milkman called every second day with a litre of milk for the lady and her cat. And sometimes she received a couple of eggs free, for the egg-seller remembered a time when Miss Mackenzie, in her earlier prosperity, bought eggs from him in large quantities. He was a sentimental man. He remembered her when she was a ravishing beauty in her twenties and he gazed at her in round-eyed, nine-year-old wonder and consternation.

Now it was September and the rains were nearly over and Miss Mackenzie's chrysanthemums were coming into their own. She hoped the coming winter wouldn't be too severe because she found it increasingly difficult to bear the cold.

One day, as she was pottering about in her garden, she saw a schoolboy plucking wild flowers on the slope about the cottage.

'Who's that?' she called. 'What are you up to, young man?'

The boy was alarmed and tried to dash up the hillside,

but he slipped on pine needles and came slithering down the slope into Miss Mackenzie's nasturtium bed.

When he found there was no escape, he gave a bright disarming smile and said, 'Good morning, Miss.'

He belonged to the local English-medium school, and wore a bright red blazer and a red-and-black-striped tie. Like most polite Indian schoolboys, he called every woman 'Miss'.

'Good morning,' said Miss Mackenzie severely. 'Would you mind moving out of my flower-bed?'

The boy stepped gingerly over the nasturtiums and looked up at Miss Mackenzie with dimpled cheeks and appealing eyes. It was impossible to be angry with him.

'You're trespassing,' said Miss Mackenzie.

'Yes, Miss.'

'And you ought to be in school at this hour.'

'Yes, Miss.'

'Then what are you doing here?'

'Picking flowers, Miss.' And he held up a bunch of ferns and wild flowers.

'Oh,' Miss Mackenzie was disarmed. It was a long time since she had seen a boy taking an interest in flowers, and, what was more, playing truant from school in order to gather them.

'Do you like flowers?' she asked.

'Yes, Miss. I'm going to be a botan – a botantist?'

'You mean a botanist.'

'Yes, Miss.'

'Well, that's unusual. Most boys at your age want to be pilots or soldiers or perhaps engineers. But you want to be a botanist. Well, well. There's still hope for the world, I see. And do you know the names of these flowers?'

'This is a Bukhilo flower,' he said, showing her a small golden flower. 'That's a Pahari name. It means Puja, or prayer. The flower is offered during prayers. But I don't know what this is . . .'

He held out a pale pink flower with a soft, heart-shaped leaf.

'It's a wild begonia,' said Miss Mackenzie. 'And that purple stuff is salvia, but it isn't wild, it's a plant that escaped from my garden. Don't you have any books on flowers?'

'No, Miss.'

'All right, come in and I'll show you a book.'

She led the boy into a small front room, which was crowded with furniture and books and vases and jam-jars, and offered him a chair. He sat awkwardly on its edge. The black cat immediately leapt on to his knees, and settled down on them, purring loudly.

'What's your name?' asked Miss Mackenzie, as she rummaged among her books.

'Anil, Miss.'

'And where do you live?'

'When school closes, I go to Delhi. My father has a business.'

'Oh, and what's that?'

'Bulbs, Miss.'

'Flower bulbs?'

'No, electric bulbs.'

'Electric bulbs! You might send me a few, when you get home. Mine are always fusing, and they're so expensive, like everything else these days. Ah, here we are!' She pulled a heavy volume down from the shelf and laid it on the table. '*Flora Himaliensis*, published in 1892, and probably the only copy in India. This is a very valuable book, Anil. No other naturalist has recorded so many wild Himalayan flowers. And let me tell you this, there are many flowers and plants which are still unknown to the fancy botanists who spend all their time at microscopes instead of in the mountains. But perhaps *you'll* do something about that, one day.'

'Yes, Miss.'

They went through the book together, and Miss Mackenzie pointed out many flowers that grew in and around the hill station, while the boy made notes of their names and seasons. She lit a stove, and put the kettle on for tea. And then the old English lady and the small Indian boy sat side by side over cups of hot sweet tea, absorbed in a book of wild flowers.

'May I come again?' asked Anil, when finally he rose to go.

'If you like,' said Miss Mackenzie. 'But not during school hours. You mustn't miss your classes.'

After that, Anil visited Miss Mackenzie about once a week, and nearly always he brought a wild flower for her to identify. She found herself looking forward to the boy's visits – and sometimes, when more than a week passed and he didn't come, she was disappointed and lonely and would grumble at the black cat.

Anil reminded her of her brother, when the latter had been a boy. There was no physical resemblance. Andrew had been fair-haired and blue-eyed. But it was Anil's eagerness, his alert, bright look and the way he stood – legs apart, hands on his hips, a picture of confidence – that reminded her of the boy who had shared her own youth in these same hills.

And why did Anil come to see her so often?

Partly because she knew about wild flowers, and he really did want to become a botanist. And partly because she smelt of freshly baked bread, and that was a smell his own grandmother had possessed. And partly because she was lonely and sometimes a boy of twelve can sense loneliness better than an adult. And partly because he was a little different from other children.

By the middle of October, when there was only a fortnight left for the school to close, the first snow had fallen on the distant mountains. One peak stood high above the rest, a white pinnacle against the azure-blue sky. When the sun set, this peak turned from orange to gold to pink to red.

'How high is that mountain?' asked Anil.

'It must be over 12,000 feet,' said Miss Mackenzie. 'About thirty miles from here, as the crow flies. I always wanted to go there, but there was no proper road. At that height, there'll be flowers that you don't get here – the blue gentian and the purple columbine, the anemone and the edelweiss.'

'I'll go there one day,' said Anil.

'I'm sure you will, if you really want to.'

The day before his school closed, Anil came to say goodbye to Miss Mackenzie.

'I don't suppose you'll be able to find many wild flowers in Delhi,' she said. 'But have a good holiday.'

'Thank you, Miss.'

As he was about to leave, Miss Mackenzie, on an impulse, thrust the *Flora Himaliensis* into his hands.

'You keep it,' she said. 'It's a present for you.'

'But I'll be back next year, and I'll be able to look at it, then. It's so valuable.'

'I know it's valuable and that's why I've given it to you. Otherwise it will only fall into the hands of the junk-dealers.'

'But, Miss – '

'Don't argue. Besides, I may not be here next year.'

'Are you going away?'

'I'm not sure. I may go to England.'

She had no intention of going to England; she had not seen the country since she was a child, and she knew she would not fit in with the life of post-war Britain. Her home was in these hills, among the oaks and maples and deodars. It was lonely, but at her age it would be lonely anywhere.

The boy tucked the book under his arm, straightened his tie, stood stiffly to attention, and said, 'Goodbye, Miss Mackenzie.'

It was the first time he had spoken her name.

Winter set in early, and strong winds brought rain and sleet, and soon there were no flowers in the garden or on the hillside. The cat stayed indoors, curled up at the foot of Miss Mackenzie's bed.

Miss Mackenzie wrapped herself up in all her old shawls and mufflers, but still she felt the cold. Her fingers grew so stiff that she took almost an hour to open a can of baked beans. And then, it snowed, and for several days the milkman did not come. The postman arrived with her pension papers, but she felt too tired to take them up to town to the bank.

She spent most of the time in bed. It was the warmest place. She kept a hot-water bottle at her back, and the cat kept her feet warm. She lay in bed, dreaming of the spring and summer months. In three months' time the primroses would be out, and with the coming of spring the boy would return.

One night the hot-water bottle burst and the bedding was soaked through. As there was no sun for several days, the blanket remained damp. Miss Mackenzie caught a chill and had to keep to her cold, uncomfortable bed. She knew she had a fever but there was no thermometer with which to take her temperature. She had difficulty in breathing.

A strong wind sprang up one night, and the window flew open and kept banging all night. Miss Mackenzie was too weak to get up and close it, and the wind swept the rain and sleet into the room. The cat crept into the bed and snuggled close to its mistress's warm body. But towards morning that body had lost its warmth and the cat felt the bed and started scratching about on the floor.

As a shaft of sunlight streamed through the open window, the milkman arrived. He poured some milk into the cat's saucer on the doorstep and the cat leapt down from the window-sill and made for the milk.

The milkman called a greeting to Miss Mackenzie, but received no answer. Her window was open and he had always known her to be up before sunrise. So he put his head in at the window and called again. But Miss Mackenzie did not answer. She had gone away to the mountain where the blue gentian and purple columbine grew.

SAROS COWASJEE

His Father's Medals

Ramu sat on the doorstep of his hut in a far corner of Thakur Madan Singh's compound, a good distance away from the quarters of the other servants better placed in life than himself. He spat on the silver medal and with the bottom edge of his shirt rubbed it hard till it shone with a dull lustre. 'That's better,' he said, dropping it gently into his shirt pocket and pulling out the other two – these of bronze. He again spat and polished them in the same manner. If I had only dug my little finger in the polish on the lavatory shelf, he thought, these would have glittered like gold. And nobody would have suspected, for what has a sweeper boy to do with polish?

Three medals were all that his father, Ramji Lal, had left him. Dying, the medals still on his famished chest, he fought to keep back his last breath – not that life had much to give, but that death would take even the little he had. Ramji Lal died and the prized proof of a lifetime's devotion to duty passed on to Ramu, his only child. Ramu looked fondly at the medals. They were no mere tokens of affection – a link between a dead father and a living son – but a flaming ideal towards which he must strive. He pressed them to his heart and tears welled up in his eyes; his dear, dear father had left them in his care.

Three medals! The two large ones of bronze from the British Government for cleaning the officers' latrines through the Burma Campaign, and the little silver one from the Colonel himself as a mark of appreciation that they were well cleaned. He looked at the medals intently.

Who was this bald, point-bearded man with the face of a butcher, waging wars and distributing medals? His father had often talked of him – a great king who ruled the world and did justice to all. Justice to all? What justice was done to his father? Two ribbons to decorate his breast while the heart beneath was starved of blood. Ah, but that was being too hard on the king. What could a king do but sit on a golden seat and empty his bowels in a silver pot? A silver pot – glistening like his little medal. How he would love to be a king's sweeper and handle silver pots!

Ramu shook himself. He was demanding too much from life. What God had given was good enough: it was not everybody who became a sweeper in the household of Thakur Madan Singh, BA. There were Goodan, Murari, Sona and Ravi and a horde of others sweeping the public streets from morning to night and envying him his honoured position.

The back door of the palatial house facing Ramu's quarters was flung open and Sultan Singh, the cook, clad in his yellow turban, called out: 'Ramu! O Ramu! Come here and clean this.'

Ramu dropped the medals in his pocket, jumped down the single step that led to his hut, and hurried towards the latrines. He lifted the lids off the commodes and expertly pulled out the pots. It was for the eleventh time this morning that he was cleaning them; yesterday he had had to attend to them some sixteen times, though only five people lived in this capacious house. God! what do they eat that they must go some twenty times a day? But it was good that they frequented the latrines, for were they habituated like the poor how could he have found full-time employment in a respectable home? As he gracefully carried the pots, his head thrown back to avoid the stink, he could not help musing that at least in this there was no difference between rich and poor except in its frequency; that whatever delicacies the rich might relish, it must come down to this, this that he carried at arm's length, and that kept him at arm's length from his fellow men.

Having done a good job, he sat down again on the doorstep. Once a sweeper, always a sweeper. He had given up all attempts to break through the social barrier. His life and his future must be decided by his own class, the Untouchable. Nothing could ever break through the rigid class system, no, not even love. There stood Kamala, now engaged to a lorry driver's son. He had loved her passionately, would have done anything to win her, but she had asked of him the impossible – to forget her. As children they had played together, planned together. He was not then a sweeper's son nor she a Rajput's daughter. But as Kamala grew to maidenhood, under the vigilance of her father Sultan Singh, and the providential care of Thakur Madan Singh, dignity and distance silenced her feeble pulse of love.

He remembered how he had once playfully caught her hand and the fear that had come into her eyes. 'Leave me,' she had begged. 'Oh, let me go!' He had pulled back his hand, to see her rush back to her quarters. Through the half-open door he had seen her washing herself clean. He had turned his face aside, the humiliation sticking in his throat: he was an Untouchable. A sweeper holding the hand of a Rajput's daughter! Did you ever hear of that?

No, he had never heard. He had given up all thought of possessing her, all thought and those rash promises of boyhood without a struggle. Love could live on, just as hope lives on, deep in the core of the poor man's heart. He would keep her memory alive, would keep the twisted hairpin and the broken bangles she had dropped into the litter bin close to his heart. And he would give her something: a little token that would remind her of Ramu and tell her that even a sweeper boy has a heart. A sweeper boy has a heart! Did you hear that?

A pathetic smile dissolved into anguish on his lips as he stood up and put his hands into the loose, patched trousers, which had once belonged to Thakur Madan Singh. He pulled out all the bits of copper and added them up. They made a little over two rupees. Enough to buy a handsome present, he said. If I run short I can sell off one of my father's medals. No, he would never sell his dear father's medals: not for love, not for this world – for what are love and a world to a sweeper boy.

He sauntered till he came to the market. He walked on, unable to decide where he should take his first peep. On the pavement Shivaji, notorious for his prices, had spread his fancy goods. He thought he could take a look; it would give him some idea of the things he could buy for Kamala. He came to the shop and stood in the midst of the little group that was examining the goods. His eager, boyish face beamed with excitement as he viewed the glittering array of bangles, hairpins, rings, bead necklaces, mirrors, till it came to rest on a pair of brilliant anklets. Shining silver anklets! He would put them round Kamala's ankles with his own hands, would give just a little press to her delicate feet; she would not object to that, no, not as long as he kept to her feet. But, ah, they must be expensive. Silver anklets cost a lot of money. Yet sometimes they are sold cheap, sometimes when they are false, sometimes when they are stolen . . .

'How much do you want for these?' he asked hesitantly, pointing to the anklets.

'Fifteen rupees and nothing less,' replied Shivaji.

Ramu stepped back. He felt as if somebody had given him a punch in the face. He turned to go.

'Wait,' said Shivaji. 'How much can you give?'

'I can't afford them. I don't want them,' said Ramu.

'You do, you do. Give anything and take them.'

Ramu blushed. 'No, no.'

'Can you give four rupees?' asked Shivaji, holding an anklet high to display it.

Ramu felt the weight of the copper in his pocket and taking courage said, 'Two rupees.'

Shivaji burst into a loud, coarse laugh. 'Ha, ha, ha, ha. Silver anklets for two rupees!' And turning to the group of buyers he remarked, 'Wants anklets for two rupees to put round the feet of some hussy!' Then with a malicious grin he swore at Ramu: 'By God, how much do you pay her for a ride?'

The little crowd seemed to enjoy Shivaji's remarks and pressed closer to get a better view of Ramu. One from the crowd mockingly reprimanded Shivaji: 'You mustn't be so hard on the poor fellow, Master. It may be for his mother!'

Burning rage gave him courage; the low jibe of Shivaji made him dare. He would teach him a lesson – and now. He looked to the left and then to the right. The street was surging with people. With one rush he snatched the anklet from Shivaji's hand and darted off to mingle in the crowd.

A hand lay on his shoulder. Two policemen tightly gripped him by the arms and stood on either side of him, while a jeering mob pressed around him.

'Move out of the way,' yelled one of the policemen. 'Let us take this son of a pig to the police station.'

'The pimp,' swore the other. 'Thinks we police and justice are dead.'

'That he will find out when the strap licks his bloody arse and leaves it as red as a monkey's bum,' rejoined the first.

'As a monkey's bum,' echoed one from the crowd. 'Give

him a monkey's bum. The fool is stealing in broad daylight, when nowadays it is not advisable even at night, because of our vigilant police.'

The two policemen, sensing the irony in the remark, cut through the crowd and triumphantly marched away with their prey. Having got clear off the busy street, they began searching Ramu's pockets.

'Just two rupees! That's not much,' said the first policeman. 'What's in your shirt pocket?'

'Nothing, nothing,' implored Ramu.

The second policeman dug his hand into Ramu's pocket and pulled out the medals. 'Eh, where did you get these from?'

'I did not steal them, I did not steal them. They are my father's medals. Please give them back to me.'

'Give them back to you, eh! Your father's medals! Where did he steal them from? Out with it, or my boot will be at your bottom. Quick.'

'My father was not a thief. They were given to him for his services,' wept Ramu, tears running down his cheeks.

'Services? What services? You and your father are not good enough to clean our latrines. Now march on fast,' said the first policeman, hitting Ramu across the calves with his cane, 'or you will find this creeping up your arse.'

Biographical Notes

RUDYARD KIPLING (1865–1936): Born in Bombay, at the age of seven he left for England, but owing to poor health did not go to school until he was eleven. After studying at the United Services College, Westward Ho!, he returned to India in 1882 and worked as a journalist for the next seven years. His early works, all dealing with India, come from this period. In 1890 he left India and, except for a brief return two years later, lived the rest of his life first in the United States and then in England. The publication of his first two collections of short stories, *Plain Tales from the Hills* and *Soldiers Three* (both in 1888), made India a major theme in English literature.

FLORA ANNIE STEEL, née Webster (1847–1927): Born at Harrow-on-the-Hill, she married a member of the Indian Civil Service and left for India in 1868. During the next twenty-two years she served India in various capacities and, unlike most of the Anglo-Indian ladies of the time, managed to establish relations with Indians of all classes. She returned to England in 1889 and wrote numerous novels and short stories, including a fine study of the Indian Mutiny, *On the Face of the Waters* (1896). She is equally well-known for her *Tales from the Punjab* (1894), a unique collection of authentic versions of oral legends.

ALICE PERRIN (1867–1934): Born in India, the daughter of General John Innes Robinson of the Bengal Cavalry, she was educated in England. She married a medical officer of the Indian Civil Service and spent some twenty-five years in India. Almost all her work (she wrote some twenty books) deals with India and the best reveals a gentle irony and humour rarely found in Anglo-Indian writing. Her most successful books are her collections of short stories, *East of Suez* (1901) and *Red Records* (1906). After her return from India she lived in Switzerland until her death.

BITHIA MARY CROKER (?–1920): Very little is known about her save that she was an Irishwoman who spent fourteen years in the East as the wife of an army officer. She wrote some twenty romantic novels dealing with India. Among these are *Proper Pride* (1882), *Mr Jervis: a Romance of the Indian Hills* (1894), and *Cat's Paw* (1902) – dealing with club life in South India.

LEONARD WOOLF (1880–1969): British historian, novelist and political essayist, he was born in London and educated at Trinity College, Cambridge. He joined the Ceylon Civil Service and served in Ceylon from 1904 to 1911. Returning to England, he married Virginia Stephen (better known by her married name) and became a regular contributor to liberal papers and magazines. With his wife, he founded the Hogarth Press in 1917 and the two published most of their own books themselves. His fictional work includes a novel, *The Village in the Jungle* (1913), and *Stories of the East* (1915).

JOHN EYTON (1890–): A popular writer about the Indian scene in the 1920s. The influence of Kipling is apparent in his novel *Bulbulla* (1928), which follows the general pattern of *Kim*. His best work, however, is his collection *The*

Dancing Fakir and Other Stories, first published by Longman, Green, London, in 1922, and reprinted by Books for Library Press, New York, in 1969.

CHRISTINE WESTON (1904–): Born in Unao in the United Provinces, the daughter of a naturalized Englishman in the Indian Imperial Police, she was educated at a convent school in the hills, and lived in India until her marriage to an American in 1923. She started publishing in the early forties, and her novel *Indigo* (1944) has been compared to E.M. Forster's *A Passage to India* for its authenticity and understanding of the complexity of the Indian problem.

PHILIP MASON (1906–): Educated at Balliol College, Oxford, he joined the ICS in 1928 and served in India until his retirement in 1947. After Independence he was for some years Director of the Institute of Race Relations in London, and thereafter he moved to Dorset and became a full-time writer. As Philip Woodruff he published a two-volume history of the British in India called *The Men Who Ruled India*. In fiction his outstanding works are *Call the Next Witness* (1945), *The Wild Sweet Witch* (1947) and *The Island of Chamba* (1950).

JOSEPH HITREC (1912–1972): Born and educated in Zagreb, Yugoslavia, he started working for a British advertising agency in London in 1935. He was later transferred to the agency's branch offices in Calcutta and Bombay and remained in India until 1946. From 1946 he lived in New York, becoming a naturalized citizen of the United States in 1951. Apart from several short stories, he wrote two novels about India, *Son of the Moon* (1948) and *Angel of Gaiety* (1953). The former was awarded the Harper Prize.

MULK RAJ ANAND (1905–): Born in Peshawar, he was educated at the universities of Punjab and London. Success came to him with the publication of his first novel, *Untouchable*, in 1935. Since then he has written some twenty works of fiction, including seven volumes of short stories. Best known for *Coolie* (1936), his most impressive work, nevertheless, is *Private Life of an Indian Prince* (1953). He lives in Bombay and is currently working on a monumental autobiographical novel entitled *The Seven Ages of Man*. Of these, four volumes have so far been published.

R. K. NARAYAN (1907–): Born in Madras, he graduated from Maharaja's College in Mysore. His first novel, *Swami and Friends*, appeared in 1935 and was greeted with a chorus of praise. He has since followed up his success with *The Bachelor of Arts* (1937), *The Dark Room* (1938), *An Astrologer's Day and Other Stories* (1947), *Mr Sampath* (1949), *The Financial Expert* (1952), *The Man-eater of Malgudi* (1961) and an autobiography, *My Days* (1974). The Michigan State University Press began in 1953 to publish Narayan's works and thus introduced him to American readers. In 1958 he was given the Sahitya Akademi Award for *The Guide*.

RAJA RAO (1909–): He was born at Hassan, Karnataka, and educated at Aligarh and Hyderabad. He went for higher studies to Montpellier and the Sorbonne in France, where he came to live for nearly thirty years before joining the University of Texas, Austin (USA), as Professor of Philosophy. His works include *Kanthapura* (1938), *The Serpent and the Rope* (1960), *The Cat and Shakespeare* (1965) and *Comrade Kirillov* (1976). His short stories have been collected in *The Cow of the Barricades* (1947) and *The Policeman and the Rose* (1978). A new novel called *The*

Chessmaster and His Moves will be published this year (1986).

ATTIA HOSAIN (1913–): Born in Lucknow, United Provinces, she graduated from Isabella Thorburn College – being the first woman from amongst the Taluqdars of Oudh to do so. Her short stories have appeared in British and Indian magazines and one, 'The Street of the Moon', was an *Atlantic Monthly* first. She is the author of *Phoenix Fled and Other Stories* (1953) and *Sunlight on a Broken Column* (1961), both published by Chatto and Windus. She has been living in England for a number of years.

KHUSHWANT SINGH (1915–): Novelist, historian and editor of the *Hindustan Times*, he was born in Hadali (now in Pakistan). After university education in Delhi and Lahore, he went to London and obtained his Bar-at-Law in 1938. He published his first fictional work, *The Mark of Vishnu and Other Stories*, in 1950, but it was *Train to Pakistan* (1955) which brought him into prominence. His writing includes some authoritative studies of Sikh history and religion. He has held visiting academic appointments at Oxford, Princeton and Syracuse.

RUTH PRAWER JHABVALA (1927–): Born of Polish parents in Cologne, now in West Germany, she received her MA in English Literature from the University of London. She married an Indian architect and came to India in 1951. Her first novel, *To Whom She Will*, was published in 1955, followed by *The Nature of Passion* (1956) and *Esmond in India* (1958). She has also published four collections of short stories, but it was the Booker Memorial Prize in 1976 for *Heat and Dust* that made her an internationally renowned writer.

RUSKIN BOND (1934–): Born in Kasauli, Himachal Pradesh, he grew up in Jamnagar and Dehra Dun, and did his schooling at Bishop Cotton School in Simla. His first novel, *The Room on the Roof* (1956), was written when he was only eighteen and won him the Llewellyn Rhys Memorial Prize. His other fictional works are *The Neighbour's Wife and Other Stories* (1968), *Angry River* (1972), *The Blue Umbrella* (1974) and *The Man-eater of Manjara and Other Stories* (1974). He lives in Mussoorie, a popular hill station in the days of the Raj, and the setting of his story 'A Prospect of Flowers'.

SAROS COWASJEE (1931–): Born in Secundrabad, formerly Hyderabad State, he was educated at the universities of Agra and Leeds. His published works include studies on Sean O'Casey and Mulk Raj Anand, but his own favourite is his novel *Goodbye to Elsa* (1974). His other fictional works include *Nude Therapy* (1978), *The Last of the Maharajas* (1980) and *Suffer Little Children* (1982). He has edited the revised Bodley Head editions of the novels of Mulk Raj Anand, and more recently *Stories from the Raj* (1982).